The
Fighter

SOHO

The
Fighter

★ A NOVEL ★

CRAIG DAVIDSON

SOHO

First published in Canada by Penguin Group (Canada),
a division of Pearson Canada Inc.
Copyright © Craig Davidson, 2006

Published in the United States in 2007 by
Soho Press, Inc.
853 Broadway
New York, NY 10003

Epigraph on p. v by Gary Smith reprinted courtesy of
SPORTS ILLUSTRATED: from "One Tough Bird" by Gary Smith,
June 26, 1995. Copyright © 1995, Time Inc. All rights reserved.

Epigraph on p. v by Chester Himes reprinted by permission from IF HE
HOLLERS LET HIM GO by Chester Himes, published by Thunder's
Mouth Press. Permission granted by Roslyn Targ Literary Agency, Inc.

Library of Congress Cataloging-in-Publication Data
Davidson, Craig, 1976-
The fighter : a novel / Craig Davidson. —1st American ed.
p. cm.
ISBN-13: 978-1-56947-465-5
ISBN-10: 1-56947-465-6
1. Boxing stories. I. Title
PR9199.4.D383F54 2007
823'.92—dc22   2006036363

10 9 8 7 6 5 4 3 2 1

A great fighter is a man alone on a path.
He must feel that he is the maker, not made.
He must feel that he fathered himself.

—GARY SMITH

'Cause all I ever wanted was just a little
thing—just to be a man.

—CHESTER HIMES

NOW

PROLOGUE

They say a man can change his personality—the basic essence of who or what he is—by five percent. Five percent: the total change any one of us is capable of.

At first it sounds trivial. Five percent, what's that? A fingernail paring. But consider the vastness of the human psyche and that number acquires real weight. Think five percent of the Earth's total landmass, five percent of the known universe. Millions of square acres, billions of light years. Consider how a change of five percent could alter anyone. Imagine dominoes lined in neat straight rows, the world of possibilities set in motion at a touch.

Five percent: everything changes. Five percent: a whole new person. Considered in these terms, five percent really means something. Considered in these terms, five percent is colossal.

I wake in a dark space. Blinking, disoriented, a dream-image lingers: a nameless face split down the center, knotted brain glimpsed through a bright halo of blood.

A tight bathroom. Peeling wallpaper, mildewed tiles. Stripped bare, I wash myself at a stone basin. My body is utilitarian: bone and muscle and skin. A purposeful body, I think of it, though from time to time I miss that old spryness. To look at me, you might believe I entered the world this way.

My legs: crosshatched with scars from machete wounds I took in the northern plantations harvesting sugarcane before moving south to the cities. An arrow-shaped divot is gouged from my right shank: on sleepless nights I'll run a finger over the spot, the hardness of shinbone beneath a quarter-inch of scar tissue.

My chest: networked with razor wounds, mottled with chemical burn scars. Lye fights—our fists wrapped in heavy rope smeared with a mixture of honey and powdered lye. A sand-filled Mekong bottle stands beside the cot; I hammer my stomach for hours, hardening my flesh for combat.

My hands: shattered. Knuckles split in dumdum Xs humped over in skin that shines under the bathroom light. They've been broken—how many times? I've lost count. So brittle I once cracked my thumb opening a bottle of soda.

Blind in one eye: those damn lye fights. My upper incisors driven through my gums, half embedded in soft palate. Cauliflower ears—*jug ears*, my old trainer would've said—and my hearing cuts in and out like a radio on the fritz; when it goes I'll smack the side of my head, the way you would a finicky TV to get the picture back. A raised line runs from the base of my scalp to a point between my eyebrows: my skull was split open on the concrete of an empty oil refinery. An unlicensed medic—there's no other kind around here—wrapped a leather belt around my head to keep the split halves together. This wound healed into a not-quite-smooth seam like blocks of wax heated along their edges and pressed gently together.

They say a man's body is a map of his existence.

I'm shrugging on a pair of floral-print shorts when the telephone rings. It's a warm evening; the air is heavy with the scent of something, though I can't quite place what.

The phone falls silent. I know what the caller wants. I know what night this is.

During World War II the roof of the Boeing aircraft factory outside Seattle was camouflaged to look like a fake city. There were little buildings, the same shape as regular buildings, only about five feet high. The streets were made of burlap; the trees were wire mesh topped with green-painted beach umbrellas. They even had mannequins: mannequin mailmen and milkmen; mannequin housewives pinning laundry on wash lines. A Hollywood set designer oversaw the whole thing. The buildings and houses had depth to them—glimpsed from overhead by a Japanese bomber pilot, it would look like a quiet residential neighborhood. Under this fake city was the factory, where construction went on around the clock. During wartime, a B-17 Flying Fortress rolled off the line every seventy-two hours.

I've come to realize all societies are much like this. On top you've got the world most live in, a safe and sanitary place, airbrushed, a polished veneer—a world I now find as fake as those five-foot buildings and mannequins must have seemed from ground level.

Underneath lies the factory, which few know of and fewer still venture into.

The place where the war machines are built.

The streets rage with bicycles and Tuk-Tuks and pickup trucks. An old woman skewers shark fins on a length of piano wire in the greasy light of a deli. Clusters of shirtless men crouch in fire-gutted alleys passing bottles of Mekong. One shouts as I walk past—catcall or cheer? I've never learned the language.

Young foreign men all around. Talking too loudly, spending too much, laughing at nonsense. Drunk on Mekong, some will return to their rented rooms with cross-dressing locals they've mistaken for women. There was a time when I could count myself one of their number. Their life was my life, their wants my own. But now, recalling the man I once was, it's as though I'm considering someone else altogether.

A figure stands before a metal door set into an alley wall. His face, half shrouded by the lapels of his duster coat, is netted with old razor scars. The nickel-plated hammers of a Rizzini shotgun jut through the folds of his coat.

"You on tonight?"

When I nod the man steps aside.

"What're you waiting for, asshole—the Queen's invite?"

The door is gunmetal gray, set in a brick wall touched black by old fires. I knock. A slot snaps back. A pair of dark considering eyes. The deadbolts disengage.

The hallway is lit by forty-watt bulbs behind wire screens. Cockroaches feast on mildew. I roll my shoulders and snap my neck, limbering. Quick jabs, short puffing breaths. I plant my lead foot the way my trainer instructed years ago: *Pretend a nail's pounded through the damn thing, okay? Turn on that point, now, pivot hard. Work that power up through your feet, legs, hips and arms and hands—bam!*

Another door leads into a prep room the size of a tiger cage. Wooden benches set at intersecting angles. The smell of resin and sweat and wintergreen liniment. A chicken-wire ceiling allows bettors to size us up before placing wagers. They can be real bastards: my scalp is pitted with burns from the Zippo-heated coins they flick through the wire.

The other fighters lounge on benches or pace restlessly. Scars and welts and bruises, missing ears, not a full set of teeth among them. My father once told me to never trust the word of a man whose body was not a little ruined. If there is any truth to that, these are some of the most trustworthy men on earth.

I check out their bodies. That guy's got a slight limp—his left side is weak. That guy's wrist is bent at a peculiar angle—it's been busted once and could bust again.

A fighter known as Prophet comes in. A burn scar in the shape of a crucifix marks his chest, self-inflicted with an acetylene torch. Tattooed above the crucifix: CRY HAVOC. And below: LET SLIP THE DOGS OF WAR.

This is a rough place to fight, but not the roughest. In Brazil, this whippety little bastard locked a jujitsu move on me and pulled my elbow apart—turned the joint into oatmeal. I heard they were tough in Brazil but wanted to see for myself. I won't be going back.

An ancient ragman steps into the room. He's got a bale of hemp rope in his right hand and a bucket of white powder hanging from his left. Nobody fights barehanded here; you can watch a fistfight on any street corner in the city. Spectators crave blood in torrents, disfigurement, death. We fighters oblige.

Concertina wire. Pine tar and busted glass. Turpentine. Razor blades. Tonight our fists will be dipped in *yaa baa*—Thai methamphetamine.

Numbers are drawn. I get #5.

A Spanish fighter sits at my side. His right eye is gone; a ball of knotted flesh sits in its place. He killed the guy who took it, pounding with fists of barbed wire until the other man's head was little more than red mush loosely moored to a stump. Él robo mi ojo, was all he could say afterward. Él robo mi ojo. *He stole my eye.* Sounds so much more poetic in Spanish, don't you think?

On the floor, between my spread legs: a ladybug. They look different on this side of the globe: nearly the size of a dime and bright purple. It lies upon its back, legs knitted like tiny black fingers. When I pick it up its legs unknit and it hangs, weightless, from my thumb. The floor is scattered with dozens of dead ones. What could have drawn so many of them? Whatever they were searching for, it's not here to be found.

I hold my thumb toward the Spaniard, who extends his cupped palm to catch the insect as it tumbles off my ragged thumbnail. We trade smiles—the very nick of time—and he sets it on the bench beside him, where it sits with a deathly stillness.

"Numba ei'!"

The Spaniard stands.

"Numba fi'!"

The arena is wide and low-ceilinged and packed to capacity. Stands rise in tiers from the circular arena floor in the style of a Greek amphitheater. Men in dark sunglasses and silk suits sit beside street gamblers in madras shorts and baseball caps. A blonde with cut-from-the-sky blue eyes sits in the front row; her face is specked with blood.

We fight on white sand trucked in from beaches to the south; it feels so soft beneath my feet. I snap my neck to drain the sinuses and for an instant the fear grips me—*I could die here*—but the emotion is as undefined as bodies at movement in a darkened room.

Scars tough as rawhide adorn the Spaniard's face; the surrounding skin is so tight a few good shots will rip it all apart. He catches me looking and smiles.

There are three signs you're up against a real fighter. They're not what you might think; nothing to do with how big the guy is, or the size of his fists. The three Harbingers are:

1. A calmness, almost a deadness, in his eyes.
2. That he insists upon shaking your hand and makes no effort to crush it.
3. When he asks your forgiveness for what comes next.

If you find yourself outside a bar faced up with a guy who shakes your hand and begs forgiveness before putting up his dukes, my humble suggestion is that you run.

We meet in the center of the ring. The Spaniard bows like a toreador. The crowd's chant is familiar though I've never understood the words. It feels as if I'm dreaming and the dream is also familiar: a dream shot through with the smell of blood.

Sometimes I'll think—often right in the middle of a fight, when I've made a mistake and loosened my guard, in the instant before that fist opens up a part of me—I'll find myself thinking, How? How did I get here? How does a man fall off the civilized slope of the earth, and how far down does that slope go? I'll think of those men I'd see every so often, nameless strangers stepping off a Greyhound bus in the witching hours with nothing but a duffel bag, men with no family or friends who must have made their way down to the factory that is constantly running under the veneer of polite society. I'll think about how every factory needs its workforce.

And I often think about how it all flowed, so ceaselessly and unerringly, from there to here and then to now. I marvel at how absolutely my life was guided upon its new course and wonder: how close are any of us to those moments? How near to our hearts do they lie—behind what doorways, around which corners?

The Spaniard holds his hand out. I raise my own. We touch fists gently.

"Perdóname."

"And you me."

I breathe deep, hold it, and exhale.

And waiting. As ever, waiting.

For the bell.

Then

★

1

Paul Harris turned to catch a fist that smashed the left side of his face along the angular ridge of jaw and rocked him through a padded burgundy door tacked with tiny brass rivets. Busted hinges, a shower of toothpicked wood, and he was reeling out into cold early autumn air.

Wiry weeds touched with frost jutted from sidewalk cracks. Streetlight reflected off office windows, windshields, and beer caps sunken in opaque puddles along the curb. Paul grasped the stalk of a parking meter and hauled himself up. Shock-sweat fused his hand to the chilled metal: when he pulled free, pinpricks of blood welled on his palm.

A pair of rough hands gripped the back of his camel-hair coat and shoved him up against the canopy of a late-model Jeep. His face mashed to the translucent window, Paul's nose filled with the anti-septic, plasticky smell of inflatable pool toys.

A clubbing blow sent him to the ground again. He backed away on his palms and heels, skittering like a sand crab. The world acquired a pinkish tinge, the buildings and streets and cars spun from cotton candy.

His attacker's shoulders were broad and dense with muscle, tapering to a supple waist and lean hips. His boots boomed like hooves on the broken cement.

"Gonna split your wig, bud."

Paul struggled to understand how all this had happened. He'd been to the club before; it was as classy as could be found in his hometown of St. Catharines, a depressed shipbuilding community sprawled along the banks of Lake Ontario. He and his date had come from a production of *The Tempest* in Niagara-on-the-Lake; neither had enjoyed or even quite understood it, but everyone they knew had seen it and they felt compelled. Faith, his date, was skinny, her eyes cored too deeply into her face; the pair of sunken pits between her collarbones were deep enough to collect rainwater. He found her about as interesting as an outdated periodontal health brochure, the sort he might have flipped through in his dentist's waiting room, and he was certain she felt the same about him—not that it mattered, as she was the daughter of one of his father's business cronies. Like feudal times: a sack of gold coins and ten head of cattle to take my daughter off my hands. Except nowadays you got forty percent equity in a chain of gelato parlors and the summer place on Lake Muskoka. How did it all end? Paul could guess: with the bloodlines all fucked, with runny-nosed mongoloids kicking big red balls around the offices of Fortune 500 companies. That's how.

Point being: the club was upscale. A well-stocked wine cellar. A tastefully understated tapas menu: Oysters Rockefeller, Wild Mushroom Croustades with Fennel. And yet here he was being slammed up against an aluminum shopfront, water trickling off the eaves and soaking his hair. This bastard's knuckles pressed into his throat, this asshole's knee driven into his crotch so hard he puked a gutful of single-malt scotch.

And here were heads popping from apartment windows, people occurring in shadowed doorways and from bars.

"Gonna bash your face to fucking pulp."

Strung together into a single word: *Gonnabashyafacetafuckinpulp.*

How the hell did this *happen*? Walk it back to the beginning.

After he and Faith had secured a booth Paul excused himself to take a piss. He ran into Drake Langley, an old prep school classmate. Drake wore a suit of lush dark fabric—padded velour?—that made him look like a sofa cushion. Drake worked for his father, same as Paul worked for his father, same as just about all the guys from school worked for their fathers.

"Hey, hey, hey . . ." Blasted, Drake pawed Paul's jacket like a needy golden retriever. "Did you hear the one," he gulped, "about the guy?"

Paul replied that no, he hadn't heard the one about the guy.

Drake slopped half a mouthful of Macallan down his shirtfront; no matter how expensive the liquor, Paul thought, a cheap drunk is still a cheap drunk. "So this guy, he's living at home with his sickly widower father and he needs a woman to keep him company. Okay?"

Paul nodded, irritated. Did Drake think he was giving a lecture on astrophysics and needed to pause so that Paul could absorb this complex information?

"So he goes to this bar and sees this chick with a rack like—*bam!*" Drake held his hands out a goodly distance from his chest. "And an ass like a Polynesian dancer. So the guy goes up to her and he says, *Right now I'm not much to write home about. But in a month or two my old man is going to kick the bucket and I'm gonna inherit millions.* So the woman goes home with him that night—and four days later she becomes his stepmother!"

Paul managed a weak chortle. Drake's face froze with mortal fear: it was as though he'd come to understand the full implication of the joke and it terrified him. He grabbed Paul's elbow. "You know what I'm gonna do tonight, Harris? I'm gonna take one of these slags home"—the liberal sweep of his arm suggested that the club was brimming with said slags—"and I'm gonna eat her ass like French vanilla ice cream. What do you think of them apples?"

The bathroom attendant was black. Why were they always black? Dressed in a faded olive-tone suit, the guy's skin looked like cheap chocolate—like a fine layer of chalk dust had settled over it. His eyes were yellowed and Paul felt he ought to be home in bed. He looked like an Uncle Tom. Not that Paul would ever call him that; he only meant that if you put the bathroom attendant in a lineup with a bunch of other black guys and asked anyone to pick the one who fit the stereotype, well, this poor guy hit about every note. After pissing he felt poorly for thinking this and left ten bucks in the tip jar.

He returned to find his date in conversation with some townie asshole. The guy blocked the booth; he leaned over the table like a hillbilly tycoon buying up cheap real estate.

"Introduce me to your friend, Faith?" Paul said, slipping past the townie to sit down.

"We've barely introduced—"

"She's being coy." Paul offered his hand. "Paul Harris."

"Todd."

Todd was a stocky unshaven shitkicker. Paul hadn't bothered to look at his feet but assumed they were clad in steel-toed boots; when he moved on, Paul was certain he'd leave a pile of debris behind. He pictured Todd's home: a trailer jacked up on cinderblocks. Engine parts laid out on oil-sodden newspapers. It struck Paul that he was infinitely richer and more successful than this poor slob; the knowledge actually filled him with a bizarre kind of pity.

"You with her?" Todd wanted to know.

"That's beside the point, Todd."

"Paul—"

He raised his hand, shushing her. "Well, Todd—what were you two confabbing about?"

"That's between me and the young lady."

Paul smiled indulgently and drew Faith down to the far end of the booth. "You can't be serious. This troglodyte's got as much personal flair as an unflushed toilet."

She laughed and tugged at his lapel, pulling him close. "Shhh. He'll hear." She was so skinny: cheekbones were shards of flint. A Madison Avenue stick insect.

"You should be ashamed of yourself," he chastised, "for encouraging him. For shame."

Todd the Shitkicker stood there like a goon. As if in expectation that Faith might—what? *Leave* with him? The image of Faith with shitkicker Todd was so absurd that Paul could only visualize it as occurring in a Salvador Dalí painting; in it, Todd's head would be replaced by a pocket watch melted over a tree branch.

"Hey," Todd said to Faith, "I was thinking maybe you'd—"

"Isn't there a toilet that needs snaking somewhere in this city?"

"Paul!"

"I'm kidding. He knows I'm kidding. You know I'm kidding, don't you, Todd?"

"Sure, Paul," the shitkicker said in a voice gone deathly soft. "I love a good joke as much as the next guy."

Paul raised his hands as if caught in a bank heist. "Listen, she's my date—what do you want? I saw you talking and got a little jealous."

A half-truth, if that. Faith was welcome to return tomorrow, find Todd, head back to his trailer, and fuck him senseless on a pile of discarded TV dinner trays.

"Us being buddies now and all," Todd told him, "figure I should tell you to watch your mouth. Otherwise, y'know, someone's liable to stuff a boot in it."

"Are you threatening me, Todd?"

"I'm saying words have consequences, Paul. Like, if I were to call you a faggot cocksucker—that would have consequences, wouldn't it?" He rapped his knuckles on the underside of the table; the sharp *bang* straightened Paul's spine. "Wouldn't it?"

It came then, fierce and unbidden: fear. It stole over the crown of Paul's head, moving under his scalp behind his eyes, cold and hollow. It oozed down his spine into his chest, his groin, pooling in his gut like dark dirty oil. He glanced about to assure himself of his location. Yes. Still this club, these people: *his* people. So why did he feel all shredded inside, shriveled and paralyzed?

Todd nodded to Faith in a way that suggested he'd lost all interest. "I'll leave you to it."

Paul was pissed to have it end on that note. But a larger part of him was just glad to have the shitkicker gone, relieved to find the fear dissipating.

"Why did you talk to him that way?"

Paul ignored Faith's question as one too obvious to merit a reply. He glanced over at the shitkicker's table. Todd and his pals looked like janitors who'd arrived early, waiting for the place to clear so they could break out the mops. He flagged down the waitress and ordered a round of Sex on the Beaches for Todd's table.

"—I'm sorry." He was dimly aware of Faith saying something. "What?"

"A teacup Chihuahua," she said. "I'm getting one."

"Is that so."

"They're adorable. And Versace makes this cute carry-bag for them."

Paul had seen the dogs. Frail, sick-looking things, all papery-eared and bulge-eyed. They looked delicate enough to die of a nosebleed and shivered all the time; perhaps being cooped up in handbags made them petrified of natural light. But if the cover of next month's *Vogue* featured a model with a ferret wrapped around her neck several women of Paul's acquaintance would soon be wearing one. Prada would probably design a ferret-tube to cart the silly fuckers about.

They finished their drinks and stood up. Faith excused herself to use the ladies' room. Paul deliberated whether he should fuck her. Conventional wisdom decreed he snap up whatever was on offer, never knowing when the opportunity might come around again; to do otherwise would be as stupid as a desert wanderer who passes over one waterhole in hopes of finding another when he's thirstier. But it would be the sexual equivalent of a lube job. Pure maintenance.

Such was the pattern of his thoughts when a hand fell upon his shoulder like a rough knighthood, a hand so insistent Paul had no choice but to obey and, turning, saw the shitkicker's face captured in clean profile, that calm and easygoing look on his face as his fist filled Paul's retinas, a flickering ball that burst like a white-hot firework to rock him back on his heels, his hands flying to his face, and when he looked down his fingers were clad in blood. He'd never been punched—maliciously, viciously *punched*—in his quarter-century-plus of life on this planet and all he could do was stare, with a stupid bovine look on his face, at the man who'd popped his cherry.

Todd hit him again. A blinding explosion went off just in back of Paul's eyes as though his brainstem had been dynamited. He had this terrifying sensation of his nose and cheeks crushed into an empty pocket behind the cartilage and bones, a fist driven so deep into his face the pressure pushed his eyes from their sockets to allow a frighteningly unhindered view of his surroundings.

His skull struck the padded leather door with its tiny brass rivets and he was outside, reeling onto the sidewalk.

And even now, with Todd slamming him against the aluminum shopfront, a vestigial part of him refused to believe this was actually happening. Desperately, like a bilge rat to a chunk of flotsam, he clung to the notion of some innate social mechanism whose function should be to prevent all this.

Paul was struck a blow that caught him on the neck; his head caromed off the shopfront. Two teeth thin and smooth as shaved ice pushed between his lips. He was terrified in the manner of a man with absolutely no frame of reference for what he was experiencing.

Run, he told himself. *Just run away*. But he couldn't even move. His mouth flushed with a corroded rusty taste and his bowels felt heavy, as if he'd swallowed an iron plug that was now forcing its way out of him.

His body slid down the aluminum, ribbed metal rucking his shirt up his spine. He spread his hands before his bloodied face.

"I give, okay?" A glistening snot-bubble expanded from his left nostril and burst wetly. "No more, okay? No more." Quietly: "Come on, man—*please*. I'm begging you."

Todd prodded his ass with the steel toe of his boot. "Aren't even going to try? Christ."

The look in Todd's eyes: as if he'd split Paul open and caught a glimpse of what lay inside and it wasn't quite human—everything gone soft and milky and diseased. Todd cleared his throat and spat. Gob landed on Paul's pants, sallow and greasy as a shucked oyster.

Todd strolled back to his buddies lounging at the bar door and exchanged rueful high fives. "Not much fun fighting when you're the only one willing." He was perspiring lightly, every hair in place save a blond lock fallen between his eyes.

Faith exited the bar and spotted him slumped against the shopfront. She reached out to touch him and he shoved her hand away. She studied his face, his lips bloated like sausages set to burst. "Your teeth," she said, casting her eyes about as though to retrieve them. Rock salt had been spread across the wet sidewalk: *everywhere* looked like fucking teeth.

"We should call the police," she said.

"Don't be an idiot."

He spied a pale lip of fat hanging over his trousers—Jesus, was that part of him? Looked like the skin of a maggot. If he unbuttoned his shirt, would he spy his lungs and the pump of his own wasted heart through that rubbery, candle-white skin?

He wanted to find something sharp and go back into the club and slice the shitkicker. Slip up behind him and stab him in the neck. He saw the shitkicker's body laid out on the smooth stone floor of the bar, blood all over everything, over every shape, his face slashed to pieces and one bloodshot eye hanging out, withered like an albino walnut. But he could never do that and the realization served only to deepen his fear, so toxic now it coursed through his veins like battery acid.

"What are we going to do?" Faith asked.

Paul did the only thing that made sense. Standing on legs that trembled like a newborn foal's, sparing not a backward glance, he took off down the sidewalk. She called after him—he distinctly heard the word "chickenshit"—but he didn't let up or look back.

2

Paul dreamed he was lying facedown in stinking mud. He rolled to a sitting position and saw he was in a bunker. He wore a cheap suit and shiny loafers and cufflinks shaped like golf balls. A decapitated head sat on a pole jabbed into the mud; the head was rotted or badly burned and a pair of novelty sunglasses covered its eyes. He peeked over the bunker and saw a field burst apart by artillery shells. Everything was blown through with smoke, but he could make out shapes draped over the razor wire and huge birds with boiled-looking heads pecking at the shapes. He was numb and sore and wanted to puke. A man stepped from the shadows and relief washed over him—it was John Wayne. The Duke wore a flak jacket and pisscutter helmet; a cigar was stuck in the side of his mouth. "We're going over the top. You with us, dogface?" Paul's body went rigid. His nuts sucked into his abdomen like a pair of yo-yos up their strings. "No, I have a . . . business lunch." The Duke got salty. "We got a war to win, peckerwood." "I'd love to make a charitable donation," Paul assured him. The Duke looked like he was staring at a piece of ambulatory dogshit. Paul got scared again. "Is there an orphan I could tend to," he asked, "one who's been wounded by shrapnel?" The Duke stuck his chin out and glared with dull disdain. He pulled a pistol from his holster and shoved Paul into a corner and told him to face it. That's when Paul saw dozens of corpses stacked atop one another by the other wall; they all wore suits and their hands were clean and soft and they had very nice hair. Each had a frosted hole in the perfect center of his forehead. "Can't trust a man who won't fight," the Duke said without much emotion. "This is a mercy."

When the gun barrel pressed to the back of his skull, Paul woke up with a jerk.

Frail angles of rust-colored light fell through the venetian blinds to touch Paul's face. His head felt broken and weak, like it'd been smashed open in the night and its contents spilled over the pillow. His mouth felt blowtorched and the tendons of his neck stretched to their tensile limit, seemingly unable to support the raw ball of his skull. He lay in his childhood room in his parents' house. Surfing posters were tacked to the walls. A glow-in-the-dark constellation decorated the ceiling.

In the bathroom, he consulted his reflection in the mirror: skin dull and blotched, right eye a deep purple, swollen closed like a dark blind drawn against the light. Elsewhere his skin was sickly pale, as though marauding bats had drained the blood from it while he slept. He spread his split lips. Two teeth gone: top left incisor, bottom left cuspid. He poked his gums with his pinkie until blood came.

He stood under the showerhead. The knobs of his spine were raw where he'd slid down the shopfront. He tried jerking off in hopes it might unknit the tension knotting his gut, but it was like trying to coax life out of a rope. In the blood-colored darkness behind his eyelids all he could see was this huge fist, this scarred ridge of knuckles exploding like a neutron bomb.

He carefully patted dry his various lumps and abrasions. He found an old pair of Ray Bans and adjusted them to cover his puffed eye.

The kitchen was a monotone oasis: white fridge and stove, alabaster tile floor, marble countertops. A bay window offered a view of Lake Ontario lying silver beneath a chalky mid-morning sky. The backyard grass was petaled with the season's first frost.

He cracked the freezer door, relishing the blast of icy air that hit his face. In fact, he liked it so much he stuck his entire head in. Frozen air flowed over the dome of his skull.

He rummaged through the fridge. His mother was on the Caspian Sea Diet. Dieters must subsist upon edibles found in and around the Caspian basin: triggerfish, sea cucumbers, drab kelps, crustaceans. The diet's creator—a swarthy MD with a face like a dried testicle—cited the uncanny virility of Mediterraneans, evidenced by the fact that many continued to labor as goatherds and pearl divers late into their seventies.

Paul's search yielded nothing one might squarely define as edible: a quivering block of tofu, a glazy-eyed fish laid out across a chafing dish, what looked to be bean sprouts floating in a bowl of turd-colored water.

He shoved aside jars of Cape Cod capers and tubs of Seaweed Health Jelly. "What the . . . *fuck*." He slammed the fridge door. On the kitchen island: Christmas cards.

His mother got cracking on them earlier each year. She sent off hundreds, licking envelopes until her mouth was syrupy with mucilage. The cards were pure white with gold filigree and the raised outline of a bell. A stack of pine-scented annual summations sat beside them: SEASON'S GREETINGS FROM HARRIS COUNTY!

His own summation read:

Paul is still living at home and we're so happy to have him, but lately he's been talking about finding his own place, leaving Jack and I empty nesters.

That was it? A year gone by and all his mother could say was that he was looking for his own place? A cowl of paranoia descended upon him; he considered scribbling something else, a flagrant lie if need be—*Paul was voted one of Young Economist's "Up and Comers Under 30"* or *Paul recently returned from a whirlwind seven-city business junket* or *Paul is in talks with Singapore Zoo officials to bring Ling Si, a giant panda, on an exhibition tour of Niagara's wine region*—anything, really, to prove to all the distant aunts and uncles, the unknown business acquaintances and second cousins twice removed, that he was going places.

He headed into the living room. The sofa was white, like the rest of the room and like most of the house. Soothing, artful white. His mother and father's sofa in his mother and father's living room in his mother and father's house, where he still lived. The floors were new, the appliances so modern as to verge upon space age: no creaks or ticks or rattles. Paul sat on the sofa in the deadening silent white.

Closing his eyes, he pictured shitkicker Todd's trailer—Paul wasn't sure he lived in a trailer, but it seemed entirely plausible—aflame, the cheap tin walls glowing and bowling trophies melting like birthday candles until suddenly the bastard crashed through the screen door, a burning effigy. Next he saw the entire trailer park on fire—why the fuck not?—occupants smoked from their mobile shanties, their macaroni-casserole-*TV-Guide* lives, running around waving flame-eaten arms and the air reeking of fried hogback.

A flashback from last night tore the fragile fabric of his daydream: a huge fat fist the size of a cannonball, the skin black as a gorilla's, rocketed at his face.

"God*damnit!*"

He struck the sofa cushion. The punch was weak but ill-placed: his wrist bent at an awkward angle and he yelped. He hopped up, shaking his hand; he booted the sofa but his kick was clumsy and he jammed his toe. Gritting his teeth, grunting, he lay upon the Persian carpet. His body quaked with rage.

Paul often found himself in this state: anger bubbling up from nowhere, a teeth-clenching, fist-pounding fury. But it was undirected and one-dimensional and lacking either the complexities or justifications of adult anger. More like a tantrum.

He nursed his hand and drummed his heels on the carpet. His cellphone chirped. One of his asshole friends calling to dredge the gory details of last night's misadventure. Or his father, wondering why he wasn't at work yet.

Paul headed to the kitchen, popped his cellphone into the garburator, and flipped the switch. The gears labored, regurgitating shards of shiny silver casing into the sink; a sharp edge of plastic shot up and struck Paul's forehead. He twisted a spigot and washed everything down, then picked up the kitchen phone and dialed a cab.

Paul followed the cobblestone path alongside a boxwood hedge past a marble fountain: an ice-glazed Venus riding a conch shell sidesaddle. Early autumn fog blew in off the lake, mantling the manor's roofline. It was much too large for its three inhabitants, but Paul's father held a tree-falling-in-the-forest outlook with regard to wealth: *If you're rich and nobody can tell, well, are you really rich?*

The cab picked him up outside the estate grounds. Paul gazed out the window as they headed downtown to retrieve his car. They drove along the banks of Twelve Mile Creek, the squat skyline of downtown

St. Catharines obscured by fog. Roadside slush was grayed with industrial effluvia pumped from the brick smokestacks of the GM factory across the river.

Paul's car, a 2005 BMW E90, was parked around the corner from the club. The car was his father's gift to him from last Christmas. There was a parking ticket on the windshield. He tore it in half between his teeth and spat the shreds into the puddle along the curb.

He stopped for a red light on the way to the winery, idling beside a Dodge pickup. A junkyard mutt was chained to the truckbed. Paul locked eyes with the dog. The mutt's muddy eyes did not blink. Its lips skinned back to reveal a row of discolored teeth. Paul looked away and fiddled with the radio.

He accelerated past big box stores and auto-body shops and gas stations out into the country. The land opened into vast orchards and groves. Peach and apple and cherry trees planted in neat straight rows, trunks wrapped in cyclone fence.

Ten minutes passed before it hit him.

He'd looked away. He'd broken eye contact first.

He'd lost a stare-down . . .

. . . to a *dog*.

The Ripple Creek winery was spread across fifty acres of land overlooked by the Niagara Escarpment. Paul's folks had planted the vines themselves some twenty-five years ago.

Paul's father, Jack Harris, had fallen in love with Paul's mother, Barbara Forbes, the daughter of a sorghum farmer whom Jack first saw slinging sacks of fertilizer into the bed of a rusted pickup at the Atikokan Feed'n' Seed, and whom he saw again at the annual Summer Dust-Off, where she danced with raucous zeal to washboard-and-zither music. He fell in love with her because at the time he felt this

coincidental sighting was fateful—later both came to realize that
they'd lived little more than thirty miles apart, but in northern
Ontario it was possible to go your whole life and never meet your
neighbor two towns distant. They had made love behind the barn
while the Dust-Off raged on, in a field studded with summer flowers
on a muffet of hay left by the baling machine. Afterward they lay
together with hay poking their bodies like busted drinking straws,
feeling a little silly at the unwitting cliché they'd made of themselves:
gormless bumpkins deflowered in a haypile. Even the dray horse
sharing the field with them looked vaguely embarrassed on their
behalf.

After graduating high school Jack spent the next year tending his
father's cornfields. He married Barbara and she moved into the
foreman's lodgings on Jack's father's farm. Barely a month had passed
before Barbara began to chafe under the deadening monotony.

One night Jack returned from the fields, filthy and itching from
corn silk, to find his wife in the kitchen. The table was piled high with
books on wine making.

"What's all this?"

"What else would you have me do all day," Barbara wanted to know,
"crochet?"

Jack knew not a thing about wine. He favored Labatt 50 from pint
bottles.

"You want wine, I'll head to the LCBO and pick up a bottle."

"I want wine, *I'll* head to the LCBO and buy *myself* a bottle."
Barbara closed a book on the tip of her finger, keeping the page
marked. "We might try making our own."

She told him that the soil of southern Ontario, much like that of
southern France, was well suited to grape growing. But wine . . . it
conjured images of beret-wearing Frenchmen zipping down country
lanes in fruity red sports cars. An altogether foreign image, Jack

thought, leagues removed from his tiny foreman's cabin on the edge of
the Ontario cornfields. Then again, why not? He knew how to grow
corn; why not grapes? And a gut instinct told him that a curve might
be developing; if they hopped on now they might land a few steps
ahead of it.

One afternoon they headed down to the Farmers' Credit Union and
applied for a small-business loan. With it they purchased a homestead
on fifteen acres in Stoney Creek, a farming community in southern
Ontario. Fruit country: local farmers grew peaches, cherries,
blueberries. Jack was the only one growing grapes; this incited a
degree of neighborly concern. *Concords?* other farmers asked. *Juice
grapes?* When Jack told them no, a Portuguese variety called Semillon,
the farmers shook their heads, sad to see a young fool leading his
family down the path to financial ruin.

Jack was in the fields every day that first spring, pounding posts
and stringing vines. He was out in the cool dawn hours with scattered farmyard lights burning in the hills and valleys. He was out
in the afternoon as the sun crested high over the escarpment, its
heat burning through the salt on his skin to draw it tight. He was
out in the evening with the wind wicking moisture off the soil until
it was like tilling shale. Jack's boots became so worn he padded
them with newspapers; his feet turned black from the ink. For
weeks they ate nothing but peaches: at night, Jack snuck into his
neighbor's groves to fill his jacket pockets. At night, they collapsed
into bed, newlyweds too exhausted to do what might have come
naturally.

That first winter Jack made the rounds of local bars and restau-
rants. Though many owners expressed skepticism at the idea of southern Ontario wine—*What's your next plan*, one said, *growing taters on
the moon?*—Jack's salesmanship resulted in a flurry of orders.
Springtime found them back in the fields. When Barb saw that first

yellow bud flowering on the vine she broke into a giddy jig that collapsed her husband into reckless laughter.

It was a success from the outset. The wine was clean and crisp, made distinctive by the soil of a virgin growing region. The first vintage sold out by mid-winter; retail orders tripled. Word of their success spread, and the farmers who'd scoffed at Jack's plan were soon selling their own farms to those hoping to copy Jack's business model. Ripple Creek became the first, and was still the most successful, winery in Ontario.

Paul was four years old when the family moved from their tiny home in the field—which was really no longer a field but rather an estate—into their massive gated manor.

The winery offices were built on the foundation of Paul's childhood home: his father, no teary-eyed nostalgic, had had it bulldozed. The foyer was paneled with oak slats bellying outward: visitors often remarked that they felt as though they were inside a wine cask—indeed, the intended effect.

Their receptionist, Callie, was pale with long blond hair, skinny but in a good way and cute. Her perfume held the bracing aroma of a car air freshener. Paul often fantasized about her: passing each other in the narrow hallway, their bodies brush accidentally-on-purpose and next thing they're on each other, kissing and clutching, ducking into the supply room where he gives it to her bent over the photocopier.

"Mr. Harris," she said. "Are you all right?"

"Not to worry. A mild misunderstanding."

"You were in a fight?"

Paul didn't care for her tone of voice: incredulous, as if he'd told her his night had been spent spinning gold out of hay.

"There was a . . . an altercation."

He couldn't quite bring himself to say *fight*. The word implied an exchange of blows, mutual bloodshed. *Beating* better expressed the reality. Mauling. Shellacking.

"Are you hurt?"

"It's nothing much. You should see the other guy."

"Is that so?"

Paul was filled with a sudden dreadful certainty that Callie had been there last night. She'd witnessed the whole sad affair and now could only smile as he stood there lying through his teeth.

His office was located off the lobby. On the desk: Macintosh computer and blotter, German beer stein, three high school rowing trophies bought at a thrift store. These were his father's idea, whose own trophies—for wrestling, and legitimately won—sat on his own desk in a much bigger office down the hall. His father thought athletic trophies accorded a desk, and by proxy its owner, that Go-Get-'Em attitude.

The nameplate on his desk read PAUL HARRIS, and under his name, in small engraved letters, his title: ORGANIZATIONAL ADVISER. When he'd questioned his father regarding the precise duties of an OA, he was told it was crucial that he "keep his fingers in a lot of pies, organizationally speaking." But since his father had his own fingers in every important pie at Ripple Creek, Paul's were relegated to inconsequential ones: the "Refill the Toner Cartridge" pie; the "Reorder Staff Room Coffee but Not the Cheap Guadeloupian Stuff Because It Gives His Dad the Trots" pie.

His nameplate may as well have read TOUR GUIDE. Every so often a buyer happened by and Paul was ordered to show him around. He'd lead a tour through the winery with its high cathedral ceilings and halogen lights, pointing out the presses and pumps and hissing PVC tubes, rapping the stainless steel kettles and commenting on their sturdy craftsmanship. He'd lift the lid on a boiler and stir its dark contents with a stained wooden paddle, remarking how the process had come a long way from some Sicilian bambino stomping grapes with her dirty feet. This usually elicited a laugh and soon the tour would wind back to the foyer, where his father was waiting to usher the buyer into his office.

How was he expected to learn anything—osmosis?

When bored—this was every day, vaguely all day—Paul would shut his eyes, lay his head on the blotter, and craft elaborate fantasies. Most frequent was the one where his mother and father were slaughtered by vicious street thugs, spurring Paul to embark upon a *Death Wish*–style killing spree. Except instead of affluent winery owners his folks were hardworking firefighters, and Paul became Rex Appleby, a tough-as-nails cop hardened by the mean streets of his youth. In the final and most satisfying scene, Paul/Rex staggers from the gang's hideout with a switchblade sticking out from his shoulder and his shirt torn open to display his totally buff abs. He's carrying a gas can, trailing a line of gasoline across the lawn. A thug crawls to the front door, his face bashed to smithereens, and, snarling like a dog, he aims a pistol at Rex's back. Rex flicks the flywheel on a burnished-chrome Zippo and drops it in the shimmer of gasoline. A line of fire races toward the house and the thug screams *Nooooo!* as a fireball mushrooms into the twilight. A cinematic pan shot captures Appleby striding from the wreckage in super-slow motion, unblinking and *ultra*-cool.

"Son, oh son of mine."

Jack Harris stepped into the office. He paused in the doorway, a framed daguerreotype: tall and thickly built, dressed in a suit that hung in flattering lines, jaw and cheeks ingrained with a blue patina of stubble.

He tapped the Rolex Submariner strapped to his wrist. "Make sure the damn thing's still ticking," he said. "Or perchance you're operating on Pacific Standard time, in which case you're hours early and I applaud your dedication. But if, like me, your watch reads eleven-thirty, you, child of my loins, are late."

It was laughable, the very suggestion that it mattered whether Paul arrived early, late, or at all. What was the point of his being there—were break-room coffee supplies running at dangerously low levels?

Paul removed the Ray Bans. "Extenuating circumstances."

"Yee-*ouch*. That's a beaut."

Jack tilted his son's head up and poked the blackened flesh with the tip of a blunt, squared-off finger.

Paul pushed it away. "Lay off, will you? I'm not a grape—don't need to squeeze the juice out of me."

"That's a blue ribbon winner." Jack set a haunch on the desk's edge. "How'd it happen?"

"Fell down a flight of stairs."

"Those stairs knock your teeth out, too? That's one mean-spirited staircase; tell me where it is so I can avoid it."

Jack, veteran of many a low-county barfight, was evidently unmoved by his son's state. Sometimes a man needed to get out there and chuck a few knuckles—it was cathartic. Afterward the winner bought the loser a pint.

"You planning to see a doctor?"

Paul waved the question off. "I possess inner resilience. I am Zen."

Jack nodded. "Well, it's like they say in poker, son: can't win them all, otherwise it'd be no fun when you did."

"Who says I lost?"

Jack laughed. Over the years he'd developed what Paul thought of as his Businessman's Laugh: boisterous and patently phony, it began as a Kris Kringle-ish chortle before segueing into an ongoing staccato hack that sounded like a Nazi submachine gun. *Oooohohohoho-aka-aka-ak-ak-ak!* His father turned it on and off at will, like a faucet. On those rare occasions when Paul found himself among businessmen with every-body's fake laughs ricocheting off the walls, he got the feeling he was deep in the forest primeval surrounded by screeching monkeys.

Jack's mirth subsided. "Well, if the other guy lost I guess the police'll be showing up any minute now—you must've murdered him."

"You're a laugh riot."

"Speaking of laugh riots, that client you showed around yesterday, did you say that bambino line—the dirty feet thing?"

"I guess."

"Well then that was awful dumb. The guy's Italian."

"He say something?"

"Yeah, he said something—why'd I bring it up, he didn't say some-thing?"

Paul shrugged. "Some people like the joke."

"Who, some people?" When Paul didn't reply: "Idiots, that's who. It's a lead balloon."

Paul was getting pointers from a man who trafficked heavily in knock-knock jokes and dried-up puns: *Hey, did you hear about the guy whose whole left side was cut off? He's all right now. Oooohohohoho-aka-aka-ak-ak-ak!*

"Ah, what does it matter?" Paul wanted to know. "Some pissant buyer who owns a pissant boozer in Welland." He snorted. "Who drinks wine in *Welland*? Grape juice cut with antifreeze is more like it. I fail to view it as a big loss."

His father kept his gaze on the floor for several seconds before tilting his chin toward him. His eyes were a pair of hard wet stones.

"We exist but for the grace and patronage of our buyers. Whether it's a hotel chain or a family-run restaurant, we treat them all with the same respect—you get me?"

Paul nudged his Ray Bans down over his eyes. "I get you."

"Take those off while I'm speaking to you."

Paul leaned back in his chair and knitted his hands behind his head. "Take those . . . *off.*"

Paul took the sunglasses off. "There. Satisfied?"

Jack's expression attested he wasn't at all satisfied. "Now tell me: who do we work for?"

"Oh, come off it."

"Who do we work for?"

"The buy*er.*"

"You got it, Pontiac."

They stared at each other across the desk. Paul saw a man who had never grown into his wealth; a man who'd never forget how his feet looked stained with newspaper ink. What did Jack see? Perhaps something he couldn't quite reconcile: his own flesh and blood, yet at the same time a deeply mystifying creature who stood outside his understanding. A son who'd been given everything—higher education, a life of the mind—and yet frequently struck him as frail and useless. And while he loved Paul deeply, Jack couldn't help but think this was not at all the son he'd envisioned.

"How was your date last night?"

"How do you figure?"

"That Faith is pretty sweet, isn't she? Her dad's done well for himself. She'll inherit quite a fortune." Jack lowered his voice on the last word, as though he were detailing some seductive quality of her physique. "Nice ass, too."

Paul groaned. "Don't talk to me about her ass."

"Take a bite out of it, like a juicy apple—*rowf*!"

"Oh, my . . . god."

Jack chuckled, easing himself off the desk. "Ah, come off it—your old man's married, not dead." He frowned. "Get your damn teeth fixed, will you? Look like you ought to be offering hayrides through Appalachia."

The offices connected to the winery down a stone corridor.

Paul walked down rows of gleaming steel tanks. Back in high school he'd snuck in here with his buddies; they tapped the spigots and guzzled Merlot until their teeth were stained the color of mulberries before stumbling out into the vineyard to reel through the darkened rows. The evidence was damning—smashed glasses on the winery floor, vines trampled by clumsy drunken feet—and surely his father had known, but his only comment was that the Angel's Share had been uncommonly high those seasons.

A door gave onto a small portico overlooking the vineyard. In the summertime it was a spectacular view: vines unfurling over the gullies and rises in lines planted straight as the hairs on a doll's scalp. On early spring nights you could actually hear them growing: a faint creaking like worn leather stretched over a pommel.

A group of men moved along the trellis lines at the vineyard's far edge.

Every spring Paul's father hired a crew of Caribbean fieldworkers. He wasn't the only one: most Niagara wineries hired crews from Jamaica, Cuba, Haiti, Ecuador, supplementing this core with university students who were generally shiftless and unreliable, prone to begging off on sunny days better spent at the beach. Paul once accompanied his father to Pearson airport to pick up a crew of pickers. They'd shared the Arrivals lounge with the owners of several local wineries, and as the pickers disembarked, calls of *Pillittieri crew, here!* and *Stonechurch, over here!* rang out while the workers stood around, dazed and jet-lagged, trying to recall the name of the winery that had hired them.

Today they were picking frozen grapes for ice wine. Winemakers waited until frosts hardened the grapes into withered purple pellets before harvesting.

"I thought you guys might like some help," he told them.

Nervous glances passed between the pickers. The owner's kid standing there in his eight-hundred-dollar suit. Was he joking? White folks had such an odd sense of humor.

Paul cinched a red kidney-shaped bucket to his hip. The black nylon strap, crusted with dirt and crushed grape skins, left muddy streaks on his jacket. A picker with a mess of dreadlocks pinned atop his head said, "Is okay, okay," a gentle dissuasion, "go on back, mahn."

The cold drew Paul's face in, thinned it down, tightened the skin to the bone. Anger twined around his brain, a thread fine as catgut slowly tightening. What the hell were they looking so damn sullen for—he was offering help. His father owned the goddamn place, he'd flown them up here and wrote their checks, and if Paul wanted to pick a few grapes he could fucking well pick grapes.

"Where should I start?"

The guy glanced at the others, shrugged, pointed to a far row.

Paul worked his way down the trellis line, stumbling over the frozen earth, knocking his bucket with a knee, wincing. Grapes hung in shriveled clusters, touched with a glaze of frost that looked like powdered sugar. They landed in the bucket with a metallic clink. Some broke open: their insides resembled a geode, all those sparkling sugars. The sweat on his back and chest cooled, sending a chill through his body. Vine ends punched through his fingertips like blunt needles.

A picker crossed over the rows and gave Paul his toque: bright orange with SUNOCO woven across the front, topped with an orange and white pompom. It stunk of dirt and sweat and of the picker himself. Paul couldn't recall the last time he'd worn clothes that weren't solely his own; he'd never worn a black person's clothes, not once. The picker made Paul hold out his hands while he wrapped strips of duct tape around his fingers to protect them from the sharp vines. He wrapped with his head down: Paul glimpsed his shaven head pitted with gouges and dents and a scar that curled halfway round his skull. He wondered how the man acquired those wounds: accidents, surgeries, fights? That night, before falling asleep, he would pass a hand over his own scalp, dismayed to find it smooth and featureless as an egg.

Wind kicked up from the west, blowing grit across the fields. The pickers bundled up in scarves and tattered parkas; one drew a pair of ski goggles down over his eyes.

He dragged his body down the rows, arms and legs and joints aching, socks glued to his feet with blood and burst blisters. He emptied his bucket into a hopper and stumbled back into the field, momentarily relieved from the constant burden at his hip. But soon the bucket filled and though he felt his will deserting he pushed on, whiting out his mind, thinking not of pain or relief or other options.

Didn't every organism by nature seek the easiest pathway to survival? Then what of the organism reared in an environment without predators or obstacles, its every need provided? Paul pictured a flabby boneless creature, shapeless, as soft and raw as the spot under a picked scab.

In some religions it was a sin for a man to die without the knowledge of how much suffering he could endure.

When the sun dipped behind the pines of the escarpment, Paul carted his final bucket to the hopper. His shoes were ruined, his pants caked in mud. He became aware of the powerful funk of his body and relished that smell.

The pickers sat around a fire stoked in the rusted rim of an old tractor tire. An urn of coffee perked on a charred grill above the flames and one of them poured Paul's measure into a beaten tin cup. They sat in the lengthening twilight enclosed by flat autumn fields. The coffee was so strong it stung his gums where they no longer moored teeth. He gave the toque back to the young man who'd lent it, then took the

Ray Bans from his shirt pocket and handed them over too. It no longer concerned him who saw his pulped eye or busted mouth.

He waved goodnight and set off across the cool evening rows. Reaching the winery he found the doors locked. Callie and his father had gone home for the night.

Paul keyed the BMW's ignition and pulled onto the road. He drove past orchards and sod farms and cows sleeping along barbed-wire fences. For a two-mile stretch all light vanished as he drove under a moonless sky. The eyes of feral night creatures flashed in roadside gullies.

He drove on across a one-lane bridge spanning the QEW, over the isolated headlights of travelers driving south into the city, a trail of taillights twisting north to Toronto. The heater's warmth restored feeling to his fingers.

Driving too fast, Paul slewed into the shale of the breakdown lane. He tromped the brake pedal but the front end slid over the culvert and slammed into an iced-over ditch. The airbag deployed: a moon-white zit exploding into his face.

Paul sat with his face buried in the silken skin of the airbag. Something was burning, wiring most likely, the smell like a blazing iron scorching linen. He considered going to sleep: the airbag made a comfortable enough pillow. But then he considered the possibility of a ruptured gas tank, pictured a greasy orange fireball billowing into the night.

He gave the door a boot and stepped out. His loafers slipped in the ditch. He went down on his ass, cracking his head on the doorframe. He sat in the frozen mud with his feet in ditch water. A rime of ice slashed his trousers and cut into the backs of his calves. The air reeked of engine coolant. The BMW's grille butted a patch of crushed cattails.

Craning his neck, he saw amidst the cattails the squat outline of the tree stump that had decimated his car. He had no means of calling for a tow truck and felt mildly regretful for having garburated his cellphone.

On the other side of the ditch lay a cornfield. He recalled a movie where the characters walked into a cornfield and into new life. It was a pleasant thought. To become something else, a whole new person. No money or name or past or worries or hunger—a solitary wanderer upon the country's heat-shimmered highways, its open-topped boxcars filled with chicken feed and baled pulp, its slashes of wilderness, its lightning storms and lost spaces. He'd befriend a dog with two-tone eyes and together they could fight small-town corruption. . . .

Then it dawned on him what a stupid notion it was. Walk into a cornfield and vanish. Ride the rails with a crime-fighting dog. What was he, an idiot?

He hauled himself from the ditch. It couldn't be more than a few degrees above freezing. He considered the possibility of dying somewhere along this isolated country lane. He pictured some gormless dirt farmer coming across his body tomorrow morning: Paul Harris in his dirt-caked suit and two-hundred-dollar loafers, frozen stiff in mid-stride with a rigor-mortis boner tenting his trousers. Ole Popsicle Paul Harris with a snot icicle hanging from his schnozz.

Shoving his hands deep in his pockets and hunching his shoulders, he set off. He had only a vague notion of how far it might be. But, if not resigned to his fate, he was at least accepting of whatever it might hold.

3

obert Tully woke in the cool exhaust-scented morning. He reached blindly for clothes he'd laid out the evening before, laced his sneakers with sleep-clumsy fingers. Coming downstairs, he misjudged the second-to-last step and stubbed his toe, cursing softly. Water pipes clattered behind the thin walls. The small bedroom off the kitchen was empty: his uncle was either pulling an all-nighter at the Fritz or already at Top Rank. He pulled a sweatshirt off its hook in the front hall, tugging the hood over his head and cinching the drawstrings.

A clear fall morning, air thick with a silvery chemical smell borne down from the SGL Carbon plant along Hyde Park Boulevard. He ran north on 24th, past abandoned shopping carts and junked cars with garbage bags taped over shattered windows, old tires and cast-off water tanks rusting in the weeds. He juked around spots where the sidewalk buckled and lapped, on past bodegas with ads for Wonder Bread and menthol Kents taped to bulletproof windows and stores without names: just neon signs blinking L-I-Q-U-O-R.

He turned west on Pine Avenue, warming up, perspiration beading on his forehead and below his eyes. At the corner of Pine and Portage a wrecker's crane sat immobile on the remnants of a pizza joint shut by the health authority. Always plenty of demolition going on: buildings torn down and rubble carted away, but nothing new ever put up. Empty lots dotted the streets and avenues, lifeless but for the profusion of weeds. It was as though a consortium of concerned citizens was buying up the neighborhood, bulldozing the homes and shops, sterilizing one block at a time in hopes that someday they might start over fresh.

Robert had a good sweat going by the time he hit Main. Running on the wet grass bordering the sidewalk, shadowboxing, flashing quick left jabs and the occasional right cross. Cars and trucks fled by on the double-lane road, people heading to work at factories or outlet malls. In the early light he made out the Rainbow Bridge as a harp of steel and concrete spanning the surging river.

He rested for a minute at the Niagara Aquarium. Ptarmigans had built nests on outcrops along the river's sheer cliff face, cobbled together from sedge grass and foil burger jackets and neon drinking straws. Closer to the falls, on the Canadian side, a sandy inlet known as Long Point sat hemmed by spidery oak trees. Rob's uncle Tommy said that back in 1858, steamboats filled with thugs, thieves, gunmen, and other so-called sportsmen crossed the river in the dead of night to watch John C. Heenan and John Morrissey fight for the American championship. They fought at Long Point since, ironically, boxing was banned in America at the time. Heenan—"The Sapulpa Plasterer"—the champ, suffered from a festering leg ulcer, which bellied the hopes of Morrissey and his backers. They fought bareknuckle, hands soaked in walnut juice to toughen the skin. The ring was pitched in the shifting sands and the men fought twenty-eight rounds. Morrissey flattened Heenan with an uppercut to open the twenty-ninth, knocking him cold; *administering the quietus*, as sportswriters of the day might've written. Rob's uncle showed him an artist's rendering of the fight: Morrissey with his wilted handlebar mustache and upraised arms, Heenan's face like a savage tomato cradled in the arms of his seconds while spectators in stovepipe hats and dueling jackets seethed outside the ring, brandishing pistols and daggers and clubs. *A Brutal Close to the Heenan–Morrissey Mill*, the caption read.

Rob continued south down Main, past boarded shopfronts and dusty antique stores, peepshow theaters with opaque windows and nightclubs advertising DRINK ALL NITE FOR ONE LOW PRICE. The sun rose over the falls, lighting the spume; it looked like the sparkling space above fresh-poured soda.

Top Rank was located in the basement of Shaw's Discount Furnishings. You will rarely find a ground-level boxing club: they're always in basements and refurbished cellars, dank subterranean chambers where men gather to study the edicts of hurt. No sign above the entryway: unless you were a boxer, knew a boxer, or paused to consider the procession of sweaty men who came and went at all hours of the day, you'd have no idea of its existence.

Rob skipped lightly down the littered concrete stairs, walking beneath exposed joists and sewage pipes padded with strips of unraveling friction tape. The walls were hung with photos of famous and not-so-famous pugilists: Ali and Holmes and Liston hung beside unknown warriors Jackson Buff, Chuck "The Bayonne Bleeder" Wepner, Mushy Callahan, Chief Danny Thunderheart.

The place was quiet at this hour of morning: a few groggy boxers shuffled around the slick concrete floor. Sickles of sunlight poured through the cracked casement windows, picking up a patina of dust motes suspended in the air. Heavybags hung like slabs of meat. A black welterweight shadowboxed in the glow of a single fluorescent tube.

Rob's uncle Tommy was getting dressed in the change room.

A few years ago, Rob went through a phase where he'd read a ton of hard-boiled detective novels. Anytime a "goon" character was introduced—a not-so-bright kneecapper with "the rough dimensions of an icebox"—Rob pictured his uncle. But seeing as how outside of a boxing ring Tommy exhibited a docility that verged on pathological, the only true similarities were physical. The story of Tommy's long and not particularly successful career was written all over his face: buckle-nosed and egg-eared, his left eyelid dropping from a dead nerve to give him the look of a man caught in perpetual half-wink. *A face hard enough to blunt an ax*, the gym bums said of it.

"Morning, lazybones."

"Lazybones?" Rob peeled a sweat-soaked shirt over his head to reveal a muscle-corded torso. "You weren't anywhere to be seen when I got up—all-nighter at the Fritz?"

"I was on a roll, Robbie. Then I pushed all my chips in on a pair of ladies when the other guy's holding kings." Tommy shook his head. "Gotta get your money in on ladies, am I right?"

Robert slipped into gym togs and stabbed his feet into boxing boots. A gloom fell over him, as it so often did at this time in the morning; a gloom brought about by the knowledge that while his schoolmates slept in warm beds he would soon step into the ring to get his nose bloodied and lips split, bashing away at some opponent until the bell rang.

Tommy said, "I thought maybe you would be tired, y'know, from staying out late with ole Katey-pie."

"You know it's not like that. We're friends."

"Friends, uh? That what you kids're calling it nowadays?"

"Who're you sparring with?" Rob said.

"Our boy wants to change the subject, I see." Tommy finished wrapping his hands, butted his fists together, rose to the sink. "Louie Scarpella, heavyweight from Buffalo. Trainer wants to work his guy against a flatfooted grinder and thought I fit the bill. You imagine that, Robbie? He says it to my face." Tommy rubbed his pancaked nose with a closed fist, pinched one nostril shut and blew a string of snot into the basin. "Right to my face like that."

"So go knock his guy's block off."

"You know that's not how it works. My job's to give Scarpella a lift—raise his spirits. I knock him on his ass, his trainer holds out on my fee."

Tommy twisted the spigot and rinsed the sink. He stared at his reflection and blinked, as if somehow surprised at the man he caught staring back. He drove a Bobcat model 13E tow-motor at the Niagara Industrial Park, a string of corrugated tin warehouses off Highway 62A. His fellow workers were fat and balding, high school heroes gone to seed. During piss breaks, standing at the long line of porcelain urinals, Tommy's nose would wrinkle at a smell that, to him, indicated dire maladies: prostate trouble, gallstones, urinary infection, sick excretions from old bodies. It drove him to the point where he'd pissed in a Dixie cup and sniffed, making sure it wasn't his own sickness he was smelling.

Tommy had boxed since the age of ten. He grew up in the gym. He loved every part of it: the training and roadwork, the sparring, the fight. He was getting older and his body didn't react the way it used to. His mind told him what moves to make but his reflexes couldn't follow through. But he trained hard and kept in fighting shape to take a match on short notice—because, hey, you just never knew.

"How many rounds you getting in?" Rob asked him.

"Five." Tommy wiped his fingers on his gray trunks. "Unless Scarpella punches himself out before that."

"He that out of shape?"

"I'll keep it light; drag it out to four, at least."

Tommy's professional record was 28-62-7. It once stood at 22-1, belted out against tomato cans handpicked by his brother and manager, Reuben, Rob's father. He'd fought in local clubs throughout the state and across state lines in Akron, Scranton, Hartford. His only big-money fight had been at Madison Square Garden, on the under-card of the Holmes–Cooney tilt in '83. Tommy squared off against Sammy "Night Train" Layne, a slippery southpaw from South Philly; Tommy's shove-and-slug style, effective against unskilled biffers, was badly exposed by the ducking and weaving Layne. By the end of the eleventh round Tommy's face was cut into ribbons, a severed artery above his left eye bringing forth blood in spurts. After that match-makers lost interest and Reuben had a rough time lining up fights.

From there Tommy turned into a trial horse, the sort of workman who'll take a stiff belt without folding. A good horse will give you ten solid rounds but never pose a serious threat to a contender. Tommy was in demand due to his rep as a bleeder: by the end of a fight he was a mess and his opponents came off looking like executioners. Until a mandatory pre-fight CAT scan showed a blood vessel had snapped inside his head. The NY boxing commission revoked its sanctioning license, citing medical unfitness.

Reuben Tully poked his head into the change room. Squat and pot-bellied, he was the polar opposite of his younger brother. He wore a rumpled button-down shirt and snap-brim hat; his short hair was shaved up the side of his head like a zek in some Russian internment camp.

"What's this, social hour?" Reuben banged a fist on the lockers, set the brass locks jumping. "Ass in gear, Robbie. And Tommy, that big shitkicker from Buffalo's waiting."

"Tell him to hold his water." Tommy snapped off a few ponderous jabs and smiled over at his nephew. "Time to make the donuts."

Rob rose to the sink and studied his face hemmed by a red hood: unbroken nose, forehead peppered with acne, eyes of such pale blue his father joked they must be unscrewed nightly and soaked in bleach. Some days he felt handsome, or at least that he was working his way toward it. Yet he knew he was one hard punch away from a busted nose or split brow or knocked-out tooth. No way you can eat leather round after round and expect to keep your looks.

Fruit bats squeaked and fluttered in the dark roost between locker-room ceiling and furniture-store floor. Rob stared down at his hands: thick and calloused, joints swollen from all the rough treatment. Old man's hands. He was only sixteen, but at times felt years older.

"Robbie!"

"Keep your shirt on," he whispered to the mirror. Then: "Coming!"

Top Rank lit up now, vapor tubes popping and fritzing as they warmed. Three huge ceiling fans with oarlike blades stirred stale air around. A pair of middleweights skipped before a long mirror. Beyond them a young Mexie straw-weight performed burpees with a fifteen-pound medicine ball. A two-hundred-pound anvil with the words THAT BITCH painted on its side sat beside him; boxers in a dick-swinging mood occasionally goaded each other, "Go on—lift that bitch!"

The gym was dominated by its ring: twenty feet by twenty feet and enclosed by sagging red ropes. The canvas stank of blood and sweat; to the best of anyone's knowledge it had not been replaced in thirty years. Spitbuckets were strapped to opposite ring posts: wide-mouthed funnels attached to flexible PVC hose trailing down to five-gallon drums once containing oleo lard. The walls were hung with cobwebbed Golden Gloves belts and framed photos of young boxers who now made their living as plumbers or foremen or short-order cooks. Handwritten signs rife with misspellings: CLUB DEWS MUST

BE PAID AT THE START OF THE MONTH!!! CLUB TOWULS ARE FOR SWET ONLY, NOT BLOOD!!! USE LOCKERS AT OWN RISK—NOT RESPONSIBUL FOR LOST GEAR!!!

Written above the wall-length mirror in neat block letters:

WE ARE EDUCATED IN PAIN.

Top Rank was operated by a consortium of managers and trainers—Reuben Tully was one of them—who collected dues to pay the rent and sent whatever was left over to an absentee landlord in Boca Raton. In exchange for this stewardship, they were given free rein to train their own prospects.

The club office was a glassed-in cube accessible by a short flight of stairs. Its door split horizontally and opened in two portions; the trainers hung out up there and kept the top portion open so that they could holler directions at their charges. Reuben sold sodas, snacks, and gum out of the office. Prices were gratifyingly archaic: 50¢ for a bottle of Coke, 40¢ for a Snickers bar, 25¢ bought you a pack of Wrigley's, and Cracker Jack set you back 35¢. Reuben iced the sodas in an ancient cooler and popped the tops off with an opener in the shape of a naked lady, cap slotted between her spread legs.

"Hit the rope, Robbie," Reuben called down. "Five rounds warm-up, then five hard."

Rob unsnarled a skipping rope from the pile and took a spot beside the middleweights. After three minutes the buzzer sounded; the middleweights rested but Rob kept on, sweat coming back now, trickling down the knobs of his spine. When the buzzer went again he kicked it up: running in place, double passes, crossovers. The middleweights matched his pace. In boxing gyms, an undercurrent of competition underlay all things: I can skip rope faster, run farther, move slicker, punch harder, fight prettier, absorb more punishment; my mind-body-heart is made of sterner stuff than yours. I can take you down any old time I want, better believe *that*.

Rob spied two of Top Rank's gym bums perched on the worn bleachers overlooking the ring. Gym bums were a common sight in boxing clubs: old trainers and managers, distinguished by their gray hair, chicken chests, and outrageous tales. You'll find the same breed in barber shops and Legion halls, anyplace men can get away with telling barefaced lies. Today's bums were a pair of grizzled fogies, one black, the other white. Rob never saw the two of them enter or leave, nor did he catch them singly: he'd break from training and see them rowed along a bench that'd stood empty moments before, huddled together as though coalesced from stale gym air.

"Now take a look at that," the white bum said, nodding at the heavyweight, Scarpella. "He's got a punch, yessir, I'll grant you. But now I trained a light-heavy, Johnny Paycheck, once knocked out a horse. Johnny had to pose with this racing horse, a photo op for his upcoming fight; he was smoking a cigar. Smoke must've upset the horse 'cause it blew snot all over Johnny's herringbone blazer. Wellsir Johnny near about knocked the poor beast into horsey heaven." He raised his right hand solemnly. "My hand to God."

Reuben Tully hammered the office window. "Two hundred sit-ups," he hollered down at his son, "and a hundred push-ups!"

Rob grabbed a medicine ball and sat on a mat worn to wafer-thinness over the years. He performed the sit-ups, twisting to work his adductor muscles. Then he flipped over and burned off knuckle push-ups, woofing out breath on each pop.

In the ring Tommy and Scarpella got to work. Scarpella was in his early twenties with ham-sized fists and a shovel-shaped head. He moved as though the ring were a town whose geography he sought to familiarize himself with, pushing his jab out with all the zip of a funeral dirge. Tommy let the kid maneuver him into a corner and bang his body before dropping his right fist, bringing it up through Scarpella's sloppy guard to thump him under the heart. Tommy was going to hit him again when the buzzer went. Like a factory worker who punches out the minute the whistle blows, he lowered his hands.

Rob couldn't help but smile. His uncle earned fifteen bucks a round as a sparring partner. He'd surrendered all dreams of boxing glory, fast cars, and HBO pay per views, the fame and pretty things. The biggest surprise was that it failed to eat at him: anytime he and Rob watched a title fight and one contender took a canvas nap, Tommy'd say, "Jeez, poor guy. Wouldn't want to be in his shoes."

Rob dropped back in on the gym bums' conversation.

"It's common knowledge," the other bum said, "that of all creatures to swim the sea or walk on land, horses have the thinnest of skulls. Thin as eggshell! Now a heavyweight of mine knocked out a donkey. The donkey head's mostly bone, brain no bigger than a walnut—takes a mighty biff. We were training down west of San Angelo and he'd been drinking. He was a Mexie and Mexies'll fight with two broke arms but are not at all keen on training. He's drunk and staggers out the gym. There's this old burro chewing cud; my guy goes to pet it—sour cuss bites him! Well didn't he smack that donkey and it tips right over, four legs twitching up at the clear blue sky. Hang me if I'm lying."

Neither questioned the other's obvious fabrications. Since every word that exited a gym bum's mouth was nearly by definition a lie, it was in their best interest to maintain an air of mutual acceptance, tolerance, or plain ignorance. Without lies, gym bums would have precious little to talk about.

"Robbie," Reuben said, coming downstairs and flicking his head toward the ring. "Quit eyeing your uncle Tommy. May as well watch a cripple fight, for all it's worth—gonna pick up bad habits."

"Well, aren't you a peach," Tommy said.

"You punch like a lollipop," Reuben told his brother. "Head down to the Legion, find some veteran to fight—some blind old biplane pilot. That's about your speed."

In riposte, Tommy laid his substantial weight on the middle ring rope and extended a beckoning hand. "Why don't you climb on in here and let's go a few rounds, Ruby? Tell you what—the first shot's free."

"I got training to do."

"You couldn't train circus fleas."

"How about you pinch that cut under your nose shut." Reuben demonstrated by pinching his own lips shut. "Give it time to heal."

"Ah . . . wah?" Tommy raised a glove to his lips, paused, then nodded. ". . . good one."

Reuben smiled, the victor. "Robbie, don't you know it's impolite to stare at cripples? Go hit a bag."

Rob pulled on a pair of sixteen-ounce gloves and approached a duct-taped heavybag. Crouched low, left foot before right, and tipped forward on his toes, he snapped left jabs. He circled the bag, breaking at the waist, shouldering it, uncorking right hooks and doubling up on body shots.

All activity in the gym stopped when Rob hit the heavybag; everyone stopped and stared. He'd hear the whispers: *Kid's got bottled lightning in those hands; a little of the ol' boom boom. Boy's so quick you couldn't hit him with a handful of sugar.* Tall and in excellent condition, Rob weighed only 164 pounds. But his body had the characteristics of a puppy dog—big bones, huge paws—that indicated he had another growth spurt in him.

Tommy's sparring session drew to a close. Scarpella was wheezing like a busted squeezebox; Tommy patted him on the head and, picking up the same tune he'd been whistling climbing through the ropes, climbed out again.

"Don't load up so much," Reuben hollered at his son. "Power thrills but speed kills, Robbie. Get that through your thick head."

"Dogging him somethin' awful today," Tommy said to his brother.

"Mind your business," Reuben told him. "Don't hear me telling you how to drive forklift, do you?"

"Just seems that, Robbie was a dog, I'd be calling the humane society right about now."

"What's he made of, glass? Throw your sweatshirt on," he called over to Rob. "We'll hit the Green Machine."

The Green Machine was an olive-green '69 Dodge pickup donated to Top Rank under dismal circumstances: its owner, an ex–club member, was currently a guest of the state at Coxsackie penitentiary. The club could've found use for used gym mats or even foul cups, but the old green beater served no earthly good; it had sat in the crushed-gravel lot out behind the club for a year until Reuben devised a novel use for it.

Bolting a wooden beam to the cab roof and suspending an old heavybag from the end, he'd created an unorthodox training device. The bag hung four or five feet in front of the truck's grille: the visual effect was of the classic carrot-on-a-stick incentive, with the bag as the carrot and the truck standing in for the donkey.

"Get the lead out!" Reuben shouted at his son. "Quit doggin' it!"

Reuben hopped into the truck. The engine yammered and chuffed. "Come on, you old pig!" The Dodge shuddered to life; the cab filled with greasy exhaust fumes. He cracked a window and said "Put up yer dukes" as he slipped the truck into gear.

Rob backpedaled as the truck came at him at five mph; he threw punches at the frost-glazed bag chained to the beam. The idea was to punch while moving back on his heels—when pursued in the ring, he could lash out and catch his advancing opponent. To mix it up Reuben would set the Green Machine in reverse, forcing Rob into the role of pursuer. Around and around the crushed-gravel parking lot they would go, Rob alternately pursuing and retreating as his father hollered instructions out the window. The engine frequently died;

Reuben would mash the gas pedal and crank the key, beseeching Rob to "keep punching, keep punching; your next opponent isn't likely to conk out like this damn truck!"

A few other trainers had added the Green Machine to their workout regimen, much to the chagrin of their charges. Boxers complained of sore hands afterward, especially when it was cold and the bag nearly frozen. Every so often the Green Machine vanished from the parking lot—it wasn't hard to steal, as the keys stayed in the ignition. It was always a boxer who'd taken it, frequently the night before his next training session. But the respite was short-lived: sooner or later the club would receive a phone call detailing the truck's whereabouts and Reuben or one of the other trainers would retrieve it.

Reuben goosed the gas pedal and the truck lurched forward. Rob ducked the bag nimbly, stinging it with a hard right hand. Watching his son through the crack-starred windshield, Reuben marveled, as he so often did, at his unstudied perfection. The way he moved, sly feints and weaves. Incremental movements, nothing frivolous or wasted. The beauty of his style lay in its geometries: the clean angular planes of his body, the straight lines by which he negotiated the distances between his opponent's body and his own. To watch Rob box was beautiful in the way a predatory cat stalking its quarry was beautiful: generations of selective breeding honed to a killing edge. Whenever he despaired that he was pushing his son too hard, Reuben convinced himself that boxing was Rob's life calling—how else could he be so damn good at it?

Of course, it never benefited a trainer to let his boxer know how good he looked.

"What's the matter," he hollered, "got lead in your damn feet? Pitiful, Robbie, just pitiful! Punch like that your next match, you better get used to the view from queer street."

Reuben's goading fell upon deaf ears. Rob knew he was a good boxer, a powerful and perhaps preternaturally skilled one: the whispers and stares told him so. But his skills also scared him. He'd never forget the first time he knocked a guy out: that bone-deep jolt traveling down his arm and his opponent's distorted face rippling from the point of impact, how his eyes closed as he fell away from Rob's glove. Afterward the fighter's trainer found three teeth embedded in the semi-soft rubber of his gumshield. In Rob's eighth fight, he broke his opponent's jaw. Felix Guiterrez was a fellow senior at his high school; he'd seen Felix in the hallway with his mouth wired shut, sucking Boost through a straw in the cafeteria. He felt guilty knowing what he'd done. But on an instinctual level it felt like something he'd practically been bred for—how else could he be so damn good at it?

Unlike some fighters, Rob was not powered by rage, fear, hatred, a desire to break living things. And while he trained hard and fought regularly, he possessed no true love for the sport. He boxed because his father had boxed and because his uncle still did; because his grandfather boxed and so on down the line back to the Heenan–Morrissey mill and beyond; because for generations the hands of Tully men had stunk of walnut juice. He boxed because the Tullys were fighting stock, and had been for as long as anyone could recall. He'd grown up in the gym among fighters; it had been a foregone conclusion that he'd become one himself.

After a half-hour Reuben parked the truck. He stepped out of the cab and booted the door shut—the Dodge's door and rocker panel were cratered with dents, the result of many years' worth of kicks. Rob didn't like it when his father hoofed the Green Machine; to him it seemed the equivalent of kicking an old trail nag who'd only done its job, albeit fitfully.

Reuben said, "You really screwed the pooch today, I don't mind telling you."

"I was concentrating on my footwork."

"And playing pattycakes with the bag. Trust me on this: no boxer's ever signed a million-dollar fight deal on account of his footwork."

4

Paul Harris sat on bleachers overlooking an empty baseball diamond. Browned grass, sky the color of stone.

His face still bore evidence of the beating. Lingering yellow traceries ringed his eye sockets. No dentist, so still the open gaps in his smile. Paul hadn't set foot in the winery for a while now; instead he'd spent his days in the field with the pickers.

He'd rise at four o'clock, dress warmly, and slip past his parents' room out into the pre-dawn darkness. The pickers were up by the time he arrived: sitting around the tractor-hub fire, they kneaded tired muscles and wrapped their fingers in tape. The men cinched buckets to their waists and stepped out into the rows. Paul would thread a bucket's nylon strap through his belt loop and grab a box cutter, testing its sharpness by running the blade over his thumb. After finding a quiet row, he'd get to work.

He'd walk in darkness for a minor eternity before the sun rose over the vineyard. The rows stretched on forever: a span of twisted vines and frozen grapes. His right thigh became one massive bruise from the constant bumping of bucket against leg. The pickers were baffled: *Wey you looka da bubu,* they'd whisper. *Nice wa'am office, fine caa and suits—ees out 'ere workin wid us!* Paul was looked out for as though he were an accident-prone child: the pickers shared their lunches and taught him to wrap hot embers in tinfoil, dropping them in his coat pocket to warm his hands.

Late in the first week his father had found him in the fields. "What the hell?" Jack Harris asked his son. "I mean, what . . . the . . . *hell*?"

Paul tugged a pair of ski goggles down around his neck; a figure eight of pale skin ringed his eyes. Jack Harris was puffing. Gobs of mud clung to his pant legs.

"This is goddamn ridiculous—mucking around in the slop."

"Thought I'd try something different."

"What's so different about it? People have picked grapes for centuries—that is until a few of us wised up and hired someone else to do it for us."

"It's honest work. The great outdoors. Fresh air."

"Fresh air? Have you been reading *Iron John* or something?" Jack looked ready to grab his son's arm and drag him back to the office. Harsh and forcible: jerk the ball-joint from his shoulder socket, if need be. But some fresh element in his son's bearing steered him off this course of action. "I know what you're trying to prove, but it's all a bit silly."

"Compared to what," said Paul, "that art show Mom dragged us to?"

"Oh, what are you bringing up that nightmare for?"

"It's the sort of thing I think about out here. Ridiculous stuff."

A few months previous they'd attended a conceptual art exhibit at his mother's request—the artist, Naveed, was the son of his mother's Pilates instructor. The opening gala was a black-tie affair at a downtown gallery; the exhibit was titled "The Commercialization of Waste." A huge vaulted chamber displayed various bodily wastes. Milk jugs filled with excrement. Jars of piss on marble colonnades. Egg cartons full of toenail clippings. A salt shaker full of cayenne pepper flakes—in actuality, scabs. Naveed was dressed in flannel jammies, the sort kids wear with the sewn-on booties. He made sure to clarify that every ounce of waste had been produced by his own body. The smell was ungodly. Everyone must have been thinking the same thing: *Sperm in Ziploc bags and turds in milk jugs—this is art?* Paul and his folks had left without a word.

"What I'm trying to say is," said Jack, "this environment doesn't suit you." He lowered his voice, as though fearful the vines were bugged. "What if someone sees you—a potential investor?"

Paul razored a grape cluster free and dropped it into his bucket. "No, I'll stay. This is real life, right? This is good for me."

"Vitamins are good for you. High colonics are good for you. This is idiotic."

But Paul felt better than he had in years. Up before dawn, ten hours of backbreaking field labor, collapse into an oblivious, dreamless sleep. The air was so cold and the labor so demanding that its effect was to flatten out his mind. Hours would pass without a single concrete thought: just empty, static wind gusting and swirling through his head, snatches of songs repeating themselves in an endless loop. The seething anger that so often manifested itself in other forms—as cold nausea, as nameless dread—was, if not erased, at least temporarily buried under the weight of physical exhaustion.

Jack grabbed the bucket at his son's waist and shook it violently. "I was out here when you were a baby," he said. "It was not *good*. It was miserable and torturous but it needed to be done so's I could get that." He pointed at the winery. "A means to an end."

"But you turned out all right, didn't you? Who's to say those days weren't the reason?"

Jack picked up a clod of earth and crushed it between his fingers. "Y'know, I said to myself, Let him go. I said, He'll come around. But you're out here all day and I may as well be living with a phantom for all I see you around the house. Your mother's worried sick—"

"Is she really?" Paul hadn't spoken more than two words to his mother in days; he wasn't altogether sure how she'd taken to his new endeavor.

"Sure she is," Jack said. "We're all worried. And I don't get it. Some shitkicker beat you up. Big deal. I never told you this, but I took a shit-kicking for a gas-n-dash years ago. This pump jockey whapped me over the head with a squeegee and had me seeing stars. Then he dragged me out behind the lifts and put the boots to me. I was in such bad shape he had to let me go: the cops would've booked me on attempted robbery, but I would've made damn sure he got booked for assault."

Paul laughed. "Why didn't you ever tell me?"

"Why the hell would I? It's not my habit to go around telling stories that cast me in an unfavorable light."

Jack looked at his son. In truth, the kid looked pretty good. He'd shed a few pounds and packed muscle onto his legs and shoulders; in all, he looked more like the son he'd imagined. Perhaps getting the stuffing knocked out of him had done him some good. Still, it was as if he'd taken a step down the evolutionary ladder—become stronger, harder even, but less cultured. Even now Jack could smell him: ripe and musky like the first whiff of a logger's shack. Problem was, his son's devolution was a threat to their shared futures. What self-respecting woman would marry a man who picked grapes all day and came at her with calloused, purple-stained fingers? How could he pass the business down to a son happy to occupy the lowest rung on the ladder when he'd been earmarked for the highest?

"Picking season's over in two weeks," he said. "I'm not sure what you plan to do then—run off into the forest and live off the land? Some hobo kick? Steal clothes off laundry lines and sleep in drainage ditches?"

"Maybe I'll pack a bindle and ride the rails. King of the open road, uh?"

Jack was appalled. "You're an infuriating little turd—do you know that? You're like a kid who runs away but only makes it to the end of the block and sits in the bushes for a few hours, coming home when it's dark and cold and he's got the hungries in his tum-tum."

His father's temper was like a busted speedometer: it was impossible to tell how fast and hot his engine was running. He could go from zero to bastard in fifteen seconds flat.

"I love you, Daddy."

"Shut up, why don't you?" Jack's temper downshifted. "If you're fixed on staying out here, you're getting paid like everyone else—by the bucket. Expect your next paycheck to be significantly smaller, old boy old chum."

"Just pay me what I'm worth."

"You're worth a lot more than what you've settled for here." Jack looked wretched, like a tank had run over him and left him lying there in the dirt. "And for god's sake get your fucking teeth looked after."

When the picking season ended the field workers went home to their wives and children to await the spring thaws. Paul did not return to the winery. He passed his days driving the city.

He would set out at dawn with the pale moon hanging over the lake and streets dark with night rain. He drove without motive or clear destination. He parked at the GM factory gates as the workers waited in line to buy coffee and Danish from a silver-paneled snack truck. He idled outside the bus terminal as drivers walked to their buses beneath strung halogens with newspapers folded under their arms. He spied on janitors sitting on picnic tables behind the Hotel Dieu hospital, chatting and laughing, dousing cigarettes in soup tins filled with rainwater. Paul felt a huge sense of disassociation watching these men, floating, unattached to anything he understood. Men whose lives he'd never considered because they were unlike any he'd ever aspired to.

What had he ever really aspired to?

He drove to Jammer's gym in his replacement wheels: a Nissan Micra, on loan from the dealership. Paul had expressly requested the crappiest loaner in the lot and the Micra fit the bill: raggedy and rust-eaten with a sewing machine engine, power nothing, K-Tel's *Hits of the 80s* lodged in the tape deck. Even once his BMW was fixed, Paul stuck with the Micra.

He steered through the lights at Church and St. Paul. "Big Country," by the Scottish group of the same name, blasted from the tinny speakers. He butted the Micra into a streetside parking spot, fed the meter, and headed into the gym.

It was sparsely populated: bored housewives going nowhere on the elliptical machines, university kids in the weight room. He donned his gym garb and hit the weights.

He'd started coming after picking let off. The only time he'd even considered working out before now was the time when, maudlinly drunk at three a.m., he'd ordered a Bowflex after watching an infomercial. But his existential despair had evaporated the next morning and the unassembled Bowflex, still in its box, was consigned to the role of mouse-turd receptacle in the backyard greenhouse.

Paul slapped a pair of weight plates on the bench press. He watched an anorexic-looking chick with fake tits run treadmill laps. Boobs bouncing, lathered in sweat, her face contorted into a look of desperate intensity unique to Olympic hopefuls and women of a Certain Age. An old dude with a toxic tanning-bed tan—his skin the diseased orange hue of a boiled tangerine—was rowing to Jehovah on an erg machine. Paul glanced away, mildly revolted, and caught the proprietor making a beeline for him.

Stacey Jamison struck the casual observer as a man who'd been given a girl's name at birth and had spent his life trying to outrun the association. At five-foot-four and nearly three hundred pounds, there was nothing on the guy that wasn't monstrous. His legs and arms and neck were like a telephone pole chainsawed into five sections. His body was networked in thick veins pushed to the surface of his skin by the sheer density of muscle tissue.

He was once a professional bodybuilder, but three consecutive heart attacks had forced him off the pro circuit. The cause of the attacks wasn't openly stated, but gym scuttlebutt had it that Stacey would pop anything that could be crammed into a syringe, including powdered bull testicle. Once he'd loaded himself up on Lasix before a show, leaching all the moisture from his body for that ultra-cut look; unfortunately the racehorse diuretic left his organs so desiccated that his kidneys tore like a tissue paper Valentine when he nailed a Double Crabbed Biceps pose during a heated pose-off segment.

"Harris, you pansy." Stacey wore a shirt with a snarling cartoon rottweiler over the legend DON'T GROWL IF YOU CAN'T BITE. "You got a hollow chest like a puffed-up paper bag. I seen ten-year-old girls with more definition."

Stacey's shtick was to stalk the gym belittling his customers' physiques: *You got driftwood arms*; *A butcher wouldn't take those stringy legs as stewing beef*; *I could fry an egg on that flat ass of yours.* While this initially struck Paul as an ideal way to alienate one's clientele, he'd grossly underestimated the average gym member's tolerance for abasement. More than a few appeared to crave Stacey's brutal assessment of their physiques, as if he were a mirror that reflected the physical deficiencies they'd long ago glimpsed in themselves. And though most of Stacey's assessments were of the critical variety, he was infrequently known to deliver faint praise: *You're not looking quite as sickly as I recall* or *You're less skeletal; I guess I'll have to tell those body farmers to look elsewhere.* Such backhanded compliments were enough to lift Stacey's regulars to a state of mild euphoria.

When Stacey wasn't berating his cowering clientele, he acted as spotter for some of the more grotesque gym denizens. These juiced-up muscleheads could bench cart-oxen weight, the bar bowed under a mass of steel plates as finger-thick veins stood out on their corded necks. Einsteins of the Body, Paul dubbed them. Some were so huge their heads looked comically small in relation. It amused him to consider the possibility that they were, in fact, fantastically tiny men who zippered into a hulking coat of meat and muscles each morning; at night they unzipped and hung their muscles on a peg. Every few weeks they got their meat coats dry-cleaned.

"Get your ass under that bar," Stacey told Paul, adding a few extra ten-pound plates. "It's go time." He slapped Paul's face, slapped his own. "*Do* this, motherfucker."

Paul braced his arms on the bar and jerked it off the pegs. His arms trembled; he entertained a giddy vision of his forearms snapping and the bar crushing his windpipe. He lowered the bar, felt it touch his chest, and pushed.

"You're in it to *WIN* it, baby!" Stacey jabbered. "Go hard or go *HOME!*"

Muscles tore across Paul's chest, fibers snapping like over-tuned piano wires. Stacey's crotch hovered above Paul's face: stuffed into lime-green spandex shorts, his package looked like a plantain and two walnuts jiggling in a grocery sack.

"Lift, bitch! Be a *MAN* for once in your life!"

Paul's strength ebbed as the bar locked inches above his chest. His muscles fluttered and bands of white fire stretched across his eyes. The strain coursed down his arms into his gut, knotting into an agonizing ball he expelled in the form of an oddly toneless fart. Stacey guided the bar onto its pegs.

Paul heaved with embarrassment. "I'm so sorry about that."

But Stacey was pleased. "Only means you gave a hundred and ten percent to your lift. You're not farting, you're not jerking enough iron. First time I squatted a thousand, I crapped my pants."

Paul couldn't tell what Stacey was more proud of: the fact that he'd squatted half a ton or that he'd shit himself in the process.

He finished his workout and hit the showers. He'd noticed how two distinct groups of men spent far more time naked than was strictly necessary: those in terrific shape and those too old to give a damn. A few struck show poses stark naked before the change room's floor-length mirror. Paul found himself scoping out their bodies: chests and arms and abs, the symmetry or lack of it, the freakish mass of the Einsteins. Lately he'd taken to picturing how elements of other men's bodies might look adorning his own: he'd take that guy's pecs, that guy's delts, that guy's pipes, that guy's soup-can cock and cobble together an idealized version of himself. Franken-Paul.

On his way out he caught Stacey behind the front desk, bent over a plate piled with skinless chicken breasts.

"Good work today, fag."

". . . Thanks." Paul nodded to the shelves at Stacey's back: tubs of protein powder with names like Whey Max and BioPure HyperPlex. Each tub featured a wraparound photo of a tanned, overdeveloped, confidently smiling Einstein.

"Which do you recommend?"

"These?" Stacey jerked a thumb at the tubs. "All shit. Chalk dust and pigeon crap." He shoveled chicken into his mouth. "No substitute for hard work, Harris." He paused with his mouth open; rags of masticated chicken swung from his teeth. "Well, that's not the literal truth."

He gave Paul a look, its shrewdness suggesting that Paul's suit-ability and trustworthiness were currently the subject of intense scrutiny. Later Paul would realize that Stacey gave everyone this look; his customer criteria was no narrower than a convenience store's.

Stacey rooted through a drawer and set an ampule on the desk. "Testosterone ethanate. We're talking the Rolls-Royce of performance enhancement."

The Einsteins made no secret of their steroid abuse—why bother, when your body was a walking billboard?—and Paul had overheard horror stories: hardened knots forming in their asses from the deep-tissue injections, excess body hair and cysts the size of corn kernels, penile atrophy. Stacey had himself developed a serious infection in his right bicep; he'd performed meatball surgery on himself in the men's bathroom, piercing the infected tissue with a heavy-gauge needle and filling a Dixie cup with a broth of blood and pus.

Paul rolled the vial between his fingers. A quarter-ounce of yellow fluid. Piss, was all it looked like. A squirt of dirty yellow piss.

"Is it safe?"

"Nothing's one hundred percent safe. You walk outta here, get hit by a bus."

Paul had always despised the well-trodden bus rationale. He asked what company manufactured the stuff. Stacey told him that medical-grade steroids were for pussies; he said Paul would be better off chugging the pigeon crap. None of this answered Paul's question, however, leaving him to wonder if it had been brewed in Stacey's bathtub.

"I hear it shrinks your dick."

"That can happen," Stacey admitted. "But here's the thing: every guy's got an extra three inches of cock rolled up in his hip cavity."

"Oh, come on with that."

"I shit you not. Rolled up in there like a chameleon's tongue. There's this operation where a surgeon makes a slit at the base of your cock and yanks out the extra bit. I got it done; my dick's not bent or anything and I piss and fuck like a champ."

Clearly Stacey had tendered this pitch a few times. Not that his salesmanship was at all necessary—despite any minor misgivings, Paul's mind had been set the moment Stacey placed the vial on the countertop.

"How do I get it into me?"

"Injection to the tushie. I'll do it for you."

"Is that the only w—?"

Stacey cut him off. "Please don't be a pussy, Harris. I was just starting to dig you."

And so it transpired that five minutes later Paul found himself in a cramped stall in the men's room at Jammer's gym, bent over the toilet with his pants wadded around his knees and Stacey Jamison's hairy caveman hands clapped to his buttocks.

Stacey kneaded roughly. "Spongier than a loaf a bread."

Paul braced his hands on the stall wall. By now sickened at his impulsiveness—why couldn't he just inject himself?—he was convinced it was too late to back out. Stacey gave his ass a rough slap.

"Christ—jiggling like Christmas pudding." He was genuinely revolted. "How can you cart those lumpy sandbags around all day? It's just . . . *gross*. Look at it—*look*!"

Paul craned his neck, angling for a glimpse of his own ass. "It could do with some work," he said helplessly.

Stacey's sigh suggested that whipping a specimen as pitiful as Paul into shape would be a mammoth chore, requiring the labor of thousands. "Don't move. If I jab too deep you'll get a knot like a monkey fist."

A steel wire of stark terror pierced Paul's heart. What if Stacey hit a vein and pumped this junk directly into his bloodstream? What if he went into anaphylactic shock and—*died*? He was horrified by how Stacey might deal with the situation; he pictured Stacey seating his dead body on the can, wrapping his dead hand around the syringe, then calling the cops and saying one of his clients had perished while geezing in the shitter. Paul pictured his body laid out on a morgue slab, raisin-testicled with a twig for a penis.

Stacey pig-stuck him and pushed the plunger. As testosterone shot through him, Paul felt . . . nothing. It might as well be vegetable oil—hell, maybe it *was* vegetable oil. He yanked his trousers up and out of sheer habit flushed the toilet—that, or he wanted to convince anyone in the change room he'd merely been taking a piss.

"Work those glutes!" Stacey hollered as Paul escaped through the change room. "Tone that saggy caboose of yours!"

Paul drove down Highway 406 following the frozen river, took the mall exit, and turned left at the lights. On Hartzell Road he passed pool halls and bars with neon signs, a foreclosed Bavarian restaurant, a train yard where boxcars rusted in the nettles.

He yanked down his pants at a red light and gave his ass a good clawing. An itchy red bump had risen at the injection site. His heartbeat was all out of whack, weird yips and baps. Reeking sweat poured from his body, soaking his shirt and running down the crack of his ass. His fingers came away bloody but the bump still itched like a bastard. He stuffed McDonald's napkins down his trousers to sop up the blood.

At the end of Hartzell a white-brick shopfront occupied the space between a knife shop and a tattoo parlor. A sign above the door read JENSEN'S PAINTS. Below that sign a smaller one, reading, in clipped red letters, IMPACT BOXING CLUB.

Paul wrenched the wheel and cut across the road, narrowly avoiding a T-bone collision with an oncoming Buick. He skipped over the curb—some vital portion of the undercarriage tore off with a shriek—into the paint store lot. The engine rattled and conked out.

He sat with his hands gripped to the wheel, wondering how he'd managed to pass these shops a hundred times without ever noticing them. He heard that up north in the provincial parks most of the trees had been clear-cut by logging companies; what they left was called a "veneer": the pines went twenty or thirty feet deep along the hiking paths and riversides, but beyond that only miles of stumps. Paul thought that if someone clear-cut this city, gutted the office buildings and homes and stores, he'd never know—so long as the veneer remained.

But he'd noticed the shops this time. Why? It wasn't like he was in dire need of a carving knife or a tattoo. What caught his eye was the small sign with its clipped red lettering.

The boxing club entrance was around back. A worn linoleum staircase and bare concrete walls taped with posters advertising a local fight card: BRAWL IN THE BASEMENT, DECEMBER 5. At the base of the staircase was another door: thick steel with an inset combination lock, the sort of thing you'd see fronting a bank vault. It was wedged open.

A short hallway hung with boxing photos in gold-edged frames: Panama Al Brown and Nigel Benn, Baltazar Sangchili, Fighting Harada, Sixto Escobar. A Spanish beer poster: Oscar De La Hoya hoisting a Budweiser over the words SALUD–RESPECTO–CONTRO. The famous George Bellow oil painting: Louis Firpo, "The Wild Bull of the Pampas," knocking "The Manassa Mauler" Jack Dempsey through the ring ropes.

The hallway led to a tiny unlit office. A shape was sprawled out on a couch. Paul knocked. The shape snuffled. Paul said, "Hello?" The shape stirred.

"How much do I owe?"

"Excuse me?"

"Don't play silly buggers. Joke's on you, asshole. I can't pay." A mirthless chuckle. "Can't squeeze water from a stone, jackass."

"I saw your sign."

"Oh." The voice brightened. "So you want to join?"

The voice assumed the aspect of a man: short and barrel-chested and wearing rumpled slacks, a short-sleeved pearl-button shirt, crack-soled Tony Lamas. Bald with deeply furrowed cheeks and a bloated nose. There was a blob of dried food on his chin.

"Caught me in the middle of naptime." His face had the haunted look of a man who'd crawled to daylight from a caved-in mineshaft. "Lou Cobb. I own the place."

Paul introduced himself.

"Ever box before, Paul?" Lou asked. "Looks it—got the build all right. You work with Ernie Riggs over at Knock Out?"

Paul said he hadn't.

"Good, that's good. Riggs is a bum. Riggs has abused more boxers than Inspector Number Twelve. He stinks. How old are you?"

"Twenty-six."

"I won't lie—bit old for a rookie. We like to get kids in the ring at twelve, thirteen tops, parents allow it. But a *young* twenty-six—now that we can work with. Sure you're not a fighter? Got that fighter's smile."

"I fell down a flight of stairs."

"We must be talking some mean-ass stairs."

Lou scraped the blob of dried food off his chin and studied it, as though straining to recall what meal it had been a part of. "Paul, you can join yearly, bi-yearly, or monthly. But you can't expect to learn anything in a month."

"Can I take a look around?"

"Not much to see." Lou seemed disappointed his spiel had not earned a quick sale. "Go take a peep round the change rooms. After I'll give you the grand tour."

The dingy change room was lit by a single bulb. Headgear and leather foul cups hung from wooden pegs. A showerhead dripped. Paul considered himself in the mirror. He'd lost fifteen pounds in the grapefields. He shed his shirt and stared dejectedly at his chest: despite the gains at Jammer's, he still looked like a human boneyard covered in a quivering layer of flab.

When he emerged, Lou beckoned him over to the ring apron. "So, ready for that grand tour?" He swept his hand in an ironic, all-encompassing fan. "Ta-daa."

It was impossible for the place to look like anything other than what it was: the basement below a paint store, with a boxing ring and a few punching bags hung from exposed girders. Paul judged its Spartan nature suitable to the sport.

A new boxer made his entrance. The guy wasn't big; his limbs jutted in raw bony outlines through his track pants and sweatshirt. His hood was pulled low to obscure his face. Only his hands were visible and they looked awful: curled into talons and terribly swollen, knuckles gone black.

"What are you doing here?" A tiny vein throbbed at Lou's temple; a note of nervous tension picked at his face. "Supposed to be home, in bed."

The guy shuffled over to a heavybag. He moved with obvious difficulty—Paul couldn't help noticing that his left leg dragged behind him like an invalid's—and set himself in a pugilist's stance, a posture he found painful judging by the grunt he let out. Paul had the uncomfortable feeling he was watching a zombie or automaton, some brainless creature driven by mere impulse.

Lou spread his hands in an embarrassed, despairing gesture. "Some guys just can't get enough of training. Like say an addiction."

He excused himself and walked over. When he set his hands on the boxer's shoulders, the guy drew away.

"Cool down," Lou said. "No need to get punchy."

The guy threw a few venomous shots at the heavybag. The bag jerked on its chain. His knuckles split open and made meaty sounds when they struck. Blood flew off the bag and splattered the scuffed floor tiles.

"No training today," Lou told the guy. He turned to offer Paul a smile that suggested such things occurred frequently in boxing clubs. For all Paul knew, they did. The guy mumbled something.

"I don't give a crap you want to," Lou told him. "Murdering your body, all this is. You're heading home and hitting the sack."

But the guy's hands flew. Blood flew. Lou's own hand snaked out and snagged the guy's wrist. After a few seconds trying to twist free, the guy relented.

"Think I'm letting you put yourself through this? Then you don't know me too well at all. You're gonna go lay your head down."

The boxer lifted his head. Light hit his face slantwise. Paul got his first real look.

The guy's eyes were swollen over, two plum-colored anthills separated by a split bridge of nose. The top portion of his head had gone dark and shiny as eggplant, impossible to tell where skin gave way to the dark roots of his hair. Strips of adhesive tape glued his broken lips together. He held one twisted hand out, tentative like a blind man or an infant reaching to touch Lou's face. Lou lowered it for him. "Ease down, Garth," he said. "You did good last night. Real good."

Laying an arm over the guy's shoulder, Lou made a clicking sound with his tongue, the sort you might make to guide a horse onward. Glancing back over his shoulder, he appeared chagrined to discover that Paul was, in fact, still present.

"I'll have to ask you to come back tomorrow. Bring your togs; I'll show you how we do things."

It was near dark when Paul left the gym. When he arrived home his parents were sitting at the kitchen table. Early-arriving Christmas cards ringed an empty bottle of Merlot. His parents' teeth had that dead-giveaway mulberry stain.

"Look who," his father said, "the goddamn wraith. *Ooooo-ooo-ooo*," he went, like a cartoon ghost.

Paul was ravenous but found the fridge stocked with the usual unappealing foodstuffs: a bag full of periwinkles, an eel wrapped in cling film, a crustacean with a price tag skewered on one spiny appendage. The damn fridge housed a bizarrely misplaced Sea World exhibit.

"Doesn't this family eat normal food anymore?"

"We figured with the way he's been acting lately, our son must be an extraterrestrial. We suspect he rocketed to Earth as an infant, moments before his world exploded." Jack tossed a swallow of wine down his neck. "We wish to cater to his alien diet. Or don't they eat that sort of stuff on your planet?"

"Alien food," his mother said derisively. "Is it alien that people should eat healthfully? I can whip you up something—how about an eel wrap?"

To Paul this sounded more like a creepy spa treatment than anything he might want to put in his mouth. "You know, I'll pass."

"Fine, mister grilled cheese sandwich."

Barbara Harris wore a black silk kimono embroidered with dragons. Paul wondered if she'd set foot off the estate all day. Years ago she'd bred Great Danes for show but quit after her prize bitch, Sweet Roses, ran off with a feral short-haired schnauzer who'd roamed the banks of

Lake Ontario. She recovered to sit on the boards of several charitable committees, but quit them and upped her Pilates and Billy Blanks Tae Bo workouts to twice daily; she'd since scaled back in favor of Thai cookery and Japanese Tea Ceremony classes—hence the kimono.

She had not always been this way. Years ago, when they'd lived on the vineyard, she'd played Nana Mouskouri or Roger Whittaker records and sang along while puttering about the house. Friends would come down from Atikokan and stay for weeks, calling her "Babs" or "Bo-Bo." They drank Blue Nun on the weathered front porch and pored over old photographs: Barbara sitting in the bleachers at a football game in scarf and mittens; at a bush party, the fire making her skin shine like Krugerrand gold. She used to laugh all the time—mildly disconcerting, as his mother's laugh sounded like a poacher machine-gunning a walrus. But Paul loved her laugh: it was a sound expressive of life and unrestrained joy, though he couldn't recall the last time he'd really heard it. Wealth hung awkwardly on some people, gave rise to perversions of taste and common sense: fad diets and Tae Bo and shit-in-milk-jug art exhibits. Some people were better off poor.

"Where were you today?" Jack wanted to know. "Working the high steel, driving a steamroller, digging ditches?"

Paul found a loaf of multigrain bread and a jar of organic peanut butter. "I was around."

"Around what—the unemployment office? Or maybe you were called back to the mothership to report to your leader."

"I'm here now, so what does it matter?"

"Hear that, Barb? Our son's off god-knows-where sticking his nose in god-knows-what and he wants to know why it matters!"

"Jack, please." Barbara's manner was that of a society doyenne calming a rowdy dinner guest.

Jack ran a hand through his hair: wild, sticking up in icicle spikes. "The other day a shipment of Cabernet bottles arrived—pink. *What the hell do you think we're bottling here,* I said to the delivery guy, *Asti Spumante? Baby shampoo?* The guy kept flapping the goddamn order sheet and the next thing I knew I had him in a headlock!" He tightened his tie—then, realizing what he'd done, tugged it loose. "I could use you back."

But Paul couldn't see himself back at the winery in his Organizational Adviser role, writing memos to his father (Subject: Cost Breakdown of Kill vs. No-Kill Rat Traps for Supply Room) and telling the bambino joke.

"You ought to hire an assistant."

"Who, some stranger?"

"Who the hell cares? There's a million guys like me, and Mom doesn't give two shits what I do—"

"I do," Barb cut in. "I do give two . . . shits. And much more. I just wasn't aware it was your aspiration to be a fruit picker."

"Guess I should have sent you to the fuckin' fruit-picking academy!" Jack roared, zero to stone-cold sonofabitch in ten point six seconds—a new record.

"Didn't know there was one, but that would've been swell," Paul said as he made for the back door.

The backyard described a shallow decline to the shores of Lake Ontario. A snowy owl perched on a tree bough, its flat phosphorescent eyes big as bicycle reflectors. The water was a frozen gunmetal sheet; the lights of Hamilton and Toronto shone upon it.

"Paul, slow up."

His mother traced a path down to the shoreline. She wore a mink coat Paul had thought flattered her, but now all he could think about was how many minks had been anally electrocuted to make the ridiculous thing.

"Can we walk a bit?" she asked.

"We can."

Wind whipped over the ice pan, tossing up fans of crystallized snow. Barbara used to walk the lakeshore for hours, calling out for her truant show dog—"Here, Sweet Roses! Here, Sweet, Sweet Roses!"— in hopes of coaxing it away from the renegade schnauzer.

"I'm not too sure what's been happening lately." Barb's face bore a wounded expression. "You were in a fight, you've picked grapes. So I guess I know what you've been up to—but I can't see why."

"You wouldn't get it."

"Care to try me?"

Paul shrugged. "Okay, say you got in a fight—"

"Man or a woman?"

"Say this she-bear of a woman kicked the snot out of you. What do you do?"

"First I'd call the police—"

"See, Mom, that's where we must part ways."

"Will you let me finish? You never let me *finish*. I think I might . . ." She sighed. "No, I'd call the police. God, Paul, what do you expect me to say? I'd embark on a province-wide killing spree?"

"You don't go to the police."

Barb's wounded expression persisted. "What you said about me not giving a shit—"

"Two shits."

"Two, even . . . that wasn't fair."

"I'm sorry," he said, meaning it. "But it's nothing to do with you."

She shook her head and shivered. "Cold as a witch's tit."

Though many things about his mother had changed, her diction had not. She still said *I could've dropped cork-legged!* when something surprised her; when Paul was young she'd tell him *Up the wooden hills to Bedfordshire* when it was time for bed. As a kid he'd purposefully misbehave to hear her holler *For two pins I swear I'd thump you!*, safe in the knowledge she'd never actually thump him.

"So what's this big problem of yours?" she asked after they'd walked for a while.

"It's bigger than one thing, more complex. I can only tell you some of the symptoms."

"Symptoms, okay."

"Okay. Last summer I was driving home dead drunk." Barb was shaking her head. "Mother, dear—did you, or did you *not*, ask? So I'm driving. If I hit a check-stop I knew I'd blow over the limit and I already had that DUI—"

"The one your father cleared up."

"Can I tell the story? I came across an accident scene. That hairpin curve—"

"At the bridge over the regatta course?"

Paul nodded. "Two cars. One crashed through the guardrail into the pond; its headlights were submerged and they looked like lights at the bottom of a swimming pool. The other one slammed into the bridge. A compact Suzuki—"

"Oh, god." Barbara drove a Lincoln Navigator, comforted by its stellar front-impact safety rating.

"—and all accordioned up. The driver had rocketed through the windshield and was laid out over the hood. His head—her head, his head; who knows?—*the* head was flattened against the bridge abutment."

His mother looked ill. "You know, I sat on a traffic safety committee years ago and that same curve came up. I voted to widen it, but the road crews were threatening a strike and . . . well, go on."

"There were cops, ambulances, fire trucks, those megawatt accident-scene spots. Everything was focused on the accident. I could have popped my trunk and rolled a headless corpse into the weeds and nobody would've said boo."

"But you didn't cause the accident. And you weren't thankful for it happening—were you?"

"Not thankful." He stomped a crescent of ice off the shoreline. "But I thought the only reason it happened was to distract the police. So I wouldn't get arrested."

"You've lost me."

"I'm saying that when I saw that person flung through the windshield the first thing that leapt into my head was that my, I guess you could say *existence*, was so vital that some god or universal force had rigged the whole accident for my benefit—a human being had been killed, just to get me off the hook. And I drove away smiling." He gave her a look: hopeless, cored out. "Smiling, Mom. Really."

"They're only thoughts, Paul. You didn't make those cars collide; you didn't hurt anyone."

"And that's basically it, Mom. I haven't done anything, ever. Good or bad."

"Nonsense. You've graduated university—"

"Whoopee. Only took six years."

"What about all those trophies in your office?"

"Dad bought them at a thrift store! Didn't you know that?"

Barb looked confused. "Really? I could have sworn . . ."

"Nothing!" The enormity of the understanding rocked Paul like a blow. "Even vicious murderers go to their graves knowing they've changed the world somehow. Murdering takes initiative; it takes *drive*. You got to get up off your duff to murder someone."

"Paul!"

He calmed down. "It's just, sometimes I feel like . . . a nonessential human being. I could be replaced with a robot that looked and dressed like me, that'd been programmed to run through the basic routines of my life, and nobody would ever know the difference."

"And you think picking a few grapes will make those thoughts go away?"

He gave a sigh. "Other suggestions?"

"Therapy, for one—"

"Jesus please us."

"—or medication. My Pilates partner told me that Stelazine brought her son back from the brink. He's grinning like a cherub all day long, never been happier. Paul—?"

He peeled away from her and walked out onto the ice. He caught his reflection in a boil of dark water: eyes as wide and scared as a horse in a barn fire.

"Do they make a drug called *Chrysalis*, Mom? You swallow one and hang from a tree branch until a cocoon forms, and two weeks later you crawl out, a whole new person. Pharmaceutical reincarnation—some egghead should get cracking on *that*!"

"Paul, come on in. You got me fluttering."

The ice pan boomed as a long fault line split its surface. Ice shattered under Paul's feet; his leg plunged in up to the crotch. His heart hammered so hard it threatened to tear his chest apart.

"Do they make pills for people who don't want to be themselves anymore, Mom?"

The water was probably fifteen feet deep beneath him, currents running swift; they wouldn't dredge his carcass up until next spring, which by then might have floated halfway to Cornwall, but he didn't give a damn and he laughed like a bastard.

I work hard so you won't have to. Parents tell their children this, Paul thought. *I will sweat and toil and bleed so you never will.*

All for love, but still, they miss the point entirely.

5

Reuben Tully worked in the bakery department at Topps Friendly Market. He rose at two a.m. weekdays, showering and dressing in the dark so as not to wake his son and brother. He caught the 2:30 Portage Express and nodded to the bus driver, who always touched the brim of his cap in reply. A woman who collected border tolls hopped on two stops later; she always sat four seats from Reuben with a coffee thermos and a lurid tabloid magazine. At the next stop the doors admitted a man in a threadbare suit who worked as night auditor for a strip of border motels; he always sat ramrod-straight—*stiff as a bishop's pecker*, the gym bums would say—with a briefcase on his lap.

Reuben had traveled with these people for twenty years. They'd all put on weight together and lost hair together, their eyesight had waned and their faces had furrowed together. They'd ridden through marriages, divorces, births, and deaths. Reuben rarely spoke to them, yet felt an odd kinship. On those rare occasions when he'd spot one on the street he'd raise a hand and they would respond with a nod or smile.

At the supermarket he'd buy coffee from an Italian with his steam cart; he'd mill with the butchers and florists and forklift drivers in the pre-dawn darkness. When the shift whistle blew he'd wheel a barrel of Red Star yeast down a row of industrial mixers. Over the years a yeasty, breadlike smell had sunk into his flesh. No amount of granulated pink industrial soap or frenzied scrubbing could erase that smell, and in his most maudlin moods Reuben could hear mourners at his funeral whispering that his corpse held the odor of fresh-baked bread.

Every few years a new man was hired fresh out of high school. Reuben wondered what he'd do if Robert chose to quit boxing and work here—a prospect that filled him with an intractable, deep-seated fear. His son was better than this town, with its crumbling tenements and bulletproof shop windows, its rusted cars and malt liquor bottles lining front stoops.

Robert Tully was destined for mythical things. Reuben Tully's only son would not die in upstate New York with the stink of bread on his hands.

The number twenty bus dropped Reuben off a block from Top Rank. He carried a grease-spotted bag of day-old bearclaws for his son. Not exactly the breakfast of champions, but Rob's metabolism ran hotter than a superconductor; he'd burn through them before lunch.

In the gym two heavies were training for an upcoming card at the armory. A pair of nightclub bouncers, they were set to square off against a couple of garrison Marines. Reuben pictured the matches: two pug-uglies in the dead center of the ring, bashing away like Rockem Sockem Robots. The war vets and jarheads on furlough would gobble it up.

Rob was up in the ring with bespectacled Frankie Jack, a retired welder who hung around the gym drumming up cut work. Frankie, with a pair of leather punch mitts over his hands, instructed Rob to turn through on his right cross, make it *sing*.

"Frank, ya fool," Reuben called, "you filling my fighter's head with nonsense?"

"Not at all, just warming him up for you." As if Rob were an old Dodge on a winter morning. "He's in fine shape, Reuben. Tip-*top* shape."

Rob spread the ropes so that Frankie could step down. Frankie jammed the punch mitts into his armpits and tugged them off; he rubbed his hands, wincing.

"I'll tell you, this kid can *hit*. He hurts just to breathe on you." Cotton swabs were pinned behind Frankie's ears like draftsman's pencils. "Hope this ain't out of line, but if you ain't yet settled on a cutman for Robbie's next fight I'd gladly step in."

"Now what makes you think he's gonna need a cutman?"

Frankie knuckled a pair of black-frame glasses up the bridge of his nose. "I'd surely like to be part of it, is all."

"Everyone wants to be part of it."

Their conversation was interrupted by the Buffalo heavyweight, Scarpella. "Seen your brother 'round?"

"I have not," said Reuben. "He owe you money?"

"Supposed to be workin' wit' him but don't see him nowhere."

"Ah, Jesus—he's over at the Fritz. Let me go grab him for you."

"I'll go get him," Rob said.

"Yeah, that's the ticket," Reuben said. "Tommy might have a tough time sparring with my boot up his ass."

The Fritz was the local appellation of a sagging row house named after its owner, Fritzie Zivic. A mooselike Croat, Zivic had had a brief and un-stellar boxing career as a mob-controlled heavyweight.

His heavily scripted run came to an undignified end when an aging Archie Moore knocked him cold under the lights at Madison Square Garden; after that, Zivic's mafia backers sent him down the river. He drifted back to his old neighborhood and parlayed his slim notoriety into a gambling den on the corner of Pine and 6th. No high rollers at the Fritz: clientele was strictly nickel and dime. Zivic sold cans of Hamms at two bucks a pop and ran a clean game: his well-known manner of dealing with hustlers was to pin the offender's fingers in a door jamb and kick till a few bones went snap.

Zivic was sitting on the porch steps in a navy pea coat. Zivic's dog, a dyspeptic bull mastiff whose blue eyes expressed a deep cunning, prowled the front lawn. It growled as Rob crossed the lawn, muzzle skinned back to bare rows of yellow teeth.

"Murdoch," said Zivic, "shut your hole."

The dog blinked its milky eyes and padded over to piss in the weeds.

"My uncle here?"

"Does the pope shit in the woods?" Zivic rubbed his smashed nose and blew a string of snot into the nettles. The skin of his face was leathery and deeply creased; razor-thin scars ran over his chin and cheeks like the seams on a baseball. "He's been here all night. I doubt he's got two pennies left to rub together." He gave Rob an appreciative up-and-down. "You're looking hale. When do you fight next?"

"The Golden Gloves qualifiers."

"Gonna win?"

"I guess, maybe."

Murdoch sat on his haunches beside Zivic. The dog yawned and broke wind against the cracked flagstones.

"You foul creature." Zivic shrugged as though to say, *Here's what boxing gets you, kid: a decrepit row house full of sadsack gamblers and a flatulent old dog. Welcome to Shangri La.*

The kitchen was empty. Padlocks on the cupboards and icebox. The place stunk like wet dog. His uncle dozed on a sofa in the adjoining room. Rob shook his shoulder. "Man, wake up."

Tommy cracked one bloodshot eye. "Robbie? Oh, god. You shouldn't be here."

"It was either me or Dad."

Tommy wiped away white lather crusted at the edges of his mouth. "In that case, I'm glad it's you."

Outside Zivic was flicking dog turds into his neighbor's yard with the toe of his boot.

"Get some shuteye," he said to Tommy. "I'll see you tonight."

"Not here you won't."

"Damn well better not—you're on at the barn, aren't you?"

Tommy rubbed his face with the flat of his hand, dug his fingers into his scalp. "Right," he said, "the barn."

They walked down Niagara Street toward Top Rank. Tommy's hair stuck up in rusty corkscrews. He shielded his sleep-puffed face from the sun.

"Feeling none too fine," he said. "We're talking ten pounds of shit in a five-pound bag, pardon my French."

"Fritzie said you were playing all night."

"Never again. It's a sucker's bet, Robbie. You remember that."

They passed a repo lot: sun glinted off the hoods and windows of derelict cars, a shining lake of metal and glass. Tommy stopped at Wilson Farms for breakfast: a box of Hostess cake donuts and a bottle of Gatorade.

"Replenish those electrolytes," he told his nephew. "So who am I sparring?"

"The heavy from Buffalo, Scarpella."

"Ah, jeez."

"What?"

"He's not worth it, is all." Tommy licked powdered sugar off his fingers. "Remember six months back I was working that young heavy, Mesi? Now that kid could *hit*—bashed me pillar to post and sent me home with a head full of canaries. But that was okay, way I saw it, because Mesi's going places—all that damage meant something 'cause I was building him up. But Scarpella's just a big kid with an okay set of whiskers. He's going nowhere. I know it, you know it, could be he knows it too. I'm not helping because he's beyond help. What does that make me? A punching bag for fifteen bucks a round."

"You trot out that line all the time."

"What line?"

"Tommy Tully, the poorly paid punching bag."

"What, now my own flesh and blood is giving me the gears?" He moaned dramatically. "I expect it from your pops, but—*et tu*, Robbie?"

Rob was unwilling to cut his uncle slack—he loved winding him up. "You don't like it, why step through the ropes?"

Tommy gave his nephew a look that said, *I might ask you the same thing.* "I read in the newspaper about this subway conductor in New York. Suicidal crazies keep leaping in front of his train. Apparently in the Big Apple they aren't satisfied with jumping off a bridge or sucking on a tailpipe—now they're flinging themselves in front of subway cars. They say a conductor can expect to have this happen two or three times in a career—this guy had it happen seven times in a month."

"Where'd you read that, the *Weekly World News*? Let me guess the next headline: Alien Love Secrets."

"Listen, I'm serious. The guy's driving merrily down the tracks and *whammo*—a body's thumping off the side of the train or exploding all over the windshield. One time the body hit so hard it busted the glass and sailed right into the driver's compartment. Imagine that!"

Rob was laughing now. It was awful, he knew it, but still.

"This guy gets to thinking he's cursed—seven in a month, who can blame him? Maybe he thinks the jumpers are plotting against him, this sect of rotten bastards hurling themselves in front of his train. But he keeps driving that subway. He's got a wife and kids and it's his job. Simple as that. So if *he* can get up every morning and face that possibility, well . . . I . . . I can . . ."

Tommy trailed off, staring at a string of boarded shopfronts.

"Tom. Hey, Tommy?"

Tommy seemed startled to be where he was, like a man who'd been caught sleepwalking. "I'm fine, Robbie. Spaced out for a minute, is all."

This happened a lot lately: Tommy's train of thought derailed, that weird thousand-yard stare. Rob feared it had to do with all the shots he'd taken in the ring. *The brain is a subtle organ,* was a saying he'd overheard at the club, *and it goes wrong in subtle ways.* He knew how postmortem examinations of dead boxers' brains often revealed severe cortical atrophy: the friction of heavy punches damaged the delicate tissue, which scarred up and sloughed away. Some boxers' brains ended up no bigger than a chimpanzee's. Sometimes he dreamed about a Monkey House for Beaten Fighters: glaze-eyed, banana-eating, diaper-wearing pugs roaming a steel cage, grunting and gibbering and swinging from radial tires.

In the worst dreams, his uncle was one of them.

Reuben got on his younger brother the moment he cleared the gym doors.

"Well if it ain't the leather-assed road gambler!"

Tommy nodded over at Scarpella. "Give me a minute to change up."

"So tell me, Amarillo Slim," said Reuben, "make out like a bandit?"

"Lay off, willya?" Tommy headed to the lockers. "Quit it with the fifth degree."

"Fifth?" Reuben said. "This is the *zero*-eth degree! You couldn't handle my fifth!"

Life in the gym took on its familiar rhythms. Trainers hollered: *Five rounds with the rope! Two hundred stomach crunches! Burn, baby, burn!* A boom box kicked on: pulsing rap beats overlaid with growling lyrics and random gunfire. Trainers held heavybags bucking against their chests and coached with their cheeks inches from their fighters' smacking fists. Managers talked on silver cellphones, arranging deals or pretending to. The buzzer sounded at three-minute intervals. *Stop playing pocket pool and HIT something!* Boxers caught their reflection in a manager's mirrored sunglasses and put a little more *oomph* into their shots. *Throw the right, baby—let it GO! He's flagging, get on his ass! Counterpunch on one and rip that shit!* Boxers finished their sparring sessions, geared down, and stepped onto the ring apron. A look on their faces like they'd exited a decompression chamber or come down from outer space.

Rob finished his circuit and sat on the risers with the managers and gym bums. Tommy worked the ring with Scarpella. He fought out of a crouch, the way Scarpella's trainer wanted. Scarpella let go with a clumsy roundhouse; Tommy let the punch slip through and took a knee.

The gym emptied out. The next wave of boxers would arrive after lunch. The gym bums swapped barefaced lies.

"Sailor Perkins could eat fifty pig's knuckles at a sitting, may god strike me blind for a lie."

"You'll never see a Mexie heavyweight champ. They just don't grow that big south of the Rio Bravo. Something to do with the intense heat shrinking the bones and that's not just me talking—that's science."

"Johnny Pushe's skin was so tough it could blunt a nail."

"Every welterweight champ in history had O-positive blood. A-negative or AB-positive welters, forget it—pack on thirteen pounds and move up to middleweight."

The walls of Robert's bedroom were hung with portraits of Muhammad Ali and Roy Jones Junior. They had been hung by his father and functioned, Reuben hoped, as a subliminal training method. Rob was working on his homework assignment—a haiku poem—while his father and uncle prepared for their trip over the river.

"Where's the adrenaline chloride, Tommy?"

"In the fridge behind the milk."

"Looks a mite yellow. Out of date?"

"How should I know?"

"Your face, not mine."

Rob had so far composed a single line: *My toenail is broken.* This had come to him staring down at his bare foot. Was that too many syllables?

"What about ice?"

"We'll grab a bag over there."

"We got any Canadian cash? Any whaddatheycallem—*loonies*?"

Robert amended: *My toenail is split.* Tommy poked his head through the door.

"What're you working on?"

"Haiku."

"Gesundheit."

"It's a Japanese poem."

Tommy strode into the room with his chest puffed out. "Why not write an ode to your handsome uncle?" He got down on one knee. "Tommy dearest, tell me true, why do all the gals love you . . ."

"Quit horsing around!" Reuben called.

"I'm helping Robbie with his poetry!"

"You wouldn't know Shakespeare if he crawled out the grave and bit you on your ass!"

"I'm a poet and you don't even know it!" Tommy hollered back. "There once was a man from Nantucket—"

"Enough," Reuben said, appearing in the doorway. "Robbie, we're gone until eleven. If your uncle's face isn't bashed so bad it'll put a man off his food, we'll meet up at Macy's."

Rob wished his uncle good luck. *Be careful*, he wanted to add, but among boxers those words were considered the father of bad luck. He could already feel the lump of fear in his belly, a lump that would persist until he received his father's call from Macy's diner.

Reuben's Dodge Shadow backed down the driveway, its rusted muffler rattling down 24th Street. Rob picked up the phone.

"Tully," Kate Paulson said from her end. "What's up?"

"Working on that poetry thing. What're you up to?"

"*Meh.*"

"Why don't you come over and help out?"

"You mean do your homework?"

"Did I say *do*? Did that word cross my lips? I said *help*." Rob tried to sound indifferent. "Or whatever."

"Or whatever," she mimicked, teasingly. "You know you need me, Tully. If poetic passion were punching power, you couldn't plow your posterior out of a paper peanut pack. Bet you don't even know what that's an example of."

"What are you talking about?"

"All those P words strung in a row—it's called . . . ?"

Kate hummed the theme from *Jeopardy*. Rob snapped his fingers, struggling to recall his last English lesson. "Alliteration?"

"Baaah! Sorry, you didn't answer in the form of a question and must forfeit your fabulous Caribbean vacation for two." Kate kept silent for a bit, then said, "Anything to eat over there?"

"Leftover spaghetti."

"Oooh, now there's a deal sweetener. No offense, but your dad . . ." She sifted various word combinations through her head. ". . . is a crummy caustic cook."

"But he's a blazingly brilliant baker."

"Not to mention a terrifically tyrannous trainer."

Rob let it slide; Kate's thoughts about his boxing aspirations were well documented, as were those regarding his father's role in them.

Kate's fingers drummed the wall beside her phone. "I'll be over in half."

Tommy and Reuben drove streets slick with twilight rain past pawn shops and discount liquor outlets and All-For-A-Buck stores. Spitting rain froze into a milky glaze at the windshield's edge. Tommy caught his reflection in the window, his forehead piled with scar tissue in the glow of passing streetlights.

Reuben paid the toll and drove out over the Rainbow Bridge. High-intensity spotlights trained on the Horseshoe Falls caused the ever-falling water to sparkle. The pines of Luna Island and Prospect Point were coated in crystallized spray.

They passed through the border toll and turned up Clifton Hill. Clusters of discount tourists peered through the darkened windows of shops closed for the season. Blinking neon reflected off frozen puddles; the road was pocked with fitful pools of blue, red, and green.

Reuben said, "A few fellas in the butcher department retired the other week. They're looking for meat cutters."

Tommy cracked his knuckles. "Maybe you think I'm blind," he said mirthlessly. "Maybe you think I missed the copy of the want ads you left on my pillow."

Reuben expressed mock surprise. "Is that where I left those? It'd be better than what you're earning now, plus it's forty hours a week, guaranteed."

Tommy opened and shut his mouth, jutting his lower jaw out until he looked like some predatory deep-sea fish: jaw limbering exercises. "I'm too clumsy. Liable to cut my pinkie off."

"Right," Reuben said, "and how would you cope without it?"

"Wouldn't be invited to any more tea parties." Tommy mimed tipping a china tea cup, his pinkie extended. "The Duchess of Windsor would be heartbroken."

The buildings and houses fell into the distance. The sawblade silhouette of a fir-lined ridge zagged above the fields.

"I thought you were done with this stuff, Tom."

"I thought so, too. This is the last time."

"The last?"

Tommy paused. "One of the last."

Reuben wasn't satisfied to let it rest. "This is how you imagined capping your career? You boxed at Madison Square Garden, in case the fact slipped your mind."

"Long time ago I did."

"So this is how you want it?"

"No, it's not." Tommy stared down at his hands lit by the dashboard, shrugging as if unable to conceive of another employment for them. "Just drop it."

"I worry about my kid brother, is all."

"Not a kid anymore."

"You know, this is about the only time I ever see you serious. And you'll always be my kid brother," Reuben said, not unkindly.

Flat frost-clad fields, fence posts, barns, the dark contours of sleeping cattle. A corduroy road cut off the rural route leading to a farmstead hemmed by a windbreak of pines. A tiny farmhouse with squares of light burning in odd windows. The dark outline of a peaked-roof barn stood east of some silos.

Vehicles were parked along a muddy fenceline: pickups and rusted beaters, ATVs and dirtbikes. Moonlight danced over the polished paint of a German sedan. Bumper stickers: SOCCER DAD AND PROUD OF IT! and MY OTHER CAR IS A BROOM.

Reuben stepped onto wooden batboards laid down over the mud. He grabbed a black valise from the back seat. They made their way through a canopy of leafless trees to the barn.

"I ought to put on one of those rubberized aprons," he said. "The kind slaughterhouse workers wear."

They were met at the barn by Manning.

On the second Thursday of each month the thick-lipped, beetle-legged cattle farmer doffed his cattleman's hat and donned his fight promoter's cap. Manning's arms were netted with old razor scars and the tip of his nose was gone: depending on which account you believed it'd been variously hacked, gouged, or bitten off his face. Tonight he wore an ankle-length duster coat, sleeves rolled to the elbows.

"Evening, lads." Starlight bent upon the barrel of a Remington over-under shotgun in his right hand. "Here to tussle or just catch an eyeful?"

"My brother's feeling frisky," Reuben said.

Manning kicked the barn door ajar with the heel of his boot. "Some fellas in there'd be happy to take that frisk right outta him."

The space under the peaked wood ceiling was as spacious as a dance hall, filled with light and smoke and milling bodies. The crowd was clotted in groups distinguished by their dress: suits and ties or flannels and work vests. Manning's buck-toothed son sold six-packs of PBR from an ice-filled trough. Bales of hay studded with pink blossoms demarcated the ring. Cows snuffled at gaps in the barn planks.

Spectators were rowed along a wooden skirt circling the barn's upper level, legs dangling over the edge. Tommy saw Fritzie Zivic standing beside a wheelchair-bound geezer with a breathing mask strapped over his face. Zivic's scrofulous old dog was chewing a wheelchair tire.

The fighters huddled in corners beyond the light. Some were washed-up trial horses and clubbers, others tavern toughs with cobalt fists. All bore the mistakes of their trade: worn-out, mangled foreheads and split brows and pitcher lips and eyes like milky balls socked into the pitted ruin of their faces.

Reuben scanned the prospects. All regulars, at least. Every so often a vagabond fighter would show up; he'd fight, collect his purse, and move on down the road. Reuben would never forget driving home after a night at the barn and seeing one of those vagabond fighters at the Niagara bus terminal: only hours ago that same guy had pinned another man's skull between bales of hay and pounded until the floorboards ran red, and now here he was stepping onto a Greyhound with blood on his hands, moving on to another town and another fight while his opponent lay on a hospital gurney with a pair of detached retinas. No remorse—everyone who stepped into the ring knew the stakes.

Men born in the wrong century, Reuben had heard it said. *Put 'em in a coliseum, fighting with spears and nets. It's all that suits 'em.* Men whose sole value lay in their willingness to absorb punishment; men in whose faces could be glimpsed an inevitability of purpose impossible to outrun. Some had no more intellect than a child. Reuben had seen one eating soda crackers spread with axle grease: his trainer insisted it thickened the blood. Later that fighter stood in the ring, his face black with blood, calling his trainer's name in a high, childish voice. Only his trainer wasn't there: he'd already hopped into his truck and driven away.

Reuben motioned his brother to a hay bale. "Gimme those mitts." He taped Tommy's hands with great care, first winding clean white bandages around and around, then placing sponge across the knuckles, then wrapping on the adhesive.

When the barn was full Manning bolted the door and crossed the wide sawdust floor. He ran down the rules, such as they were. "Fight goes until one man can't answer the bell. A man goes down, both fighters take a rest. I won't accept no outright foul play but whatever happens between two men in the course of a tussle, happens. Those men ain't got nobody to stand by them, gypsy cab's waiting to run ya to the medic need be—fare come out your purse, but."

Something tightened in Reuben's chest to hear Manning's spiel. He knew his brother never went out to make a show—he went out to get a job done. He was a boxer: a rough occupation, yes, but one governed by laws of fairness and respect. There was a refinement and cleanliness to it. You don't hit a man when he's down. You don't punch after the bell.

Here, men fought like weasels down a hole. It was dangerous and dirty and men were hurt in ways they would never recover from. Here you might see a guy staggering to his corner with his scalp split pink down the dark weave of his hair, his eyes half-lidded and tongue hanging like a dog's. Here you might see an overmatched fighter struck a blow so vicious it cracked the orbital bone and pushed his eye from its socket, the blood-washed eyeball swinging on its optic nerve like a lacquered radish. Reuben knew such things were a possibility because he had, in fact, seen those exact things on past nights.

Top Rank operated under laws. The barn was international waters. Top Rank was for boxers. The barn was for fighters.

Rob was watching TV when Kate Paulson rapped on the door.

"Ándale, Tully, ándale," she called. "Freakin' cold out here."

He opened the door and smirked. As typical, she was overdressed: blue winter shell, scarf, and mittens. "You must be looking for the polar expedition team. They're two doors down."

"I walk all the way over and you give me grief? May just go home."

"What, head back out in that weather?" He clutched his shoulders and shivered. *"Brrrrr."*

Kate lived three blocks east on 22nd. Kate's mother, Ellen, had known the Tully brothers since the first grade; they'd grown up in the same ten-mile radius, attended the same schools, caroused the same bars. She worked in the florist department at Topp's, where she and Reuben often chatted amid the daffodils and zinnias.

The Tullys and Paulsons might have existed like any two families in the Love Canal district of Niagara Falls—that is to say, distantly— if not for a pair of coincidences, one happy, the other not so. The happy coincidence was the near-simultaneous births of their first, and only, children; Robert Thomas was born Monday afternoon, Katherine Harriet during the witching hours Tuesday morning. The infants spent their first night together in the Mount St. Mary nursery, side by side in transparent plastic tubs. Tommy, the most whimsical member in either family, believed they had imprinted on each other like baby chicks; this he held accountable for their enduring closeness.

The other coincidence was that, shortly after the births, both Ellen's husband and Reuben's wife had realized parenting wasn't in their blood. Phil Paulson stepped out for a pack of Kools days after his daughter's birth and never did manage to find his way home. And speculation had it that Phil's itchy feet must have been highly contagious, spreading all the way down to Carol Tully's house; one afternoon Reuben came home to find baby Robbie at the next-door neighbor's and a note from his wife informing him she'd moved to Nashville to pursue a music career.

Following from the initial, heart-defibrillating shock of abandonment, Ellen Paulson recovered rather quickly. Her husband was a contract handyman whose keenest aspiration was to lose a digit in a work-related mishap and live off the settlement; as Ellen saw it, now she had only one child to care for instead of two. Every so often she'd receive a postcard from deadbeat Phil; these she read aloud to Reuben and Tommy in a deft imitation of her husband's voice: *I still love you, don't think for a second I don't, but the aloor of the open road, that freedum . . . its got me in its spell.* She'd point out all the misspellings and clichés and finally, cathartically, burned each postcard in the fireplace. After a year she didn't bother to read them anymore, just pitched them in the trash.

"So." Kate clapped her hands. "Where's that leftover spag?"

In the kitchen Rob set the pot of sauce on the stove. She sat at the table rubbing the cold from her hands. Her pageboy-style hair stuck up in wild spikes. She had green eyes, like her mother: *cat's eye green,* Reuben called that color.

"You want noodles," he asked, "or on toast?"

"You're kidding."

Rob shrugged. "Tommy likes it that way."

Which was true. Tommy ladled spaghetti sauce on top of bread—and not any old bread: Wonder Bread. This caused friction in the household, since Tommy preferred it to the bakery loaves his brother brought home. *Why,* Reuben harped, *would you fill your face with that crap? I doubt it's even bread; I bet it's labeled "food substitute."*

Rob set another pot on the stove and dumped in a handful of spaghetti. Kate, who'd been watching with a critical eye, asked what the heck he was doing.

"You didn't sound keen on toast."

She joined him at the stove, hip-checking him out of the way. "Got to boil the water first, dummy. Then the noodles." It was hot over the stove top and she pulled off her school sweatshirt, rucking her undershirt up. Rob caught bare skin, the dip under her ribcage, a groove of muscle down her stomach.

He was unruffled that she'd taken over the kitchen; Kate had always been alpha to his beta. Their easy acceptance of these roles was one of the reasons they got on so well. And since Rob had never seen his own father and mother interact, he'd always wondered if, in their way, he and Kate behaved as a married couple might.

She sprinkled the cooked spaghetti with Kraft Parmesan—"Cheese in a canister," she said disapprovingly, "that's what you get in a house full of men"—and slid Rob's plate across the table. He'd eaten only two hours ago, but most boxers existed in a more or less permanent state of appetite.

"Where's your pops," Kate said, "or Tommy?"

Rob kept his eyes on his plate. "Busy tonight."

Kate arched her eyebrows. "Second Thursday of the month. I didn't think your uncle was mixed up in that anymore."

Most people in the neighborhood knew of the barn; a few, desperately strapped for cash, had even tried their luck there. For all but Tommy, once had been enough.

"Tommy's shifts at the warehouse got cut back," Rob said. "He's in some to Fritzie Zivic and hasn't been drumming up much sparring work—"

She cut him off. "The supermarket's looking, and nobody's gonna try and knock his head off there—or if so, some turkey-armed fogy because he cuts the salami too thick."

Rob laughed, but he was shaking his head. "It's not the money so much . . ."

"So much as?"

All Rob could think was that boxing got into people's blood like a poison, except that the poison was the only thing that kept them alive, or at least made them feel that way.

"I mean it's a tough life for a man to leave behind, is all."

Kate looked up at the ceiling, scanning for bits of Rob's brain that clearly must have drifted out his ears. "Women find it hard to leave things, too—shitty marriages, and boyfriends, and degrading jobs. We can be every bit as pigheaded as men."

"Let me get this straight," said Rob. "You're defending a woman's right to act as stupidly as a man?"

"I'm saying men don't have a hammerlock on weakness. But it's still no excuse."

In their neighborhood, gender roles were pretty well defined. Men did this; women, that. There wasn't a lot of friction over it—just the way things were.

"Hey," he wanted to know, "are we having an argument?"

"No, Tully. We are having a discussion."

". . . Oh."

One commonly held theory in streetfighting is that you must get the first punch no matter what the price.

Christ, Tommy thought, staggering back on his heels, *I really should've known better.*

The blow struck him dead between the eyes—a poleax, in the same spot that a slaughterhouse stunner aims his kill hammer. The air shimmered with darts of white light as his mouth filled with the taste of cold lightning.

He'd been matched against a young fighter, Caleb Kilbride. The Kilbrides were a clan of ridge runners who made ends meet smuggling reservation cigs and booze across the Niagara River. Shirtless, the kid was built like the butt end of a sledgehammer. His neck and arms were mottled with burn scars; the falling light picked out further scarring on his hips, a galaxy of pale white chips.

They'd met in the middle of the ring. Tommy noted Kilbride's small, close-set eyes, the slight upslope at their outer edges that bespoke inbreeding. He looked over at the kid's corner, where Papa Kilbride swigged at a flask of triple-X; a black eyepatch gave him the look of a landlocked, hillbilly pirate. He seemed the sort of father who might force his mentally defective son into a fight, and Tommy had been considering this very possibility when Caleb Kilbride came forward and popped him in the face.

The blinding sting in Tommy's eyes told him that Kilbride's work-gloves were soaked in caustic, weed killer most likely, but it was too late for complaining and besides, there was no ref to hear his grievance. Kilbride pressed in, bashing Tommy about the head and arms; the ridge runner's breath was warm in Tommy's ears, the excited exhale of his lungs like hickory wood cracking.

"Circle out of there!" his brother called as the crowd hooted and catcalled.

Kilbride let go with a flurry of haymakers, thudding them into the dense muscling of Tommy's arms and shoulders. By then the canaries had flitted from Tommy's head and he was able to step inside one of Kilbride's looping punches, set his shoulders, and hook to the kidneys. Kilbride's breath escaped in a gust: a sweet pablum-y smell.

He recovered enough to smash a fist into Tommy's forehead. The shot lacked gas and Tommy weathered it easily, but Kilbride followed up with another in the same spot, planting his feet and dropping his fist like a guillotine blade. The blow landed with the sound of an ax chopping into wet wood and split the skin over Tommy's left eye along the socket ridge; he felt the buzzing X-ray contour of bone beneath his skin.

He dropped to one knee and Kilbride hit him going down, an uppercut fired straight from the hip that flattened Tommy's lips against his teeth. He went down with the taste of blood and Killex on his tongue. The bell rang but Kilbride kept slugging until Manning dragged him off.

Reuben helped his brother to the corner. The railbirds hubbubed and pumped their fists. Fritzie Zivic sucked a toothpick beside the wheelchair-bound fogy who looked either comatose or dead save his eyes, which were riveted on the ring above the green plastic edge of his oxygen mask.

Reuben jammed a hand down Tommy's trunks and splashed ice water on his groin. "What's the matter? He's wide open."

"Something's wrong with him. He's not all there upstairs."

Reuben cracked the seal on a vial of adrenaline 1:1000 and dipped a Q-Tip. He jammed it into the wound above Tommy's eye, down through the layers of meat, pinching the flaps of skin over the cotton tip.

"How many of these punch-drunk tomato cans do you figure are all there?"

"No, I mean . . . slow." Tommy rinsed water around his mouth and spat. "His breath smells like a baby's."

Reuben glanced at the opposite corner. Kilbride was taking pulls from a flask while Papa massaged his shoulders.

"You socked him, all right," Papa crowed. "The ole Missouri soupbone!"

Reuben smeared Vaseline over the burns left by Kilbride's gloves. "Slow or not, I couldn't help but notice that kid's only too happy to hit you."

Two bungling men in their mid-twenties, Reuben and Tom Tully's combined knowledge of child rearing could have fit on the head of a pin. To spare infant Robbie the indignity of newsprint diapers and herself the expense of a nanny, Kate's mother had come up with a solution. Weekday mornings she dropped her daughter off with Tom, who cared for Kate and Robbie until Reuben arrived home from his bakery shift; Tommy then set off for the loading docks and Reuben looked after the kids until Ellen returned from the floral shop.

The five of them knit into an odd, but oddly workable, unit. The sight of Ellen Paulson flanked by lumbering Tom Tully and Reuben in his peaked fedora became a familiar one: at the park, in the supermarket aisle, pushing prams up Niagara Street. Tommy and Reuben often took Robbie to Loughran's Park on their own; those newly arrived to the neighborhood had been overheard remarking upon the raffish homosexual couple and their adopted Serbian baby. Tommy made a joke of this perception at his prudish brother's expense: he'd grab Reuben's hand at inappropriate times, or rub his shoulder with the tender fondness of a lover. "So help me *god*," Reuben would seethe.

Kate and Rob had grown up almost as brother and sister; for the most part, they treated each other with the brusque affection of siblings. But lately Rob had been reminding himself that she was not, in point of fact, his birth sister.

"You're hopeless," she said when Rob told her his haiku began with the line *My toenail is split*. "Of all the poetic topics in our vast universe, you settle on the most revolting feature of the human body."

"You're forgetting something," he said. "The duodenum."

They were covering anatomy in biology class; everyone agreed the duodenum was one ugly organ. "Fine, second most revolting. Come on—what sort of things excite you?"

Like a lot of guys his age, Rob twigged on stories tinged with a note of morbid irony—like the newspaper article about a frozen ball of shit that was accidentally discharged from the hull of a Swiss Air flight from Geneva to New York; the pinky-brown boulder had rocketed into a house in Rochester, crushing its owner, who happened to be relieving himself at that very moment.

"Frozen balls of turd?" Kate said, after he'd been foolish enough to tell her. She put the base of her palm on the flat of her forehead and held it there for several seconds. "Roll over, Basho."

"Then give me guidance, O Poetic Spirit."

"Look around you. And a bit farther than your toenail."

"Busted syringes on the basketball court at Loughren's?" he said, after brief consideration. "The god-awful stench from the rubber plant as you cross the bridge over the polluted river, before you hit the burned-down strip mall and pass into factory outlet wasteland? Is that poetry?"

"Probably," Kate said, "to some people. But why concentrate on that? How about something you know a lot about? How about boxing?"

"No," muttered Rob. "Not boxing."

Kate was pleased to hear this. They sat for a while in silence, then Rob stood up and tapped the windowpane. "How about that?"

"What, Mr. Cryptic—the curtains?"

"The view. The maple tree, the fence, the sky. I've grown up, so my perspective has changed. But tree, fence, sky. Those have always stayed the same."

Kate clapped her hands. "Grab a pen, son—strike while the iron is hot!"

When he sat down with a pen she plucked it from his grip. She took Rob's hand, flipped it so his palm showed, and pressed it flat to the table. She licked the pen tip and touched it to a big blue vein where his wrist met the meat of his palm. "So—how does that make you feel?"

A trapdoor opened in Rob's head, dumping endorphins into his brainpan; it felt like getting hit in a sparring session, his pain centers bombed with peptides. No pain now, only the pressure of Kate's fingers on his hand. A surge of power flooded him, the kind that made him a terror in the ring, but here, now, he had no idea where to go with it.

"How about . . ." He flushed; his eyeballs must be bulging like grapefruits. Why? She was only touching his *hand*. ". . . The view out of my kitchen window—"

Her fingertip tapped beats on his wrist like a second heartbeat. "The view out of my . . . okay, that's your first line . . . kit-chen win-dow. Three more syllables."

"Remains the same . . . no, *is* the same . . ."

She wrote across his palm in smooth cursive. ". . . Is the same . . . one more line. Five beats."

". . . since I . . ."

". . . since I . . ."

". . . was a child—no, boy."

She contemplated the words spread across his palm. "Simple, but I like it."

Looking at her, he thought of a night months ago. He'd stopped by on his way home from the club and she'd been on the porch—waiting for him, or so he'd felt for a moment. She stepped into light thrown by the porch bulb and the scent of her—vanilla, remarkable only in that he'd never known her to smell this way—fell through the light, melding and bonding so that for Rob the light itself smelled of her.

Kate flipped Rob's other palm over and, with quick strokes, wrote her own haiku.

When the bell rang to start the second round Caleb Kilbride tear-assed across the ring windmilling his fists. Tommy got on his bicycle and circled away, taking a few harmless shots to the arms and brisket. Kilbride was in no kind of shape: greasy sweat shone under his eyes and where his nose met the rest of his face. The kid was used to fighting scratch-ass hill people who folded at the sight of those flatiron fists.

Tommy led Kilbride around the ring, absorbing the young man's lunging blows on hip and elbow. *Taking him into the deep waters,* any boxing aficionado would've known. *Gonna drown him.*

Kilbride threw a sloppy hook and when Tommy ducked he saw the ridge of Kilbride's wide-open torso. After a moment's hesitation Tommy lashed out with his left, banging Kilbride's liver. The bigger man bent forward at the hip; ropes of snot jetted from his nose.

Tommy grabbed Kilbride by the scruff of the neck—the hairs back there were coarse as hog bristles—and, jerking his skull forward, smashed a fist into his face. Something gave under his knuckles with a dim splintering and Tommy saw a shard of bone poking through the skin below Kilbride's right eye.

Kilbride struck out instinctively, a bone-cutting shot that sheared off Tommy's jaw. Tommy belted Kilbride's left ear, fattening it instantly. They fell into a clumsy embrace, foreheads touching, arms tangled.

"Go down, kid," Tommy whispered. "No shame in it. You're one tough hombre."

Kilbride only grunted. Blood sprayed from his fractured cheekbone into one eye but the other one held Tommy in its gaze with the belligerence of a petting zoo goat.

Kilbride pushed off and hit Tommy with a left, following up with a right. Tommy held his hands at his waist, not bothering to cover up, and the shots glanced off the crown of his skull, reopening the cut above his eye. Kilbride threw another weak left and Tommy swatted his fist out of the air and came over the top with a right hook that slammed the side of Kilbride's head and the ridge runner's swollen ear exploded, the pressure of compressed blood splitting it off the side of his head. Hanging by its lobe on a rope of skin, it looked like a crushed baby mouse.

Kilbride crumpled to his knees, cradling the side of his head. Tommy stared in horror: it was the worst damage he'd ever inflicted upon another human being. It was as though Kilbride were made not of flesh and bone but of weaker substances that broke and tore and bled at the barest provocation.

Tommy threw a helpless glance at his brother. Reuben had already packed the valise and now tossed the towel. "It's over," he signaled to Manning. "We're quit."

The crowd booed lustily. Beer cans and flaming matchbooks pelted the ring.

"We better hightail it." Reuben shielded his brother's head from the flames that rained down. "These crazies are bound to riot."

On the way out Tommy stopped before Papa Kilbride, who was weaving drunk and hadn't yet attended to his stricken son. His eyepatch had slipped down around his neck; he stared at the brothers with a pair of boozy but working eyes.

"Your boy's feebleminded and we both know it." With his face veiled in blood, Tommy's eyes were very wide, very white. "If I catch you running him out here again, you and me will have business."

"Goddamn butcher shop," Reuben said once they were clear of the barn. "Look at you carved right to hell."

"I'm fine. But the kid—"

"Some are made of flimsier stuff. The kid won't win any beauty contests, but skin heals."

Reuben grabbed a low-hanging branch and pulled it aside, allowing his brother to walk past before letting it whip back. "You're bleeding something fierce. Get you cleaned up."

He guided Tommy to a fence post and hung his valise on a point of barbed wire. With a clean towel he wiped the blood from Tommy's face. His brow was so sodden with adrenaline Reuben could only patch it with a butterfly bandage. He set two fingers under Tommy's jaw to ease the chatter of his teeth.

"What about your fight purse?"

"Manning knows to give it to Fr-Fruh-Fitzie Z-Zuh-Zivic. I owe him."

A spotted cow ambled over and jammed its blunt, ski-boot-shaped head through the wire. It snuffled loudly, rooting about under Tommy's armpit.

"Shoo," Reuben told it.

"L-luh-le-leave it be," Tommy said. "Its breath is nice and wuh-warm. You know, it was the st-struh-strangest thing." Shivering, he spoke with his eyes shut. "I'm lo-lo-locked up with that kuh-kid, his f-f-face pissing bl-bluh-blood, look into his eyes and see no way is he quitting. I could've beat on that poor boy till there was nuh-nuh-othing left that was really hu-hyu-human and he'd've kept getting uh-uh-up. So I had to quit."

"I would've been disappointed if you hadn't."

The cow chewed at the seat of Tommy's pants, pulling the material so taut Reuben saw the shape of his brother's crotch.

"Stupid animal's gonna chew your pants off."

Tommy grinned. "This is the most a-ah-action I've got in a l-luh-long time."

Reuben took his brother's head between his palms and considered it at a few angles. "Border guards ask, we'll say you fell down a set of icy steps."

Kate had bundled herself up and headed for home by the time Rob's father called.

"Come on down and get a slice—pecan's just out of the oven."

The sky coldly pristine, spokes of lightning flashing across a bank of night clouds far off to the west. Through lit windows of the houses strung down the block Rob saw familiar silhouettes watching television, preparing for night shifts, arguing, eating alone. The nature of his neighborhood was such that he knew why that woman was eating alone, the job that man was preparing for, the root of that couple's argument. To live on these streets was to know everything about those you lived among, to see inside their homes and lives and be seen in turn. Rob knew it was a big world from the books he'd read and movies he'd watched, but his own world often felt infinitesimally small: a limited orbit of opportunities and events, faces and places, friends and enemies. And the specific gravities of obligation and fear and love could keep you locked in that orbit your whole life.

Macy's was an institution. The original owner, Jefferson Macy, was a pipefitter who'd come from Altoona to labor on the bridge crews; he'd sunk down to the Niagara River in a diving bell to set foundation anchors in the stony riverbed. He'd received hazard wages: at shift's end sometimes nothing but an empty helmet was retrieved from the deeps, the diver's waterlogged body found dashed on the rocks beyond the whirlpool rapids. Most workers—Irish, Polish, Mi'kmaq, and Iroquois—bunked in clapboard shacks or tents pitched on Goat Island. On cold nights the tents frequently collapsed, weighed down by frozen spray off Bridal Veil Falls. Each week Macy's wife crossed the river by punt boat with pies for the laborers. Macy insisted his wife charge them for ingredients, if not her sweat and toil. By 1942 they'd saved enough to open a shopfront on Elmwood.

Reuben and Tommy sat in a corner booth. Tommy wasn't too bad off, considering. A few gloveburns, that old scar over his eye bust open again.

"You win?"

His uncle sipped black coffee and shrugged. "Some you win, some you lose."

Reuben clarified: "He lost."

The waitress freshened their cups. "Can I get you, Robbie?"

"Give him orange soda, Ellie," Reuben said. "Coffee'll stunt his growth."

"Old wives' tale," she said. "Your brother's been drinking it since he was in short pants and look at the size of him." She appraised Tommy's face. "Been in a scrape tonight?"

"Ran into a door, my darling."

"You're the only man I know runs into doors with a nasty habit of swinging back. Robbie, you steer clear of the doorways your uncle frequents."

Pecan pie for Reuben, pumpkin for Rob, cherry for Tommy. The slices were a good two inches thick, topped with a big ball of vanilla ice cream.

"What's that?" Reuben gestured with his chin to the words on Rob's palm. "Looks like a girl's writing."

Tommy brightened. "Kate must've been over."

Reuben pinned Rob's palm to the table and read Kate's haiku: "*Though there will always / Be those things out of your reach / Never stop reaching.*" He nodded. "I like it. Yours?"

"It's Kate's."

"She's a clever gal," said Tommy. "Pretty as her mother, too."

"Get off it," Rob said.

"What's the matter," said Reuben. "Not like she's your sister."

"I know!" Rob nearly shouted. The brothers chuckled at this.

They sat with stuffed bellies. Ellie came around with a bag of frozen strawberries for Tommy's lumps.

"You see that place up there?" Tommy pointed across the street, to the lit windows of an otherwise darkened building. "I ever tell you the story?"

Neither Reuben nor Rob wished to see the puzzled look come over Tommy's face should they say he'd told it a dozen times, so both shook their heads.

"That's the LOH on the third story—Loyal Order of Hibernians. You need a card to get in, even though it's just card tables and a wet bar. One time I was working the door and this guy showed up, didn't have no card, so I tell him to bug off. *Come on, let me in, I'm Irish*, the guy says. I tell him no card, no dice, and when he got pushy I threw him down the steps."

Tommy mopped crumbs off his plate with his thumb. "Well, pretty soon come that knock again. It's the same guy, looking a bit worse for wear. *Come on, let me in, I'm Irish*. Well, he gets a bit flagrant so I got to throw him down the steps again. A few minutes later another knock. The same guy. Well I stepped aside and let him in, saying, *You're right. You* must *be Irish*."

Tommy threw back his head and roared. Rob and Reuben joined in—not for the punch line, which they'd heard a thousand times, but simply for the telling.

6

Paul's head hit the canvas and things went dark and in the blackness he saw a chicken hatchery. The walls were ribbed sheet metal stretching into the dark, a cavernous place like a warehouse thick with an ammonia smell. A pool of light hung above a hatching pen as though a spotlight were trained on it, only there was no spotlight. The pen was constructed of small-gauge wire and filled with yellow chicks clustered at a tube spitting out cracked corn which they fought over with stunning viciousness. He saw a hen in there, too, a big sleek mama clucking and ruffling her pinfeathers as if agitated. She shifted her weight and a tiny beak poked out from under her dirty feathers, a beak opening and closing like a fish dying on a beach. A wing popped out under the hen, a wing without feathers flapping feebly, bone ends snagging the wire. The hen tucked the wing gently beneath her and kept on clucking and shifting, and finally she shook her feathers out and stepped off the pitiful thing she'd been sheltering. The chick was withered and milk-pale and one of its claws, crushed close to its body, had torn a ragged hole in its side. One eye was a swollen mound trickling pus and the other had ruptured from being sat on, a shiny ball of blood. Its wings were smeared in shit and the print of the wire was pushed into its flesh, a deep hexagonal grid over one side of its body. Paul felt shocked and terrified and all shredded up inside as the thing thrashed, its beak opening and closing but not a sound coming out. The other chicks saw it lying there. They clustered around as it struggled to stand but its legs were withered and its wings nothing more than bones and it flopped on its side, breathing rapidly. The chicks bobbed up and down and shook their wings all out and stared on with dusky wet eyes. One pecked the sick one's head and opened a hole there. One pecked at an eye and broke it. Then they were pecking fanatically and peeping with excitement while the mama watched without emotion and in the midst of the fluttering yellow bodies Paul saw that beak opening and closing, opening and closing—

". . . aul . . . Paul . . ."

The burn of ammonia filled his nostrils. He opened his eyes, blinked, squinted. The ring lights were set in steel lattices, a spot of total blackness at their centers.

He tried to sit up but couldn't. It was like someone had taken a heavy mallet and nailed his gloves and boots to the mat. His opponent— Everett, a tattooed black kid—stood with his arms draped over the turnbuckle.

Lou said, "What's your name?"

Paul worked his jaw. "Did I get . . . knocked out?"

"What's your name?"

"Paul Harris. How long was I out?"

"Long enough. Can you see my fingers? How many am I holding?"

He'd been training six or seven hours a day, including a good deal of sparring. He'd taken bodyshots that filled his mouth with bile and clubbing blows that dropped him to one knee, but this was a fresh twist.

"Sneak uppercut," Lou said. "Tickled you right on the knockout button."

Everett came over and, in a belated gesture of concern, asked was Paul all right.

"You hit pretty hard." Paul's tone was gleeful. "Let's get back at it."

Lou stepped back through the ropes. "Go to it, then."

The buzzer sounded. Everett streaked across the ring to catch Paul moving hesitantly out of his corner. Everett boasted an accurate jab, throwing it out on the end of his long left arm.

"Get down on your haunches!" Lou called at him. "You're boxing like Frankenstein!"

The morning after his first training session Paul had awakened near-paralyzed, his tendons so tight he could barely walk. But he dragged himself back to the club and, after some crass ribbing from Lou—*You look like twice-pounded shit*—kept at it. He took to running a five-mile circuit each morning, following a path along the train tracks to the Welland Canal where great shipping cranes slanted against the sky. He ran the steps connecting the club and paint store with a medicine ball; he hit the heavybag until his hands looked like ground chuck. Pushing his body, he found that it possessed limits beyond his reckoning. Muscle groups presented themselves: ice-cube-tray abs and a cobra's hood of latissimus muscle; a trickledown map of blue veins running under skin gone translucent as rice paper.

Everett's hand flashed and a polar whiteness expanded inside Paul's skull. He gagged on his gumshield but got his gloves up; Everett's punches glanced off his elbows.

"Keep your head down. You're holding it out there like a lantern in a storm!"

Paul had been surprised at how quickly his body accommodated itself to pain—not only the mediated pain of training, but the immediate and unavoidable pain of the ring. He'd been hit with such force that blood leapt from his nose like a grisly magic trick, yet he gathered himself and fought back. He discovered the miracle of adrenaline.

They circled, feinting and juking. Paul saw the curve of Everett's torso, the smooth ladder of his ribcage. His fist could fit into that space, he reasoned, into the bundle of organs below Everett's short rib.

When he threw the punch, turning on his lead foot and twisting his hips, the coiled momentum released his fist like a boulder from a catapult. The punch landed solid and the shock rebounded down his arm like the kickback of an elephant gun.

Everett made a small sound like a sigh and fell away from Paul's glove.

"Whoa!" Lou hopped up on the apron and ducked through the ropes.

Everett gulped for breath on the mat. Lou took the kid's arms and held them up. A dark patch spread over the crotch of his boxing trunks. "Breathe, now, Ev. Find those lungs."

Paul felt pretty damn pleased with himself. He envisioned Everett's blood stunned in his veins, hardening like ice. He felt the displacement of Everett's guts through his glove, the organs shifting in deference to his fist.

Lou helped Everett back to the change room. "That was some punch," he said upon his return. "Like to bring down the walls of a city."

"Just doing like you taught."

Lou scratched under the brim of his paisley porkpie, lips pursed in an effort to recall what, if any, advice he'd offered Paul. "Well, you're a good kid—you're a *listener*." He whistled. "Hit a guy that bad, you steal a piece of him forever."

"It was a lucky punch."

"Some of my prospects had half your hustle, they'd be champs. Hop in the ring."

Lou shrugged on punch mitts and worked with Paul. The kid was raw as hell, a hundred and eighty-odd pounds of flailing flesh and bone, but the sting in Lou's hands signaled one-punch power. That overhand left could scramble anyone's brain.

"What was it you said you did?" Lou asked during a break. "Businessman of some sort?"

"Worked at a winery. I quit, though."

"So why boxing?"

Paul spat on a blotch of blood marking the canvas. "I can't say," he said, scuffing the spot with his boot. "I needed to be stronger."

"Muscles? Will power? How do you mean?"

He wanted to tell Lou about a World War I documentary he'd seen, these veteran soldiers talking about mercy kills. Back then, they said, if a man in your unit was a liability, you put a bullet in his brain and made it look like an accident. The murdered men were officers, silver spooners; the killers were working-class enlisted men. Out in the trenches the degrees on your wall didn't matter, they said, nor that your father played tennis with the Duke of York. Out there it was, Do I trust this man with my life? Dog eat dog, the basic law of man, and the refinements of civilization a million miles away. The vets were not the least bit shamed by their actions—they considered it an act of mercy.

Paul couldn't help but wonder: if it ever came to it, would he be facedown in a bunker with a bullet in his skull? He'd never know, and that was the worst part—the wondering.

All he said was, "I've had it pretty cushy so far."

Lou nodded. "First time I saw you, I said give this guy a week. You had the look of a lot of guys your age—a lily. I don't quite get the things you boys get up to. Building superhero bodies at the gym and hurling yourselves off high rises with a parachute on your back." Lou snorted. "John Wayne never lifted a barbell in his life. Put Jack La Lanne and the Duke in a cage and see who comes out alive."

Lou worked Paul another round. Lordy, this kid could *hit*. His power reminded Lou of another fighter he'd trained, the young son of a carnival barker. Years back Lou had taken the kid down south of Rock Springs, where he'd fought in a dirt bowl at the base of the Rockies. July or early August and they'd fought like dogs, the barker's kid and a lanky Mexie who'd ridden boxcars up from Ciudad Obregón. Between rounds the idiots in charge had laid down a sheen of lamp oil to keep the dust down. Maybe it had been the righteously burning sun or a cigar ember—this low *whoomph,* then greasy orange fire licking from the earth. The spectators backed away but inside the bowl the Mexie and the barker's son kept swinging, their eyes bruised shut and blood coming out of them all places. Flames crawled up their arms in glittering sleeves but they kept punching as though the fight was the only thing keeping them alive or was the only thing worth dying for.

"Your generation's got a lot to prove," Lou said during the next break. "Before, just staying alive was proof. My granddad with the Depression, then the war. My pops, Big Two. Me, Vietnam. And otherwise you were poor, which is a war of its own. You guys, though . . ."

Paul pounded the punch mitts. Lou winced.

"All I'm saying is, how can you ever know sweet until you've tasted the sour? How can any of you quite know you're . . . men?"

Paul was irritated. He wanted to slip a fist past the punch mitts and crack Lou in the teeth but wasn't sure he could fob it off as an accident.

"Go change up and meet me in the office."

In the change room Paul doffed his sweaty top and stood before the mirror. The flesh of his chest was tight, pebbled, rough as pig leather. He'd gained an inch around his arms, two around his neck, and dropped two pant sizes. The steroids had done their job, but not without side effects. Paul's shoulders were pocked with greasy cysts, his scalp ringed with acne. He also suffered a case of grape-cluster hemorrhoids; the bleeding had gotten so bad he found himself browsing the pharmacy's adult diaper aisle.

In the office, Lou beckoned him to a chair that looked to be held together with surgical tape. "Let me show you something."

He set a framed print on the desktop. It was an etching of a muscular athlete approaching middle age. He had a thick beard, a flattened nose, and was balding around the crown of his skull. His breeches were held up by suspenders over his bare shoulders, which were rounded and enormous. He stood in the classic pugilist's stance: right foot forward and turned slightly inward, hands staggered before his chin. *Thunderbird Layne*, the caption read, *Itinerant Bareknuckler.*

"Years ago, fighters traveled town to town like gunfighters," said Lou. "A whole class of men lived this way; also card sharks and mariachis and snake-oil salesmen. Drifters as far as most were concerned, crazed faces who came and went in the space of a single night. These fighters would stride into some town square, toe a line in the dirt, and challenge any man to cross it. If that town happened to be full of serious brawlers he might fight ten, twelve men—whole families, uncles and brothers and sons. If that town was wrathful it beat the fighter down and ran him out on a rail. And if that town was kind it gave him a warm bed and sent him on the next day.

"They fought for money, yeah, enough to get them down the road— but that wasn't why they did it. Men like that, they were born for fighting, the way other men are born for the sciences or high finance. Alone on a dusty street, squared up against some burly native son with pissed-off townsfolk screaming for his scalp . . ." A dramatic sigh. "But then along came the Marquis de Queensberry with his rules of fair play and soon nobody remembered the drifting bareknucklers. I got nothing against boxing—a more noble sport you will not find—but those men were gladiators, or the closest we've seen since those times."

Lou opened a drawer and pulled out a bottle of Bell's whiskey and a pair of waterspotted glasses. He poured a respectable two ounces into each and handed one over.

"Guys like Thunderbird here," he tapped the photo with his glass, "they're still around."

"I've never seen anyone like that."

"Oh, you probably have. Just didn't know it."

Paul thought of the boxer who'd come in that first day—the guy with his eggplant-colored head and anthill eyes—and remembered thinking no way could that damage have come from a legitimate boxing match.

"There are places where you'll find them, still . . ."

"You know any of those places?"

"Oh," Lou said innocently, "so . . . you're interested?"

Paul felt springs coiled under his skin waiting to lurch out. "Do me a favor, Lou, and don't jerk me around."

Lou's face changed like still water brushed by a breeze. "I know a place, yeah. It's illegal, obviously. Take you sometime, you want."

"I'd like that."

"We'll see." Lou leaned back in his chair. "Can't promise anything."

He scribbled an address on the back of an unpaid hydro bill. "I noticed you're a bleeder. One little biff and you're gushing. That's gonna hurt you in the ring." He handed the address over. "The guy's name is Sandercott. A lot of my guys see him."

The address led to a housing project in the Western Hill district.

The house occupied the final lot on a treeless lane. Its faded paint was the color of boiled organ meat. A Datsun B-210 jacked up on blocks on the front lawn, windows smashed, interior gutted.

Paul's knock was answered by a man in his late fifties. Balding and rotund, he wore a ratty housecoat cinched with a yellow extension cord.

Paul said, "Lou sent me."

Sandercott said, "Nose or brows?"

Before Paul could answer Sandercott reached out and ran a nicotine-stained thumb over the curve of his eyebrow. "Brows look okay. So, by process of elimination, nose."

The place stunk of deep-fryer fat. The carpet was so threadbare the nylon underweave showed through in spots. Paul had seen houses like this only in movies, desperately grim movies where unfit mothers nodded on heroin while their urchins splashed in the scummy gray water of a Mister Turtle pool.

"Head on into the shitter," Sandercott said.

The bathroom was bright and not particularly clean. A framed needlepoint slogan over the toilet read IF YOU SPRINKLE WHEN YOU TINKLE, BE A SWEETIE, WIPE THE SEATIE. Sandercott came in with a Plano tacklebox. When he opened it on the sink's edge, Paul saw that each compartment was stocked with gauze and iodine and burn salve.

"What are you planning on?"

"Lou didn't tell you? Typical." Sandercott motioned to the toilet. "Siddown."

He showed Paul a slender brushed-aluminum tool. It looked like the soldering rod that'd come with Paul's Unger Industrial wood-burning kit.

"Electric cauterizing wand," Sandercott told him. "A spark gun, in layman's terms. Fuses veins during emergency surgery."

He pushed a silver button; a cold blue spark snapped between the conductors. The hairs on the nape of Paul's neck stood on end.

"What I do is cauterize the soft tissue in your nostrils. Once you scar up you'll never bleed again, even if someone whacks your schnozz with a ball-peen hammer."

"Can't this be done at a hospital?"

Sandercott shook his head. "Falls under the umbrella of non-essential surgery. Plus there'd be questions—with me it's don't ask, don't tell." He considered Paul, his cheap white T-shirt and knocked-out teeth. "No offense, but you don't strike me as the type who's got much choice."

He spread Paul's nostrils with a pair of nasal retractors. After trimming the bristly nose hairs, he took a leather thong from the tacklebox and rinsed it under the tap.

"Bite down hard," he said. "Not going to lie, son: this'll sting like a motherfuck."

Paul drove through a light snow, big flakes dissolving on the windshield like spun sugar. Plugs of blood-soaked gauze were shoved up his nostrils. His brain felt swollen and monstrous and threatened to split his skull.

When Sandercott had eased the spark gun up his right nostril, Paul felt the contact points butt the ridge of cartilage, then—*tsszzzap*! His mouth filled with an ozone taste; blue sparks spat between his fillings. His spine straightened as a rope of blood geysered from his nose. The spark gun *tsszzzzapp*ed again. His nose lit up like a Chinese paper lantern. Paul puked and passed out. When he came to, Sandercott was Q-Tipping his nostrils with petroleum burn salve.

"All done," he said. "You did good. I'd give you a lollipop, I had one. Got Vicodin."

"I'll take two." With Paul's nose swollen, this came out: *I dake doo.*

He arrived home shortly after nine o'clock. The house was festooned with Christmas lights, thousands of them. Cars lined the horseshoe drive: Lexuses and Mercedes, Cadillacs and Porsches.

He crossed the front lawn past a carved-ice nativity scene. Faint music from inside: Bing Crosby's "Silver Bells." The Harrises' annual Christmas function was in full swing.

He crept in through the back door; his ambition was to slip down the hall into his room and avoid the party altogether. But his mother corralled him as he breezed up the back stairs.

"Paul, dear." Barbara wore a strapless black dress with fake-fur trim; stuffed reindeer antlers were tilted askew on her head. She was distracted, her gaze lingering on the living room and her guests. "You *must* come in and mingle, darling."

He realized he was dealing with Socialite Barb, an altogether different creature from his mom. Socialite Barb had her own lexicon— *Darling* and *Oh my* and *Nonsense*—and her every mannerism was exaggerated: privy to a juicy bit of gossip, Socialite Barb would flap a hand before her face and swoon like a silent movie actress. Socialite Barb wouldn't be caught dead uttering "Cold as a witch's tit."

He sat on the stairs. Taking a seat beside him, Barbara flinched at the blood on his shirt, the toilet paper jammed up his nose. "Oh, Paul . . ." The socialite veneer slipped. "What have you done to yourself?"

"I aw'ight."

She smiled sadly and went to touch his face, but could not quite bring herself to. "You can't come in looking like that."

"Why oo I hab to cub in a' aw?"

"Paul, please. Your father and I want this to come off well." Worry strobe-lighted across her face. "We want everything to look nice."

"'Appy fambly."

"Yes, a happy family. Aren't we?" She touched his shoulder; Paul thought she was going to hug him but instead she plucked a hair off his shirt. "You've been losing a lot of it, lately."

Another side effect of the steroids. His shower soap was furred with so much shed hair it looked like some headless, amputee rodent. He went upstairs and changed, shoved fresh toilet paper up his nose, and soon found himself in a room full of people he didn't want to talk to.

Tall, full blue spruces decked with twinkling lights and tinsel stood on either side of the fireplace—which, instead of an actual fire, contained a thirty-four-inch TV playing a DVD of a crackling fire. Rita MacNeil Christmas carols on the CD player. Guests milled about in sleekly cut dresses and dinner jackets, sipping martinis or Seabreezes or Danish beers. Broken conversations washed over him, so unlike the patter of the boxing gym it was nearly a foreign language.

. . . got my money in at 34¼ and got out at 56¾—zoom! . . .

. . . four hundred thread count. Anything less, you may as well sleep on sandpaper . . .

. . . Oh no. Can't do it Thursday. Herbal wrap. But how's Friday? . . .

. . . East Timor. Who will consider the downtrodden shepherds of East Timor . . .

His father tended bar, dispensing Chardonnay and Veuve Clicquot with typical Jack Harris swagger. Seeing his son with those racoon eyes and corkscrews of toilet paper jammed up each nostril, a flinching expression crossed his face.

"Ah, god," he said. "Have you been boxing—seriously *boxing*?"

By now Jack knew that his son had taken up the sport. The glove-burns on his face and the bruised state of his hands, the smelly boxing shoes in the front hall.

"Whaa 'id oo 'ink?"

"I thought you were training," Jack told him, "not actually fighting. Looks like you got popped one—how you feel?"

"Grade," Paul said truthfully. "Riddy, riddy grade."

"Great?" Jack touched his son's face, traced with thick fingers the slope of Paul's nose. "Keep it up, son, you're gonna wind up with a face like a catcher's mitt."

"I'b 'ine."

"Fine, he says!" Jack spread his hands in an appeal to some unseen jury. "Twists of TP up his nose and a pair of matching shiners—not to mention those teeth—*this* guy's telling me he's fine." A snort. "You're too old to be a fighter. You'll never earn a dime. Might as well teach Esperanto lessons!"

Paul was unsurprised that, to his father, it came down to dollars and cents. He took his bottled water to a chair in a corner of the room. Guests roamed about in bovine patterns. Businessmen's laughs boomed like awkward thunder: *Oooohohohoho-aka-aka-ak-ak-ak!* Everyone was so fat and satisfied. Sausagey fingers grasped at canapés; fleshy goldfish lips sucked at cocktail glasses. The older men, the fathers, still bore traces of a hardened life: facial scars and roughened features, a certain tautness around the eyes indicative of past toil. But their sons' faces were scrubbed rosy and unmarked, their manicured hands smooth as glass.

"Young master Harris. How do, how do?"

He'd been accosted by Drake Langley, whom Paul had last seen the night of his beating.

"'Ello, Drake."

Tonight Langley wore a checkerboard-patterned jacket with a ludicrous bow tie flared beneath his jaw. His insubstantial frame was balanced on a walking stick with a silver dog's-head handle—a Dachshund—which Drake leaned on like a vaudeville performer at the cusp of a song-and-dance number.

"You and I should set up a meeting . . ." Drake was saying, ". . . relative merits and demerits of corporate reconfiguration . . ." he was saying, ". . . that new Porsche 911 Boxster made my dick hard just looking at the brochure . . ." he was saying.

Drake's thin lips formed a stream of inane jabber. Paul was amazed that Drake hadn't bothered to comment on his frightful appearance—he'd nearly forgotten how self-absorbed his old chums could be, with their spectacular ignorance of all things outside their tiny sphere of existence. He felt he was in the presence of an alien life form unsuited to existence on this planet: a creature to whom oxygen was poison and water acid.

". . . Asset allocation . . . Cohiba coronas and their impact on bistro culture . . ."

A wave of cold nausea ripped through Paul's guts. The room lurched, its reds and whites transposing so that, for an instant, the spackled ceiling became an expanse of curdled blood. An intense loathing welled up at the sight of these sons and daughters of privilege. He saw them all lying facedown in the mud with slugs riven through their skulls. He saw their bodies heaped pell-mell in a mass grave with a dusting of quicklime eating their bones. He saw them not as bodies but as vague unformed *shapes*, featureless faces smooth as eggshell.

". . . Cambodian sweatshop sanctions . . . tennis elbow . . ."

Then Drake's body swelled and bloated until his face tore in two like sun-rotted fatback to reveal the head of a massive quivering maggot. Paul's eyes went big; he choked, averting Drake's gaze, and saw that *all* the children had turned into maggots. Giant greasy tubes sheathed in Donna Karan dresses with nautilus-whorl hairdos and redwood-framed glasses and clutch purses, tubes peristaltic-flexing across the lush white carpeting. A guest leaned down and kissed his maggot-daughter and his lips came away with taffy pulls of mucus clinging to them. A guest fed her maggot-son a stuffed olive canapé, fingers disappearing into the dilated asshole of its mouth. Drake the Maggot stood on its tail like a cartoon worm, body curled like an S and, revoltingly, it continued to speak.

". . . white-chocolate truffles . . ." Maggot-Drake said. ". . . Jerry's Kids . . ."

The puckered balloon-knot of Maggot-Drake's mouth blurped and blorped and spewed snotlike goo that stuck to Paul's face like gobs of gelatin.

"*Yakka-yakka-yakka,*" Maggot-Drake laughed, "*Hohohohohoho HOOO!*"

Paul's own hysterical laughter ricocheted off the walls, so deafening all other conversations ground to a halt as he gagged *HO-HO-HO* like a demented Père Noël. The toilet-paper plugs rocketed from his nose and his body quaked and the television fire crackled and Rita MacNeil sang "O Tannenbaum"—

Paul punched Maggot-Drake in its butthole mouth. His arm sunk in to the elbow and Drake's maggot body went *sssssss*, deflating like a ruptured parade balloon. Paul blinked and there was Drake Langley, crumpled up on the hearth.

The DVD skipped. The TV fire went black.

Paul sat on the back porch. He'd broken Drake's jaw. The sound of young Drake moaning, the sight of those strings of saliva dribbling from his unhinged puppet-mouth—it spoiled the seasonal *joie de vivre*. The party broke up quickly, despite Socialite Barb's best efforts: "Please, everything's fine! Let's all roast chestnuts!"

He'd watched Drake Langley transform into a maggot. The Vicodin Sandercott had given him—blotter acid? That, or he'd gone temporarily delusional. At this point, either scenario struck him as completely possible.

His father joined him with a bottle of scotch. "Well, thank god that kid's dad isn't the litigious type." He sat, took a pull from the bottle, and set it between his legs. "Maybe I should consider it lucky you didn't punch him, too."

"It may end up being the best thing anyone's ever done for him."

"You know," Jack said, peevishly, "most people who get beat up aren't changed for it. Blake will ice his jaw tonight and go to work in the morning."

"His name is Drake."

"I've been calling him Blake for years. Drake. Isn't that a sort of bird?" Another gulp. "So why'd you do it?"

Alas, dear Drake had turned into a quivering blubbery maggot.

"How's Mom?"

"How would you figure?"

Paul reached between his father's legs for the bottle. Inside, some china shattered.

"I should sleep somewhere else tonight."

"Tonight? Think more like a week," said Jack. "So, figured out how all this is benefiting you yet?" When Paul said nothing his father persisted. "Why you're decking party guests?"

Paul took a swig. If there was one thing he missed lately, it was good scotch. "Dad, did you ever think, even for one fleeting moment, that maybe I didn't want the life you'd staked out for me?"

Jack looked like he'd been knifed in the guts. "Staked out for you? Is that what you think? I only wanted you to be happy. I wanted you to go to a good school—you did. I wanted you to go to university—you did. I wanted you to work at a job you'd be happy with . . ." He trailed off, confused. "I thought you'd found that." Jack slugged scotch, breathed deep, another slug. "But . . . you never showed the slightest ambition. Sports, academics, jigsaw puzzles, ships in bottles—nothing."

"Fair point. I'm a late bloomer."

"Blooming into what? Into something that belongs up in a friggin' *bell tower*. Jesus, and now you're . . ." Jack hung his head. ". . . bleeding."

Paul wiped under his nose; his fingers came away bloody. He thought about the cleanliness of Sandercott's instruments and considered the prospect of staph infection.

"So this is all my fault?" Jack went on. "You're blaming me?"

"Give me a break. Self-pity doesn't suit you."

"I'm drunk." More shattering noises from inside. "And in a few minutes I have to go deal with *that*. So let me wallow, will you?"

Paul softened. "It's not your fault. I don't think you gave it any thought, is all. You had a sense of how things should be, and I didn't make any waves, so . . ."

"And this is how you want it?"

"I'm happier."

"No you're not. You just think you are."

Inside: stomping, another crash.

"Good thing I got a snootful to keep me warm," Jack said dourly. "Conjugal bed's bound to be a mite frosty tonight."

His father went inside. Raised voices, a spectacularly loud crash, what might or might not have been weeping. Paul shivered, coming down from the adrenaline buzz.

"That was quite a performance."

It was Callie, his father's receptionist. She wore a puffy parka over a peach blouse, short black skirt, nylons.

She sat on the porch stairs. The smoke from her menthol cigarette mingled with the smell of jasmine perfume. "Haven't seen you around the office. Jack thinks you're having a breakdown. Quarter-life crisis."

He reached out, suddenly, and set his hand on her face. She didn't flinch; her eyes did not release from his. He ran his thumb down the center of her face to her chin. Convinced she was not liable to split apart as Drake had, he let out a shuddering breath and smiled.

"What was that all about?"

Paul brushed her question off. "What do *you* think?" he said. "Am I having a breakdown?"

"I can't say, exactly. You're . . . different. You've changed. Definitely."

"For the better?"

"I think so." The rapid beat of her heart pulsed her neck vein. "You really popped that poor guy. Never seen anyone hit so hard. It was . . . wow."

She butted her cigarette on the porch steps, leaning over to do so. Her blouse was sheer and low-cut, her breasts just bigger than medium and firm. They were about the most beautiful tits Paul had ever seen. This was his first sexual stirring since his steroid cycle began and it broiled through his veins in a galvanizing, all-consuming, full-barrel rush. She studied him with a knowing half-smile, a few wisps of cigarette smoke curling from the sides of her lips.

The two of them in the greenhouse with its long dusty tables, trowels, and boxes of expired slug poison. Paul's hands clutched at Callie's ass as she bit his lower lip, small pink tongue slicing the gaps between his teeth. He tore her blouse off, buttons popping, his hands and mouth on her tits, groping her with all the subtlety of an orang-utan. Their bodies glanced off the glass; a pane fractured in spiderweb cracks. She tugged his fly down and jerked his cock, her strong farm-girl hands pulling so hard it was as if she were trying to yank a stubborn weed; he shook her hand away and crushed his mouth to hers with such force he thought their teeth would splinter. They maneuvered amid sacks of cacao shells and blood-and-bone meal; Paul's toe struck the old Bowflex and he bellowed like a gorgon. She moaned unintelligible words as he picked her up and dropped her on bags of peat, the white plastic splitting in puffs of dust, and when their lips met again they could taste the earthy grit of it on their tongues.

Callie's pussy sopping, wet satin molded to her labia, and Paul hiked her skirt up, hands and teeth shredding her panties and Callie's box neatly shaved, clitoris poking from its hood hard as a polished pebble and she gripped his cock but when she tried to contort her body to fit it into her mouth, panting ravenously, he pushed her down and rubbed his cock over her pussy, which was tight and hot and wet and when a flicker of dismay crossed his face she ignored it completely, impatient now, grasping his cock and digging her nails into his shaft—he went "Aaaah!"; she went "Come on, move *it* . . ."—she slipped him in and then Paul was pushing hard and fast, gasping and dizzy as tree pruners and Garden Weasels shook off their hooks, the two of them rocking together and Paul's fingers puncturing bags of peat—

And there, under the tepid glow of a sixty-watt bulb with soil crumbling in his bruised hands, Paul Harris saw a sleepy hillside village. Clapboard houses, horses and mules yoked to hitching posts. He stands alone in the street, warm breeze scrolling dust and dry leaves across the lane. With the toe of his boot he drags a line in the dirt. Men come from the saltbox shacks rolling shirt-sleeves to their elbows, swiveling their arms and cracking their necks. The first man is huge but slow: Paul ducks his ponderous fists, answering with stinging rights and lefts to his boxlike face, splitting it open until the man goes down and is dragged away. The next guy fights fiercely, crushing blows to Paul's liver and pancreas until Paul catches him a sneaky right on the temple and he goes down twitching. He fights another, then another and another and another; log-boom stacks pile up in the gullies. They fight in a ring of blood and Paul breaks noses and crushes eyeballs from sockets. Hot blood coats his hands the way nacre forms around a speck of grit and soon his fists are the size of bowling balls, hard and heavy, yet he swings them with ease, crushing ribcages and cracking skulls, pulverizing spinal cords and splattering faces like rotted fruit, the men reduced to sticky pulp, to horrible wet noise, but they keep coming, dozen upon dozen, and Paul dispatches them all without mercy, reducing their bodies to chunks, to gristle and bone, sunk knee-deep in gore and he's screaming for more, Bring it on, Bring it on, *Bring . . . It . . . On.*

7

The Upper New York Golden Gloves qualifying tournament was held in the basement of St. Michael's cathedral at the corner of Niagara and 12th. The day was December 31, 2005.

The dressing room boiled with voices and bodies, bodies of men and boys, naked chests and shoulders, black, white, brown, beige, yellow. Altar boy smocks and votive candle holders were hung on hooks beside the weigh station.

Rob stripped to his underwear and took his place in line. Irish guys with freckled arms, Mexican flyweights who looked made of braided rope, black cruiserweights with superhero bodies—muscles where there shouldn't be muscles—Cuban street kids with scars marking their faces, Italian bruisers with marbled forearms and squashed noses. They'd come from all over the region: Lockport and Erie, Lackawanna and Tonawanda, a few driving north from New York City looking for softer brackets. They eyed one another cagily, sizing each other up, laying their own private odds.

Rob stepped onto a scale. His torso shone blue in places, the shaped muscles touched with shadow. An official scribbled "164" on the cover of his boxing book. A fight doc shone a penlight in his eyes and listened to the *thack-thack* of his heart.

Rob's US Boxing book was tossed upon the heap at the match-makers' table. Three officials were tasked with matching fighters according to weight and experience. As they sorted through books, the trainers assembled on the sidelines voiced their opinion:

"Make it fair, boys, make it fair . . ."

"Aw, no, man! That boy's dead for a ringer—no *waaaay* we taking that match!"

"We'll fight anybody. Any*BODY!*"

Rob was matched against a twenty-five-year-old amateur from Bed-Stuy: Marty "Sugar" Caine. Caine had recently qualified for a berth on the Olympic squad.

Reuben and Rob sequestered themselves in the temporary trainer's quarters: a rubdown table bookended by flimsy hospital screens. On either side could be glimpsed the shadows of trainers wrapping their fighters' hands, massaging necks and shoulders.

"Won't be a cakewalk," Reuben said. "Caine's got skills. But his knockout ratio's piss-poor. You gotta get inside his head, Robbie. I want him thinking, *This kid's got bricks in his chin.* I want him thinking, *This kid drinks kerosene and breathes nitrous oxide flames.* Got it?"

Tommy poked his head through the hospital screen.

"Where've you been?" Reuben said.

"Bus broke down on the side of the highway." He smiled at Rob. "How you feeling, champ?"

A boxing official stopped by to watch Reuben tape Robbie's hands; New York boxing commission rules stipulated that an official must observe the pre-fight hand wrap to ensure it was done by the book, no lead slugs or mustard-seed oil. The official initialed Rob's wraps and Reuben had his son lie down on the training table, working winter-green liniment into the muscles of Rob's back.

"How you feeling?"

"Nervous," said Rob.

"Hey, if you don't have butterflies, there's something the matter with you. Just remember: cowards and heroes feel the same fear. Heroes react to it differently, is all."

But his father didn't understand. Rob wasn't scared of being hit or even getting knocked out. Rob was scared for Marty "Sugar" Caine.

"Fear has been around for centuries," Reuben said. "It's old, and it's good."

The basement of St. Michael's cathedral was cloaked in shadow save for a halo of spotlights above the ring. Rows of folding chairs hosted mothers and fathers, local fight enthusiasts, boxers and coaches, the odd talent scout. The canteen was staffed by the nuns of St. Francis. Fighters skipped rope or shadowboxed in darkened corners. A folding table behind them supported a glittering cargo of trophies, each crowned with a brass boxer with arms upraised.

Rob sat between his uncle and father in a black robe. In the ring a pair of middleweights went at it. That they were the same weight seemed insupportable: one a thick-necked fireplug, the other a lanky beanpole. The fireplug pursued the beanpole, hoping to blow a hole through his willowy opponent with one solid punch. The taller fighter kept him at bay, snapping hard jabs, avoiding those bullish charges as smoothly as a toreador.

When the bell rang, the judges scored unanimously in favor of the beanpole. The decision received scattered boos, most of them coming from the fireplug's cheering section. The beanpole's supporters jeered back and before long two women—the boxers' mothers, in all probability—were screaming hysterical threats at each other. "Hold me back!" the fireplug's mother cried, "or else I'll pound her!" She took her husband's arm, braced it across her chest, and again cried, "Hold me back, so help me *god*!" Once things settled down, Reuben said, "We're up."

Marty "Sugar" Caine was lean and tapered, his every muscle visible under a thin stretching of flesh. Rob noticed a pair of star-shaped welts on Caine's torso, one between the second and third rib, another above his right nipple. Gunshot wounds. When Caine turned around in his corner, kneeling to bless himself, Rob saw the exit wounds on his back: scar tissue like lumps of bubblegum smoothed across the underside of a table.

The fighters touched gloves over the referee's arm. The bell rang.

Caine skipped lightly, appearing to float a half-inch above the canvas. Rob stalked, hands low, gloves poised and rotating. Caine snapped out a pair of jabs, fast but merely pestering; they glanced off his headgear. Rob bulled in and, as Caine hooked behind a left jab, slipped the second punch and threw his own hook, a submarine right to the body.

Caine managed to take a piece of Rob's punch on his arm, but the shot was thrown with such force it drove the point of his elbow into Caine's abdominal wall. Caine bent sideways at the hip, lips skinned back from his gumshield. The ref—dressed in white trousers and a vest like an English estate butler—hovered nearby to call the mandatory eight-count.

"Follow up!" Reuben hollered. "Get *on* it!"

But Rob did not get on it. He threw another hook but pulled short, feinted left for no reason at all, and drew away.

Caine recovered enough to throw a series of jabs coming off the ropes. Rob held his hands low and let the punches hit him flush in the face. Caine came through with a wrecking-ball right that caught Rob under the chin; his head snapped back. He closed his eyes and . . . *wished*. But when his eyes opened a split-second later he was still standing. He'd taken Caine's best shot and knew—right then, *knew*— that Caine didn't have the *oomph* to put him away. This cold fact filled Rob with a measure of desolation the likes of which he'd rarely known.

The bell rang.

In the corner Reuben slapped his face.

"What the hell? You had him. Christ, Robbie—*had* him."

Reuben offered instruction but Rob's attention was focused on the opposite corner: Caine sat on a stool, face shiny with Vaseline, gumshield socked in the crook of his mouth. Caine's eyes darted into the crowd. Rob followed his gaze to a slim, beautiful woman in the third row. Girlfriend? Wife? Someone who cared for him, obviously— Rob could see the lines of worry on her face. An infant girl sat on the woman's lap.

For an instant the fighters' eyes met across the hunched backs of their trainers. Caine nodded, a nearly imperceptible motion of his head.

The bell rang.

Caine sprang in slugging, was jolted by a flurry and backed off, dancing high on his toes. They came together again, Caine pepper-potting jabs until a right cross sent sweat flying from his headgear. Spurred by the crowd, he followed two precise jabs with a straight right that Rob slipped by an eighth of an inch, Caine's hand finding only empty air above Rob's shoulder. Pivoting on his lead, Rob ripped a body shot under Caine's ribcage that sent the other boxer into a flutter-legged swoon.

"Go on! You got him!" Reuben yelled.

Caine's eyes were unfocused; yellow bile foamed the edges of his gumshield. Rob saw the gunshot wound on Caine's chest, a tight pink asterisk spread like the petals of an ice plant. Where had he gotten it? Here was Marty Caine with a wife and a kid and dreams of big paydays and here was Rob fucking it all up—what earthly right did he have to fuck it up for anyone? He knew Caine would fight until his eyes filled with blood and his arms grew numb, until he was a senseless wreck on the canvas. Caine would fight until there was nothing left because he was fighting for more than just himself, and because the complete sacrifice of his body was everything he could possibly surrender.

They went two more rounds. Though Rob controlled the tempo, Caine kept busy and landed some flashy shots. The judges ruled it a split-decision draw. The decision split the crowd: half cheered while the other half booed.

Rob and Caine fell into a loose embrace in the middle of the ring. "Lordy, did you ever hit me," Caine whispered in Rob's ear. "Nobody should have to be hit like that."

"I'm sorry," Rob said.

"No sorries, man." Caine patted Rob's head. "Never sorries."

Reuben was at the judges' table, vowing to challenge the decision. "Hung from the highest bough!" he yelled. "The . . . highest . . . *bough!*"

From the ring Rob watched his opponent walk to the locker room. Supported by his trainer, Caine stopped beside the woman. His taped hands moved tenderly on her shoulder, tenderly over the infant girl's cheeks and hair.

It was dusk when they left St. Michael's. The dark air quivered in funnels of light cast by gooseneck streetlamps.

Reuben and Rob sat in the idling car while Tommy brushed snow off the windows. Rob drank from a liter bottle of bubblegum-flavored Pedialyte to jack up his electrolytes; a jar of Gerber's baby food sat between his legs, the only stuff his system could tolerate after a fight. A warrior twenty minutes ago, now he ate like an infant.

"Tully's Record Sullied," Reuben said. "That's what the headline'll read in the Sports section of the *Gazette*. They'll love the goddamn alliteration."

"That's not alliteration," Rob said from the backseat. "Just rhyming."

"Don't get smart. I don't get it," Reuben went on. "You had him, and not once—three, four times. The hell happened?"

Rob wanted to tell his father how, when he had Caine staggered, he'd thought of his first knockout—those teeth winking like bloody pearls in a black rubber gumshield. He wanted to tell his father that he couldn't hate a stranger, even for the short time they shared a ring together, even when that stranger's intent was to inflict harm.

"We might not make it out of the preliminaries." A mystified shake of the head. "Robbie, you were the favorite. The odds *on* . . . favorite."

Nine o'clock, New Year's Eve.

Rob skipped lightly down the stairs. He wore workboots, faded blue jeans, a clean white T-shirt. Reddened slashes marked his cheeks and chin: burns from Caine's gloves.

"I'm heading out."

Reuben sat at the kitchen table with a bottle of Jim Beam. He stared at the Formica tabletop as though, were he to fixate his gaze long enough, the random mica chips might disclose some earth-shattering epiphany.

"Go on, then." He flicked his hand. "Home no later than twelve-thirty or I'll be dragging you home by the scruff."

The party was hosted by Felix Guiterrez—Felix, the guy whose jaw Rob had broken a year and a half ago. He answered Rob's knock wearing a shiny costume top hat.

"Tully, my man." Rob noted the dimple scars on Felix's jaw and felt a pang of regret. To Felix's credit, he didn't hold a grudge. "Come on down. My folks are partying upstairs."

Thirty-odd people filled the unfinished basement, standing or sitting on lawn chairs. Earlier in the night the place had been decorated but now all that remained were shreds of crepe paper and rubber balloon-rings taped to the beams. Bottles of rum and vodka liberated from parents' liquor cabinets passed amongst the throng.

He spotted Kate with Darren Gregory. Darren was a willowy senior who favored ripped jeans and Goodwill corduroy; thick dark hair fell over his handsome features. His mother was a border toll–taker who, unbeknownst to Rob, had ridden the same bus as his father for the better part of twenty years. Last month Darren had won a poetry competition; his love sonnet had appeared in the Sunday *Gazette*. He and Kate sat on lawn chairs, knees touching. Darren made flourishes with his hands as Kate's mouth formed words—"Yes! Absolutely!"—and she laughed. Watching them, Rob felt strangely cold, *gutted*, blood running thin as copper wire in his veins.

Felix sidled up with a jug of Comrade Popov's potato vodka. "Heard about the draw at the Gloves. Who the hell did you fight— King Kong?"

"Could have gone either way," Rob told him. "I could've lost."

Felix appeared upset, or let down. Rob wondered if, sometime in the future, Felix had wanted to tell people he'd had his jaw broken by a world champion. He drank from the jug and winced.

Felix's mother knelt at the top of the basement steps. She wore a pair of novelty glasses: red plastic shaped in the year 2006, eyeballs set like boozy marbles in the middle of each zero.

"How's everything down here? Need more grape sodas—Cheez-Its?"

"We're fine," Felix said. "Go a-*way*."

Rob took another pull. He was a lightweight when it came to drinking, plus his body was worn out from the fight; the basement took on a warped convex, as though he was viewing things through a busted telescope. At some point Kate was standing next to him. She wore a red sweater: a spray of pale freckles, the dovelike sweep of her collarbones. Rob wasn't sure if she smelled of vanilla or if, in the stark basement light, he only imagined that smell.

"Tully," she said, "you look a bit greased."

"And so what? Not like there's a law against it."

Kate *tsk-tsk*ed. "Golden Boy, drunk as a sailor. Taking that draw pretty hard, aren't you?"

"I couldn't care less. A few more draws, a loss, get knocked out, and I can hang it up for good."

"Or you can hang it up before all that."

Rob gave her a look that said they both knew better. "And don't call me that, either."

"What?"

"Golden Boy."

"Touchy, touchy."

Rob was still rankled at seeing Kate and Darren together, and Comrade Popov did his mood a further disservice: level-headed and warm-hearted while sober, it appeared that Rob could be a nasty jealous drunk.

"What were you and Shakespeare talking about?" he couldn't help asking.

"Schools," Kate told him. "Darren applied to UC Santa Cruz, me to Santa Barbara. I'll need a scholarship, but Darren's got a plan to make ends meet."

She detailed Darren's can't-miss moneymaking scheme: he planned to scour the sands of Monterey Bay with a metal detector, cleaning the beaches of debris and paying his tuition at the same time. It struck Rob as a childish plan, even by a teenager's standards. What did he expect to uncover—antique bottle caps? A trove of Nazi gold?

Kate said, "Darren's so eco-conscious."

If Rob had been a little drunker he might have remarked that if "eco-conscious" were a synonym for "corduroy-wearing wiener," then by all means, Darren Gregory was as eco-conscious as they came. Rob saw Kate and Darren on a beach, barefoot on the sand. A beach so far removed from the weed-strewn lots, tumbledown row houses, and terminal bleakness of Niagara Falls it might as well be another planet. They bent together over an object glinting at the rim of a tide pool, touching and smiling and laughing.

Darren Gregory materialized, bony and stoop-shouldered with hair like a bear pelt. "Robert, my fine friend," he said. "You're looking worse for wear."

Darren wore his artsy-fartsy heart on his corduroy sleeve; to him, boxing and cockfighting were distinguishable only in that one involved animals who didn't know any better.

"Any job comes with its lumps. And you know what they say— women dig scars."

Darren placed his hand on Rob's wrist as though they were sharing a close personal confidence. "And here I was thinking they *dug* sophistication and intelligence. And as for a job—I didn't know amateur boxers got paid."

Rob figured amateurs could at least pawn their trophies, earning them more than most beachcombers. "How much did you make for that sonnet in the *Gazette*?"

"I do it for the love of words." He slipped his hand off Rob's wrist and set it on Kate's. "She and I were just talking about that, as a matter of fact. We're going to collaborate on a brace of poems."

Rob saw the two of them on the beach again, except now Darren was composing poetry for her, dipping a quill pen in a pot of ink. Rob jammed his hands in his pockets, afraid of what they might do.

"You're lucky, then. Kate's a great poet. She helped me with that haiku assignment."

Darren chuckled—indulgently, Rob thought. "Yes, and what did you come up with?"

Rob was certain his own poem would be met with derision; with an apologetic look at Kate, he recited hers instead. "It went, *Though there will always / Be those things out of your reach / Never stop reaching.*"

"It's admirable, Robert; an admirable effort. Quite good for a fledgling attempt."

Kate crossed her arms. "What would you say marks it as a fledgling attempt?"

"The meter's sloppy, for one. And the sentiment is, should I say . . ." He gave Rob a sorry-to-be-the-bearer-of-bad-news look. ". . . a tad juvenile."

"You're right," Rob said. "Juvenile, through and through."

"Buck up, chum." Darren clapped Rob's shoulder. "Not everyone's made for the world of letters. Some of us are better off . . ." he shrugged, ". . . on another of life's paths."

Kate looked embarrassed at Darren's preening, and Rob had had enough. He'd drag the flapping loose-lipped bastard out into the snow and smash him. That blown-glass chin would shatter in one shot.

"Why not say what you mean; let's not sit here attacking each other on the sly."

"You recited your poem," Darren said flatly. "I told you what I thought. If that's attacking—"

"You know what you're doing and so do I. You're not half so clever as you think. You want to talk about juvenile sentiments—" He flicked the sleeve of Darren's corduroy jacket. "How about a guy from around here wearing this shit? Professor Plum in the study with the candlestick."

Overhearing this, a few partyers voiced their drunken approval.

"Your ma's a *toll-taker*," Rob went on. "Your pops works a wrecking crane. Look in your fridge and I'll find a pack of Helmbolds bologna, same as in mine."

"Rob, come on—"

He cut Kate off. "You're the same Darren Gregory who took a shit on the floor in first grade. Remember that? Mrs. Frieberger stepped out and you couldn't wait for her to get back with the hall pass so you squatted next to the goldfish bowl. So go on wearing your jacket and writing sonnets—you'll always be the kid who shit on the floor."

Darren jerked a glare of solid malevolence at Rob, then gave Kate a you-see-how-it-is look. "When was that?" he said quietly. "Ten years ago? It's okay. One day I'll leave here and end up someplace where people have no memory of what I did as a six-year-old; I can start over, fresh. But you'll never leave, because your best and only hope is right here." He reached over Rob's head, pantomiming, like his hand was hitting something solid. "Feel that? It's a glass ceiling, and you're about to slam into it."

Rob was jolted. "Who cares? I'm not ashamed of where I come from—"

"And it's not just a ceiling—it's a box with glass walls, and you're never going to grow out of it because you never tried to when you had the chance. And the rest of your life you're going to wonder, Robert."

It was the *Robert* that did it. Blinding rage. "I swear, for a nickel I'd smash you—"

Darren rummaged through his pocket. "Here's a dime." He bounced it off Rob's chest and jutted his chin out. "If you leave a scar I can lie and say it isn't from some Love Canal bully, because I'll be someplace where nobody knows any better."

Bile rolled up Rob's stomach and spread into his mouth. He'd never been called a bully before, and was proud of the fact. But next his hands were wrapped up in Darren's jacket and he was shaking him so hard his teeth rattled. He yanked Darren's jacket until their noses touched.

"You don't know anything," he growled. "You're not getting out of here. You're not—"

Felix Guitterez jammed his body between them. "Take it outside, guys."

The rage drained out of Rob; in its wake only regret at the hollowness of his actions. He smoothed Darren's jacket. "Sorry," he mumbled. "No, no going outside. Sorry, sorry."

Kate grabbed his hand. As she dragged him up the basement steps, Rob caught Darren looking at him, giving him the most sympathetic smile he'd ever seen.

Outside, Kate dropped his hand and marched down the sidewalk toward her home.

"Idiotic, Tully," she called over her shoulder. "Grade-A asshole material."

The night sky was salted with stars. Rob walked down the street on snow packed hard from car tires. Revelers headed to their cars—wives supported drunken husbands; husbands cradled drunken wives. He felt awful for what he'd said about Darren. He shouldn't have recited Kate's poem, either.

Tommy sat on the porch steps; he raised a hand and shook his head, a wry, guilty gesture.

"Your dad's still up. Don't think I can face him right now."

Rob said, "You lose at cards?"

"Yuh."

"The whole Christmas bonus?"

"Yuh. So what happened this afternoon?"

"I wasn't on."

Tommy scratched his neck, winced. "I don't know . . . looked to me you had the guy."

"Don't know what else to tell you."

"It's just, y'know, boxing is rough business, Rob. If you're not very, very good, you can get killed or made over into a vegetable or what have you. Anyone who doesn't have his heart in it can get himself hurt." His memory jogged. "I ever tell you about Garth Briscoe? He was this light-heavy used to train at the club. Good fella; a give-you-the-shirt-off-his-back kind of guy . . ."

Fritzie Zivic's bulldog rounded the corner at 22nd Street, followed by Zivic himself.

"Put that hell-hound on a leash," Tommy called. "Damn thing nipped my toes tonight."

"Were your toes under the table? Under the table is a dog's domain."

"So where you want they should go?" Tommy wanted to know. "Maybe you nail boots to the ceiling and let us all hang."

Zivic came up the walk. "Your uncle, uh?" he said to Rob. "Always the bitch and moan. And to think, I come bearing gifts."

He produced a few sawbucks from his navy peacoat and shoved them at Tommy.

"What's this?"

"Yours, dummy. Dropped them under the card table."

Tommy, skeptical: "Another guy could've dropped 'em."

Fritzie cut a glance at Rob, like he wished he wasn't here to see this. "They were under your seat, okay?"

Tommy's big hand reached out and covered Zivic's; when they came apart, the bills were gone. "Thanks, Fritzie. Ought to be more careful."

"Tell me something I don't know. Ah jeez . . . I'm sorry, fellas."

Fritzie apologized on behalf of Murdoch, who had chosen to bestow his nightly movement on the Tullys' lawn.

Tommy said, "Looks like he's enjoying himself. Bring a bag with you?"

"Ah, come on, Tommy. It's nature's way. Whaddayacallit—biodegradable."

"Yeah, and so are corpses. Doesn't mean I want one—"

"—on your front lawn, yeah, yeah." Fritzie kicked snow over the load. "Did I hear you talking about Garth Briscoe? Sad story, was Garth."

"What happened?" said Rob. "He get hurt in the ring?"

"That was his problem," Fritzie said. "He couldn't get hurt *enough*."

"Let me tell it," Tommy cut in. "Fritzie tells it, we'll be here come next New Year. Briscoe was a good guy; he taught English composition down at St. Mary's of the Sacred Heart—"

"The Professor, is what the guys around the gym called him," said Fritzie. "And in the beginning, he did have that professor-like air about him."

"But he had a problem," Tommy said. "He was one of those whaddayacallems—like to hurt themselves?"

"Punch pugs," Fritzie supplied.

Rob said, "A masochist?"

"Right," Tommy continued, "so a masochist. Briscoe took punishment the likes of which I'd never seen. He'd hardly protect himself. His ribs were always bruised, face always bristly with catgut."

"His old lady left him," Fritzie said. "Took the kids. Briscoe kept on fighting."

Tommy said, "Don't get me wrong—I respect a man who sucks it up and can give as good as he gets for a few rounds and, when it comes down to it, takes his beating like a man—"

"You should," Fritzie cut in. "Made a career of it."

"People in glass houses, Fritzie . . ."

Fritzie gave Rob a pointed look. "Some of us, that was the only way to go. We didn't have such talent."

"I asked Briscoe one time," Tommy said. "*What exactly is the point?* He told me his aim was to get hit so hard and so often that, y' know, *not* getting hit became its own pleasure."

"*Euphoric* pleasure," Fritzie said, pleased with himself. "Thought if he dealt with pain on a nonstop basis, when that pain was taken away, his body would exist in this state of constant bliss. Crazy, but . . ." He shrugged.

"God, it was awful watching him fight after hearing that. And the problem was he never reached that state of grace, so after a while the pain became an end in itself. A guy can get addicted to pain, just like anything. Get so his body craves it."

Rob pictured a man taking that sort of punishment—*eating leather*, the gym bums called it: *That poor palooka ate leather till his face was full.*

Murdoch was now chewing on the wooden steps. Gnawing with rotten yellow teeth, a meringue of foam slathering his chops.

"Can you stop him doing that, Fritzie? First he turds in the yard, now he's like a beaver on the steps. You'd think he was sent by the realtors' board to drive house values down."

"Yawh!" Fritzie prodded the dog's haunches. "Scit!" Murdoch wheeled and nipped Fritzie's boot. "Miserable devil. He'll be dead soon." Feeling poorly for having wished his sole companion dead, Fritzie picked the old dog up and kneaded its ears.

"Briscoe . . ." Tommy went on, ". . . ended up not entirely human. Your dad booted him out of the club: guys felt ill staring at his bashed-in mug. I saw him a few years ago, walking down Ferry Street. His face was so scarred I barely recognized him. And this *nothing* look in his eyes—like he was dead and hadn't quite figured it out yet. Boxing's a wonderful thing, Robbie, but it's not the only thing. It wasn't the thing for Garth Briscoe. It isn't for everyone."

Murdoch squirmed and whined. "Fine, you loveless brute," said Fritzie, setting him on the ground. The dog's hips gave out; his rear legs crumpled under his haunches.

"It's why he's so mean all the time." Fritzie's eyes glassed over; Rob was worried he might start sobbing. "A dog gets old, it doesn't understand why it can't do the things it used to. Makes a creature ornery."

"That thing was ornery as a pup," said Tommy.

"Poor Murdoch . . ." Fritzie went on, ". . . doubt he'll see another year."

Inside the house: a crash, a drunken roar.

Tommy said, "Reuben's pissed as a jar of hornets."

Fritzie said, "Sounds like he's just plain old pissed, too."

Tommy nodded. "Yuh."

"Come on, Murdoch." Fritzie slapped his thigh. "I'll leave you men to it."

Reuben Tully's forehead lay on the table like it had been glued there. The bottle of Jim Beam was empty. At some point in the evening he'd taken Rob's boxing trophies out of their display case and arrayed them across the tabletop.

The sound of Tommy's and Rob's feet squeaking on the linoleum jerked him from his stupor. "If it isn't my two favorite people in the whole . . . wide . . . world."

"You look like shit, Ruby. The drunkard style doesn't suit you."

Reuben's eyes were red-rimmed. "You're not wearing a rain barrel. You win, Tommy?"

"I did not."

Reuben nodded, as though expecting it. "And you," he said to Rob. "The great white hope." He gulped air and slurred, "The *pacifishht.*"

"Head on up to bed, Robbie. I'll get him squared away."

"Uh-uh-uh." Reuben held his hand out like a traffic cop—*halt.* "I wanna talk. Discuss the . . ." His head bobbed. ". . . happened today."

Rob said he only wanted to go to bed.

"Well, I want things, too. I want to know . . ." Reuben's hand cinched around the golden boxer on top of a trophy, his finger tapping its little golden head. ". . . why you tanked the goddamn match today."

"I didn't tank it, Da—"

Tommy cut in. "Don't answer him. He's loaded and talking nonsense."

"I wasn't loaded this afternoon! And I been around long enough to spot a piss-tank!"

Tommy guided Rob toward the stairs. "Okay, you're off to bed."

Reuben jerked up, knocking the table with his knees. Trophies bucked off and hit the linoleum, their cheap metal heads and arms busting off. The bottle shattered, spraying shards. He lost his balance and collapsed onto his chair; a metal leg buckled, spilling him onto the floor.

Tommy grabbed his brother's sweater and yanked him up. "Goddamnit, get your hands off me!" Tommy shoved his brother up against the fridge. Reuben swatted Tommy's face, a glancing shot that drew blood above his eye. The fridge rocked on its casters; the jar of quarters Tommy collected for the laundromat tipped off and smashed. Rob was surprised at how easily Tommy was able to manhandle his father. "Let *go,* you prick!"

But Tommy pinned Reuben's wrists and jammed his head into Reuben's shoulder. "You're in sock feet and there's busted glass all over. Damned if I'll let go."

Reuben closed his eyes; he couldn't seem to catch his breath. When he opened them they were focused, with calm intensity, on his son.

"In the ring," he said, "you hit a man, you earn his respect. Other places—the office, the boardroom, wherever—that man does not have to respect you. But in the ring, it's the law. And sure, it's rough. And no, I can't say you won't ever get hurt. But that pain is temporary, Robbie, and better than the pain of a wasted life, the same faces and places and heartbreak for seventy, eighty years."

"I don't care about getting hurt, Dad. What worries me is that this"—he nodded to the broken trophies—". . . is all there'll ever be."

"It won't be. Listen, we want the same thing—for you to get out of this town." He shoved against Tommy, who didn't budge. "Boxing is your ticket. You see the ring as a trap, but it's not: it's a doorway. You got to step through." He sighed. "I'm done, Tom. You can let go a me."

Tommy kicked stray bits of glass away so that Reuben could make the stairs without slicing his feet. Supported by the railing, Reuben ventured into the unlit darkness of the second floor.

Tommy wiped at the trickle of blood rounding his eye. "That went about as good as you could expect."

"He doesn't listen. Never has."

"What'd you say?" Tommy threw an arm around his nephew's shoulders, hugged him close, kissed the top of his head. "I'm kidding. Listen, the sauce turns your pops into a comic book villain—the Asshole from the Black Lagoon. Let's hit the sack; the Asshole can clean this mess up tomorrow morning."

8

P aul was in an unnamed metropolis with sunlight trickling between the high rises. He was naked, his muscles sleek and oiled, and at the end of one arm hung a snub-nosed revolver. Up and down the sidewalks walked businessmen in identical suits and ties and glossy shoes and briefcases with their hair cut in the same style. They wandered aimlessly, bumping into one another and apologizing, tripping and falling and getting up and falling again, running as if to catch a departing bus only to smash headlong into the spotless facade of a skyscraper. He turned and found one at his side and his breath caught because its only feature was a huge mouth like a puppet's stretching halfway round its face. This thing grabbed Paul's hand and shook it but Paul couldn't feel any bones, a wash-glove packed with chilled lard, and the thing's oversize mouth opened up and said, "You're missing the big picture." It said, "Uh-huh, uh-huh, yup-yup-yup-yup-yup-yup-yup—" and Paul's other hand, the one with the revolver, came up and the muzzle fitted under the thing's chin and when he pulled the trigger the thing's hair fluttered and it fell and Paul saw the hole in its head where the bullet went through but no blood just a sound like wind rushing through a tunnel. And he turned to find another right next to him, noseless and earless and eyeless and Paul wished for a razor blade to slit the milky bulbs where its eyes should be and peel back the skin and see if anything stared back. This one also grabbed his hand and shook it and said "The bubble has burst" with great sadness and its teeth were the size of shoe-peg corn, hundreds of them on account of its mouth being so big, and Paul put the gun to the spot where its heart should be and pulled the trigger twice, the sounds ricocheting between the skyscrapers and echoing along the street and its body curled up and turned to white flakes like instant potatoes that blew away. Paul cracked the chamber and checked the cylinders but each one still had a bullet so he flicked it shut and shot another one and another, laughing like hell, but they spun through the office building's revolving doors without end and his exultation was replaced by hopelessness and he began to wither and shrink, his body dwindling to half-size, then quarter-size and smaller as the sun vanished behind a high rise so black it ate all light and Paul was no bigger than a toy solider, naked and terrified as he fired at legs the size of giant redwoods and fear exploded in his chest as a huge soft-soled loafer came down to crush him . . .

He woke in the backseat of Stacey Jamison's Humvee, wedged between two giant Einsteins. The Humvee—Stacey had painted GET YOUR JAM ON AT JAMMER'S on the side—jounced down a washboard road; silver maples arched their branches overhead.

Stacey's hands were clad in weightlifter's gloves; his shirt read PRAY FOR WAR.

Twice a month Stacey and his Cro-Magnon gym buddies engaged in paintball warfare. "It's serious business," Stacey had told Paul before becoming wistful. "They've outlawed it—outlawed *war*. There'll never be a Big Three, Paul," he'd said desolately. "Not unless those ragheads get hold of a few more 747s." Convinced it was nothing more than an exercise in tactical grab-ass, Paul had accepted Stacey's invite out of curiosity.

They pulled into an open field. Sport-utes and pickup trucks, Einsteins in camo fatigues smearing lampblack on their faces. Late afternoon sunlight glittered on patches of unmelted snow.

Stacey popped the trunk and doled out ordnance. Paul got a paintball gun and a faceshield. He realized he'd be easy to spot: his puffy white parka made him look, as Stacey remarked, "like a faggot cloud drifted down to earth."

They divvied up into teams. Paul was selected second-to-last, one ahead of Pegs, an Einstein so nicknamed because he'd lost his feet in a childhood combine accident. Nobody liked to play with Pegs because the hinges of his prosthetics creaked in chilly weather and betrayed his team's position.

The squads made their way into a forest of maple, oak, and black locust. Stacey captained Paul's team. "Fan out," he told them, "and keep your heads on a swivel."

Paul found a spot behind a rotted log. An air horn went off to start the match. Seconds later paintballs were whizzing through the air all around him, slamming into trees with pops and splats.

Paul spied an Einstein blundering through the brush like a crazed boar. He took aim and fired. A *phut* of compressed gas and his paintball curved through the air to splatter harmlessly in a nettle thicket. He ducked as paintballs jack-hammered the log, *pok-pok-p-pok!* His jaw and chest muscles seized up—taking heavy fire!

Paul's hopes that the Einstein would hump off in search of less elusive quarry were dashed when he heard, "I got all day, goat-fucker! I smell your fear, and it *fuels* me!"

Most Einsteins spoke the same patois of intimidation and degradation. Paul tried to imagine them at the supper table: *Pass the margarine, Mom, you turkey-armed weakling; Dad, make with the salad or I'll poke your eyeballs out with a toothpick and serve them to you in a nice dry martini . . .*

Paul would settle for one-for-one. He wasn't Rambo; nobody expected him to mow down an entire regiment. He jammed two fingers under his faceshield and wiped away the condensation; then he jumped up, unleashed a primal scream, and charged the Einstein.

He squeezed off a few rounds before his visor exploded orange. Once he cleared the paint away his heart took a giddy leap: he'd hit the Einstein. Not lethally—his left foot. Had it been Pegs, he probably would've been allowed to play on. But he was not, and since any hit counted, he was out.

"Flesh wound!" the Einstein cried. "If this were a real war, I'd keep fighting."

"So would I," said Paul, tetchily.

"What," the Einstein wanted to know, "with a hole through your head? Wait a sec—what team are you on?"

"The Log Jammers." Stacey's brainchild.

The Einstein hurled his facemask to the ground. "We're on the same team, you retard! Killed by friendly *fucking* fire—I should rip your *face* off and wear *it* as a mask!"

Paul and the other KIAs assembled back in the field. A gasoline-stoked fire raged; a boom box played "Hatchet to the Head" by Cannibal Corpse. *Slit open crushed eyeballs dripping hanging / A life of beheading I must have.* Einsteins walked around shirtless, flexing, their chilled flesh marbled like Kobe beef.

Paul kept his shirt on. Stacey had him on Androl, Winstrol, and Human Growth Hormone—a dog's breakfast that bloated him up like a dead cow. He sloshed like a wineskin; he could bench-press two-fifty but looked like a walrus. With his liver values out of whack, his skin had gone the color of dried lemon rind. The HGH, concocted from the pituitary glands of cadavers—"The best stuff," Stacey told him, "comes from aborted third-trimester fetuses"—had given him the swollen forehead and elongated jaw of those giant heads on Easter Island. "Think of it as a cocoon," Stacey had told him. "You puff up, look disgusting for a month, then I put you on Lasix to leach the fluid out—a whole new you."

The boom box kicked out "Skull Full of Maggots," "Sanded Faceless," and "Fucked With a Knife," and by the time "I Cum Blood" hit its final note the other players had made their way back. The Einstein sought Stacey out and started bitching about Paul's gaffe.

"Is this true?" Stacey asked. "You killed your own man?"

Paul glared at the Einstein, who stood behind Stacey like a tattletale behind his headmaster. "I didn't kill anyone. It's a game."

Stacey bristled. "Shooting your own man is the most disgraceful act a soldier can commit."

"Nail on the head, Stace," the Einstein spat. "He's a fucking disgrace."

"What were you doing in front of me?" Paul asked.

"He was probably running an end-around flanking pattern." When Stacey sought confirmation on this, the Einstein gave him a "what else?" look.

Paul's teeth clenched the length of his jaw; it felt as if someone had slapped a jellyfish on his scalp, stinging, stinging. If the Einstein bitched once more, Paul resolved to punch his nose down his throat.

The players loaded up fresh paint and headed out for round two.

"Paul," Stacey said, "you take point."

Paul had watched enough *Tour of Duty* to know that point was not anywhere a soldier wanted to be. But he was sick of these over-muscled jackasses and their war games; the prospect of getting killed early wasn't a heartbreaker.

He hunkered down behind a tree stump. The air horn sounded. Paul scanned the woods for any sign of movement, keeping his eyes sighted down the gun barrel. He spied a body crashing through the underbrush and opened fire. His target dodged and wove; Paul cursed as his shots went wide or fell short. He managed to pin him down behind a tree.

"I got all day!" he cried out. "I can—"

A paintball slammed into his head—the *back* of it, above the trim of fine dark hair. His skull snapped forward like he'd been donkey-punched. He'd been shot at point-blank range and expected to find the back of his head blown apart: bone fragments, spattered brains. But his fingers came away clown's-nose red: only paint.

He turned and saw the Einstein he'd shot in the foot. The guy's body was locked in an action-hero pose; CO_2 smoke curled from his gun barrel.

"Mercy," was all he said.

A flashpot went off inside Paul's braincase, a tiny superheated sun that scorched the walls of bone; the light froze in thin sharp icicles that dangled, luminous, from the roof of his skull.

He clawed himself up and shot the Einstein. His gun went *phut*: a bright Rorschach appeared over the Einstein's heart. The Einstein returned fire. They were less than two feet apart. *Phut-phut-ph-phut*. The air was alive with twisting, curiously static strings of paint.

Paul gripped his gun by the barrel and swung it at the Einstein's head. The CO_2 canister struck his jaw and the guy went down in the sedge grass.

Paul sat on his chest and rained blows. Fierce chopping punches, left-right, left-right. Dark arterial red plastered the inside of the Einstein's faceshield; red bubbled through the mask's airholes.

Left-right, left-right. A fist cracked the faceshield: needles of red, pulped skin. Left-right, left-right. Things crumpled and snapped and split and tore loose. A shockingly bright ring spread across the grass. The Einstein wasn't moving; his left leg twitched the way a sleeping dog's will. Paul's shoulders throbbed. His fists dripped.

He tore a bush from the ground. It came up easily, root system clumped with dirt. He replanted it: now the bush appeared to be growing up out of the Einstein's face.

Back in the field Paul opened car doors until he found one with keys in the ignition. His paint-splattered parka left carnival smears on the leather interior. He gunned the engine and careened through the fire and scraped up the side of Stacey's Humvee; sparks leapt through the open window. He lined up the boom box and hit it dead center: it exploded in a spray of cheap plastic and a woofer glanced off the windshield as he accelerated out of the field howling like a banshee.

He kept an eye on the rearview and even pulled over, idling at the roadside for a minute. Nobody came after him.

Paul dropped the vehicle at Jammer's, where he'd left his own car, and grabbed a tire iron from the Micra's trunk.

The gym was empty save for an old guy on a treadmill plodding along like a prisoner on the Bataan death march. Paul took the tire iron to the locked drawer behind the front desk. He filled his pockets with Deca, HGH, two 500-count jars of Dianabol. He was amused to find that the drawer also held Polaroids of Stacey in naked bodybuilding poses. He sported a boner in one shot: the thing looked like a whippet's backbone. Paul emptied out his locker and departed Jammer's for the last time.

Back in the Micra he wiped his face with fast-food napkins; red paint was still grimed into the creases at his eyes. He gobbled a handful of Dianabol and a live-wire jolt thundered up his spine. His skin was yellow and tight and infested with a bone-deep itch, as if his skeletal system were constructed of pink fiberglass insulation.

He drove down Geneva to Queenston then on to Glendale past a stretch of shipyards. He got the little car up to eighty, sparks hopping off the muffler like flaming crickets. Popping the cap off an HGH syrette and plunging it into the hard-packed muscles of his trapezium, he wondered if he'd shot himself with quality fetal brain tissue or run-of-the-mill cadaver.

Had he killed that guy? The silly fucker who shot him—was he dead? Paul pictured the Einstein on the frosty earth with that fucking shrub growing up out of his face. Had he been breathing? Probably. Human organisms are tough and it's hard for them to die. He tried to concentrate—had the guy's lungs been pumping, even a little?—but the image dissolved, his mind unraveling in messy loops.

People were jogging and dog-walking along the canal. He thought how easy it would be to skip the curb, accelerate across the greenbelt, slam into one of them. He pictured bodies crumpling over the hood or rupturing under the tires with red goo spewing from mouths and ears and assholes; he saw smashed headlight glass embedded in faces, saw windshield wipers flying at murderous velocity to sever arms and legs.

He was doing sixty-five when he wrenched the wheel and sent the Micra over the curb. His skull hit the roof and the seatbelt cut into his porcine, fluid-filled body.

His target was riding one of those idiotic recumbent bicycles. He wore a shiny metal-flake helmet, royal purple, like the paint job on a custom roadster. Paul figured he'd hit him broadside and crush him against a dock pillar, or else clip his wheel and launch him into the ice-cold sky, a flailing purple mortar crashing through the canal ice. The Micra shimmy-shook as he gunned it over the greenbelt; a tree branch tore the side-view mirror off. The cyclist caught sight of the car barreling down and pumped his pedals as if to outrun it. Paul had a hearty laugh—what bravado!

He slewed onto the pedestrian footpath, his heart palpitating madly. He popped an ampule of Deca-Durabolin into his mouth, crushed the light-bulb-thin glass between his molars, and swallowed it all down.

An old man was seated on a bench scattering bread crusts to pigeons; his eyes became cavernous white Os at the sight of the onrushing car. Paul considered grazing the bench, severing his legs at the knees, but the old man didn't deserve it half so much as the cyclist so he swerved through the pigeons instead and had to admire their reluctance to pass up a free meal, even in the face of death; their gluttonous shapes bounded over the hood leaving blood and shards of pigeon skull on the windshield. One bird's beak got jammed in the windshield-wiper arm—its body sailed over the roof but its knotted rag of a head, with its calcified beak and diseased eyes, *that* stayed put. This unsettled the hell out of Paul; he flicked the wipers but the damn thing just flapped side to side across the glass.

The cyclist glanced over his shoulder and saw Paul twenty yards back; his legs were pumping like a pair of sewing machine needles. Paul checked the speedometer, saw he was doing nearly forty klicks, and felt grudging respect. He pictured himself in a courtroom, defending his actions to a powder-wigged judge. *Mitigating circumstances, your honor: not only was the deceased riding a recumbent bicycle, but let the record show he also wore a fruity purple helmet.* He inched up on the bike tire, close enough to see the cyclist's terrified reflection in the bike's rearview mirror—*Your honor, he had a* rearview mirror *bolted to the handlebars! I throw myself upon the mercy of the court!*

Paul was charged up, galvanic, rocket fuel coursing through his veins, but at the last possible instant he jerked the wheel and the Micra went skipping back across the greenbelt, the front bumper clipping a trash can and sending the car into an unchecked swoon. His head cracked the dashboard and stars, whole constellations, blossomed before his eyes as the car spun across the frictionless grass, one revolution, two, three, then he was back on the street as the windshield filled with the blaze of oncoming headlights, tires screeching, horns bleating, and Paul, still woozy, hit the gas and cut across lanes into the parking lot of an insurance broker, mercifully closed. He lay draped over the wheel until he heard angry voices nearby and veered onto the street again.

In a supermarket now, pushing a shopping cart down the aisles. The industrial halogens stung his eyes. In the produce section he picked a ripe peach, took a bite and grinned as sweet nectar dribbled down his chin.

He bagged up a dozen tomatoes then swung down the next aisle and picked up six cartons of extra large Omega 3 eggs. He spied a pack of firecrackers in the discount bin and chucked it in the cart.

He passed down the household gadgets aisle. He saw the Remington Fuzz Away; phone attachments with 200-number autodial memories; something called the Racquet Zapper, an electric flyswatter that promised to make "pest control a *zap*." It was funny, Paul thought, how we do it to ourselves. He thought of all the inventions over the past fifty years and figured ninety-nine percent were of the "quality of life" variety. Inventions to make life easier, lighten the roughness of existence—as if an electric flyswatter could somehow ease the stress of daily life. So now everyone's got a houseful of these dopey gadgets, mountains of cheap plastic and wiring, and can't possibly live without their juicers and pepperballs and hands-free phone sets and—he scanned the shelves restlessly—yes, their cordless Black and Decker Scumbuster 300s, couldn't visualize life before any of them—god, how did the pioneers manage it?—when all they really did was make everyone weaker, more reliant, less able to do for themselves until they were nothing but puddles of mush.

"Remember your own damn phone numbers," he muttered. "Roll up a newspaper to swat at flies," his voice rising. "Pick lint off your fucking sweater with your *fingers!*" he screamed.

In line at the checkout he scanned newspaper headlines. The *Weekly World News*'s top headline read: CLONED HITLER TURNS SEVEN YEARS OLD! The *Toronto Star*'s seemed equally absurd: SHOT IN THE DARK: BLIND STUDENTS TREATED TO DEER HUNTING TRIP. He felt much calmer now, having settled on a plan of attack.

The cashier eyed his purchases skeptically. "Looks like you've got an evening all planned out."

"Yes," said Paul. "I'm baking a pie."

She waved the firecrackers over the scanner. "Missing a few ingredients."

"It's mostly meringue."

She handed him the bags with a rueful shake of her head. "Hope you're not planning to bake this cake in my neighborhood."

In the parking lot with his gonads kicking out toxic levels of testosterone some biological imperative made him drop to the tarmac and burn off push-ups; his mind whited out at two hundred reps and when his senses returned he was crouched behind the Micra with his hands gripping the bumper, straining to lift the rear wheels off the ground, but merciless pressure built up in his abdominal cavity and he feared a hernia or a prolapsed colon so he walked to a payphone at the lot's edge and dialed Lou Cobb.

"That . . . that place you were . . . talking about . . ."

"You been out jogging, kid? Sound puffed."

". . . Gladiators . . ." Paul was picturing arms and legs rupturing from excess mass, hyper-developed muscles splitting biceps and thighs. ". . . Thunderbird Layne and all that . . ."

"How's your schnozz?" Lou wanted to know. "Healed up yet?"

Paul felt his own muscles twitching, the tendons hard and tight as a condom packed with walnuts. "My nose is fine. So, about that place—"

Lou laughed for no reason: *Bhar-har-har!* Or was Paul hearing things; was it some odd distortion on the line? "We'll work something out. Sounds like you're ready."

He hung up and drove to Bayside, a neighborhood strung along the banks of Twelve Mile Creek. In the dusky evening light he saw million-dollar homes, topiary gardens, pool houses. Paul stomped on the brakes and stepped out. The house was gaudy: ornate columns, three-car garage, his-and-her hunter green Range Rovers.

He tucked the tire iron down the back of his pants—cold steel slid between the crack of his ass and he shivered—and grabbed a carton of eggs. He eased through the open gates up the drive and found a spot on the front lawn. Methodically, with great relish, he started chucking.

Eggs broke over the mullioned windows and the stained-glass door. Eggs broke with the sound of brittle bones, so richly rewarding.

A soft terrified face materialized in a second-floor window. Paul threw an egg and that face vaporized. Egg dripped off the eaves. Egg coated the Range Rovers.

The mailbox was shaped like a dog: an Irish setter. Paul stared at this grinning dog with a metal pole shoved up its ass and found himself unsettled on a sub-cellular level. He drew the tire iron from his trousers and whacked the fucking thing's head and put a satisfying dent in it; another whack tore its mouth off its hinges. He jammed the tire iron down its throat and pried it off its moorings. A kick sent the mouthless thing skittering across the driveway into a flower bed.

A buttery face poked out the front door. The face hollered that Paul was an unhinged crazyperson and that the cops were on their way.

"I *am* the cops!" Paul screamed. "My name is Rex Appleby—part of that thin blue line separating you from the unadulterated *scum* out there!"

"Get off my lawn, degenerate!"

"Your mailbox was resisting arrest. I'm well within my rights!"

When the guy reappeared at the door, relating Paul's physical description to 911 dispatch, it was time to hit the dusty trail.

Back in the car he crushed Dianabols on the dashboard and snorted the pink powder. The Micra started with a shudder; he punched the accelerator and blatted down the street singing along to the stereo, slewing around a hairpin curve, getting the shitbox up on two wheels.

He drove a few blocks before pulling up beside a gold Lexus SUV. Paul had once wanted one of these so badly—he'd planned on asking for one for Christmas. Now the very sight of it made him queasy with rage.

He got out and checked the door: unlocked. He grabbed a handful of eggs and pelted the mahogany instrument panel. With the tire iron he stabbed holes in the fragrant leather seats and jammed Roman candles into the stuffing. He lit the fuses and slammed the door. The soundproofing was top-notch: only brilliant intermittent flashes behind the tinted windows. Acrid gray smoke seeped from the door seams.

He hopped in the Micra. His heart trip-hammered wildly; he pictured aortic valves spun from carnival glass on the verge of splintering. He lit off some Magic Black Snakes on the passenger seat but they were unrewarding, dirty little turds, so he fired up a Screaming Devil and puttered down the street with gobs of shrieking orange fire spitting out the windows.

At some point he noticed the flashing cherries in his rearview and pulled over.

The cop was old, with the skittery-dodgy gait of a man clearly terrified of being shot or otherwise incapacitated so close to retirement. He scanned the car's interior. An arresting officer's wet dream: busted eggs, squashed tomatoes, the reek of gunpowder.

"And how are you tonight, sir?"

"Feeling jim-dandy *fine*, officer."

"I'll ask you to put both hands on the wheel . . . yup, like that."

The officer walked around front of the car. "You've got a busted headlight. And what looks to be a . . ." He hunkered down for a better look. ". . . bird lodged in the grille, here."

"That came with the car."

"Funny option, I'd say." He returned to the driver's side. "We received a call about a disturbance. You wouldn't happen to know anything about that?"

Paul scraped at a shard of eggshell stuck to his chin. "I did see a suspicious fellow—a prowler, you might say—a few blocks back. He was tall and skinny, with rolls of fat hanging off his squat frame. And he was sitting astride a gryphon."

The cop sighed heavily. "A gryphon, huh?"

"Yes, the mythical creature. Half lion, half eagle. Quite rare, I can assure you."

"And you haven't been making mischief tonight—throwing eggs, batting mailboxes, and the like? Nothing illegal?"

"My understanding of the law is fuzzy, officer—is driving drunk illegal nowadays?"

"Telling me you're intoxicated?"

"Yo ho ho and a bottle of *r-r-r-r-r-ruuum!*"

The cop looked as though he'd dearly love to drag Paul to the precinct and interrogate him with a phonebook. "You've got some restitutions to make, son—though by the looks of this heap here, the offended parties may have to satisfy themselves with an apology. License and registration."

Paul rooted through the glove compartment and handed them over. The officer's brow wrinkled. He glanced at Paul, the license, back at Paul.

"You're not ..." confused, "... Jack Harris's son? The winery owner?"

Paul nodded.

The officer leaned down to get a better look. "Lord," he said, "it *is* you."

Paul tallied up his offenses over the past hours: assault, petty larceny, attempted vehicular manslaughter, drug abuse, vandalism, tendering false statements to an officer—how many years in the hoosegow was he looking at here?

"I want you to put this car in gear," the cop said evenly, "then I want you to drive up to that main street there and get yourself home."

"But I egged the almighty fuck out of that house."

"Just a boy being a boy, s'far as I'm concerned."

"I'm twenty-six!"

"Simmer down. I'm doing you a favor." The officer headed back to his squad car and pulled up beside Paul. "You drive safe, now. And tell your pops Jim Halliday sends his regards."

With a sunny smile and a toot of his horn, he drove away.

Paul tightened his grip on the wheel and butted it sharply with his head; the horn issued a strangled honk. His ... fucking ... *father.* He butted the wheel again and again; blood trickled down the sides of his nose. He jerked the car in gear and trod on the gas.

A thump; a strangled yelp. The back tire skipped ever so slightly, then settled.

He got out in time to see a little dog running frantic circles around its own head, which had been flattened under the Micra's rear wheel. A teacup Chihuahua; it must've gotten under the car while Paul and the cop were talking.

He knelt on the street and looked around for its owner. The dog's legs got tangled up and its body tumbled over its own head in a maneuver circus acrobats call a "flic flac" and stayed that way.

The streetlamp's acid glow was stark, merciless. The dog was mangy-looking, with clumps of hair falling off; maybe it had been abandoned, maybe they weren't hot fashion items anymore. Its head was intact only in the way a light bulb wrapped in layers of masking tape before being stepped on could be considered intact. The dog's eyes were closed; what looked like burst bath beads were pinched between each eyelid. A quivering red worm poked from the soft beige skin of its pelvis.

Paul's guilt curdled into rage when no owner appeared: what sort of asshole lets his little dog run around unattended? Rage soured into fear: what was he going to do? He sat there in his sheath of muscles wondering what the hell any of it mattered because he still felt terrified, weak, and worthless—he didn't even know what to do about a *dead dog*.

The dog's body was as loose and warm as a boiled hen, its legs Tinker Toys wrapped in moleskin. He pulled gently but realized that if he pulled much harder he'd disconnect its head from the rest of it. Hunting through the trunk, he found an ice scraper and tried to lift it off the cement, but he was crying by then and the chest hitches made him so clumsy he ended up folding the dog's muzzle over its eyes, folding the poor thing's head like an omelet, and the desecration reduced him to racking sobs and his tears, pattering the cold street, were yellow like his skin, yellow from the poisons he'd shoveled into himself, the mashed-up fetal brains funneled into his veins, and then he realized he had nothing to put the dog into and found himself back in the car hunting under the seats until he located a crumpled Burger King bag.

He returned to the dog, which he'd managed to scrape up without further damage. He dropped it in the bag and felt a sadness that bordered on the existential to discover that a dog's body could actually *fit* in a paper bag.

The Chihuahua's collar lay on the street. Pink, no thicker than a shoestring. One of the tags, shaped like a bone, read KILLER. Another one said IF I AM LOST, PLEASE RETURN ME TO . . . followed by an address. He stared at the address for a long time before hurling the leash into the bordering yard. He rolled the bag closed like a sack lunch and set it on the passenger seat.

Ten minutes later he was in the country. No streetlights, one headlight busted: he hurtled through the night in near-total blackness. Fruit fields rushed past as the car bounced along a corduroy road, wind howling through the windows and his mind out of sync, destination forgotten until like a desert heat-shimmer the winery appeared, dozens of security lamps fighting off the darkness. He sped through the parking lot and hit a speed bump and the muffler finally tore loose as the car crashed through a chain-link gate in a spray of blue sparks and shot into the grape fields, flying between the tight rows as a re-energized Paul Harris sang over the un-mufflered roar of the engine until an irrigation pipe rose up and he had just enough time to picture himself on a hospital bed with tubes running in and out of him before he hit the pipe dead-on, his body thrown against the windshield.

He came to dazed but remarkably unhurt. The windshield was smashed, webbed, but still of one piece. A wave of cold nausea rolled through his chest and he jerked forward and vomited between his legs. The crash jarred the tape from the cassette player; silence except for a slow hiss of steam from the rad.

The door was crimped shut. Paul wiped strings of bile swinging from his lips, grabbed the tire iron and paper bag, and clambered out the window.

A clean, still night, dark though he could still make out the contours of the fringing hills. The Micra's hood was crushed halfway down the middle. The headlights nearly faced each other.

From summer through early fall the pickers bunked in shacks on the easternmost edge of the fields. Small and spare—they reminded Paul of Boy Scout cabins. He made his way to the nearest one and used the tire iron to pry the padlock off. Meticulously winterized: mattresses wrapped in tarps, the stove's flue tightly stoppered.

He stoked a fire in the potbellied stove. The pickers had left a box of canned food behind; Paul brushed away mouse turds and found a tin of sardines. His hands were grimed with blood and dog fur but he shoveled the fish into his mouth and licked the oil off his fingers. God, he'd never tasted anything so good. The warmth awakened pain he hadn't felt all night. Shoulders and arms and neck: every part of him ached.

The shack creaked as fire-heat flexed the joists. He relished the isolation, miles and miles from another human being. He sensed he was on a collision course, though with whom or what he didn't yet know. There was no doubt about it. Something *was* approaching. The tracks he stood on vibrated with the force of it, yet he was powerless to move so much as a step.

He stirred the fire and set the paper bag on a bed of embers and shut the grate. The shack filled with the stink of burning hair. Sizzlings and spatterings; a sharp pop.

Paul lay on the planks and shut his eyes.

He dreams he is in a cave with another man. There is a sense of being miles underground; above is a vast and empty darkness. He sits on a wooden chair, lashed at the wrists and ankles with copper wire. The other man is huge, three hundred fifty, four hundred pounds, not fat but thick-gutted; he's wearing a rubberized butcher's apron and a belt hung with delicate tools like dentist's instruments. He dances forward awkwardly, as though he isn't in control of his own limbs; the effect is shocking and awful because he is so large. "Are you scared?" The pitch of his voice is breathy, babyish. Paul says no and so the man plucks a sharp tool from his belt and reaches two fat sluglike fingers into Paul's mouth, taking hold of his tongue, and Paul bites the man's fingers only to find they're hard as wood, then the tool is in his mouth, the taste of metal at the back of his throat, and his tongue is severed deftly and the man stares at it with fleeting curiosity before casting it into the darkness. "Are you scared?" he asks. "Oo," says Paul. The man looks confused or even scared but he reaches to his belt and picks a long steel rod and, setting a hand on the side of Paul's head to steady it, pushes the rod into Paul's ear until a stereophonic crunch fills his skull, followed by silence. He does the other ear, too, until Paul can hear only a soft hiss inside his head, the sound you'd hear on a cassette tape between songs. The man's lips move: *Are you scared?* Paul shakes his head. The big man's look of confusion deepens as he unhooks a walnut-handled meat cleaver from his belt and hacks Paul's legs off with a few brisk strokes, sawing through strings of gristle, and there's no blood, not a single drop. The insides of Paul's thighs are full of dark coils, like age rings on a tree. *Are you scared?* Paul says he is not—and he *is not*, none of this scares him—and when the man shakes his head Paul sees there are filament-thin strings attached to the man's skull and arms and legs, to his fingers and every joint, strings threading up into the darkness, and the man is moving under their influence like a marionette in a dumb show. With a tool like a sharpened spoon he slits the skin around Paul's eyes and draws Paul's head down until his eyes fall from their sockets and Paul feels something for the first time—a bracing icy coldness all along his optic nerves—and just before the man snips the nerves with a pair of silver scissors Paul sees his own fingers, sees the thin black threads tied around each fingertip moving the huge man to his bidding. The world goes black and though he cannot see the man's mouth he knows what words are being spoken because he is making the man say them, and his answer is unflinching: *No, No, No, No, No . . .*

Paul awoke in the shack. Cold and dark, the fire dead. When he tried to sit up, fishhook spiders seized his spine; he gasped and curled up again. Parts of his body hurt so badly he wondered if they were ruptured. He dragged himself to the stove and hugged its cast-iron belly, grateful for the warmth.

A hesitant edge of light skirted the hills to the east. Clutching the sardine tin into which he'd swept the fire's ashes he made his way up the nearest rise. Dawn broke over Lake Ontario, tinting gold the undersides of low-lying clouds. The sun provided no warmth yet was beautiful in a way he could not recall ever seeing; light clung to frost-glazed pussy willows as it poured over the flattened grass. Were he a painter, he might have spent his whole life in search of such a scene.

The lake was a few miles away, and while the possibility of ashes traveling quite that far was remote, he figured, Why not? But the wind shifted when he shook the tin and the ashes blew back into his face, up his nose and into his mouth. He sneezed and spat dirty gray gobs, shaking his head at this dismal failure. Then he saw that some ashes were still stuck to the oil at the bottom of the sardine tin and resolved that they would receive a proper burial.

He set off across the plateau, away from the winery, down toward the lake.

9

Fight night.

Tommy Tully bounded down the stairs into the kitchen, pushing off the bottom stair to glide awkwardly across the worn linoleum in his sock feet. Reuben and Rob sat at the kitchen table. The black valise lay open at Reuben's elbow; he inspected rolls of gauze and white tape, strips of sponge and vials of adrenaline chloride. Rob sat with a bowl of hard-boiled eggs and a cup of lemon tea.

Tommy stalked over to the Amana fridge and threw jabs at its white unmoving bulk. He hooked to the icebox, puffing through his nose, *"Yip! Bing! Thwack!"* shuffling his feet Muhammad Ali style, *"Biff, Bing, Pow!"* raising his arms, dancing, grinning. "You better check the warranty, 'cause the fridge is *toast.*"

"Stop clowning," said Reuben.

Tommy grabbed a loaf of his beloved Wonder Bread off the counter and hefted it above his head like a trophy. "I dedicate this win to

Gummy Sue and Stinky Mulligan and ol' Armless Joe down at the VFW hall—we did it, guys!"

Rob found a wooden soup spoon and put it to his uncle's mouth, assuming the folksy bearing of an interviewer. "Gee golly, Tom Tully, that was some fight. You and the Fridge exchanged heated pre-fight words—you remarked that the Fridge didn't have the legs to make it through the late rounds. The prediction seems to have rung true."

Tommy said, "First of all I'd like to thank God almighty, without whom no things are possible. The Fridge put up a hell of a fight. I respect the Fridge as a fighter. But this was Tom Tully's night." He hugged the loaf of bread to his chest. "If the Fridge wants a rematch, okay, fine, but it'll have to get in line. The Stove's my mandatory challenger, and the Toaster Oven's been flapping its gums. Tom Tully don't duck no appliance! None!"

Rob said, "Stern words from a stern man—Tom 'Boom Boom' Tully."

Tommy and Rob dissolved into snorting giggles. Reuben wasn't laughing.

"Pull yourself together," he said.

Tommy patted his brother on the back. "Lighten up, killjoy."

Reuben finished packing while Tommy fetched their coats and boots.

Tommy returned with their gear. "What're we waiting for?"

"Waiting for you to wise up," said Reuben. "But since there's about as much chance of that as there is me sprouting fairy's wings, guess there's no use wasting our time."

Tommy said, "That's the spirit."

"Meet at Macy's after?" Rob said.

"If your uncle's face doesn't look like ten pounds of ground chuck."

Rob wished his uncle good luck. He felt the lump lodged deep in his belly.

Tommy winked. "Another day in the salt mines."

★

Two men drove the southbound QEW in a rattletrap Ford.

They crossed the Niagara overpass, high over freighters plying the Welland Canal. The highway cut west, curling around a Christmas tree farm, on past wrecking yards and discount tire outlets.

Weeks had passed since the paintball incident. Nothing had come of it all, aside from an article in the *St. Catharines Standard*: CRAZED MOTORIST RUNS AMUCK ON CANAL FOOTPATH. (A quote from the recumbent bicyclist: "Thank heavens the maniac was driving a small foreign car and I was able to outrace it.") He'd seen no headline titled MUSCLEBOUND IDIOT FOUND DEAD IN FIELD and so assumed the Einstein was okay. He had moved out of his parents' house the next day; his nights had been spent on the couch in Lou's office.

Lou drove with both hands on the wheel, a prudent five miles below the speed limit on account of the icy roads and his driving license being suspended. Between them on the front seat: a black leather valise stocked with gauze and tape, adrenaline chloride, ferric acid.

"You're off that shit, aren't you?"

Paul nodded; he'd quit the 'roids cold turkey following his binge. And though he'd surrendered muscle mass, he was streamlined and agile and his skin had lost its yellowish tinge.

"Let me tell you something about muscles," Lou told him. "They look good and I guess they'll frighten off a lot of guys; nine out of ten—ninety-nine out of a hundred—take one look at a pair of sporty arm-cannons and walk the other way. But muscles aren't skill or heart. So your problem is when you run across the one guy in a hundred who recognizes that—and *that* guy is going to hurt you a hell of a lot worse than those other ninety-nine would've. Hurt you half for spite."

They drove along the river. The spiraling coils of a hydroelectric plant reared in solitary abandonment against the night sky. Farther on, a rutted dirt path rounded into a sprawling farmstead. Cars were parked along a barbed-wire fence.

At the barn door they were met by Manning in his long duster coat. He dragged on a corn-husk cigarette and said, "Who we got here?"

Lou hooked a thumb at Paul. "From the club. Tough kid. The guts of a burglar."

Manning sized Paul up. His eyes were obscured by a haze of smoke spindling the cigarette. "On you go, then."

The barn was packed. A highway work crew in bib pants and reflective vests; high rollers with narrow silk ties and suits of exotic cut; tattooed, bandanna-wearing members of the local Hells Angels chapter—one sported a tattoo that read I'D RATHER SEE MY SISTER IN A WHOREHOUSE THAN SEE MY BROTHER ON A JAP BIKE. The dark, dumb eyes of cattle peered through knotholes in the barn walls. Fighters stood on the peripheries, clustered in pockets of shadow beyond the lit ring.

"Wait here," Lou said.

Paul sat on a hay bale. A fighter sat on the floor beside him. Not too tall or short, thin or fat, lean or muscular. He wore a deerstalker tugged low over his lumpen features and a pair of boxy black-rimmed glasses. He sat there, rocking. Paul had heard that schizophrenics gave off a stink that often got so intense doctors claimed to see colors— scarlet, aquamarine, magenta—wafting off their patients. An imbalance in their bodily makeup, the enzymes being out of kilter or otherwise fucked. This guy stunk like rotting peaches.

"Fight like a dog," Paul heard him say.

"What's that?"

"It's the best mindset to put yourself in." In the stark white of the barn lights, the guy's sockets looked like they were packed with dry ice.

"You're a dog. A dog isn't frightened by pain. A dog is frightened by thunder and fireworks and the vacuum cleaner, all the things its tiny brain can't quite comprehend. But a dog—and I'm talking a *real* dog, here—is not the least bit frightened of pain. So: fight like a dog."

Paul considered this man closely. He looked as though, in some former life, he might have been a doctor or a professor. Paul felt like he'd seen him before, somewhere.

"Makes my dick hard." The fighter gestured to his jeans, the rigid outline of his cock swelling the denim halfway down his thigh. "It's the anticipation."

Paul had no response to this—he was fairly certain the guy wasn't looking for one. And he was utterly certain he'd rather not fight the bastard.

Lou returned. "You're on as an alternate. But we should get your hands wrapped in case it turns out you're called in."

Reuben looped bandages over and around, pressing gently the oft-broken bones of his brother's huge hands. Tape next, over and around, a thick encasing layer. How many times had they done this together, in preparation for training, sparring, title fights? A few thousand, surely. The act held an underlying ease, a familiarity: their heads bent and almost touching, they resembled lovers sharing some sweet intimacy.

Reuben scanned the barn. The dark peripheries hosted seventy or eighty spectators. Fritzie Zivic stood beside a withered ancient in a wheelchair; Murdoch was chewing the codger's slippers off his senseless feet. Reuben nudged his brother.

"Look who's here."

Tommy followed his gaze and saw Garth Briscoe sitting beside a young guy. Garth was wearing a pair of boxy glasses and looked repulsive; he rocked back and forth like someone suffering a neural disorder—as could be the case.

"Huh," said Reuben. "Least he's alive."

"Take a break, Ruby. You don't have to be a prick every day of your life."

"That wasn't very nice," he admitted. "I always liked Garth; everyone liked him, till he went off the rails. But what does it say that you and him are in the same place?"

"Ruby . . ."

"All right, forget it, I'm laying off. You ready?"

Tommy punched himself under the jaw. "Time to make the donuts."

Manning singled out Tom and Paul for the evening's fourth bout. He recalled the rough time Tommy had had with the Kilbride kid and thought he'd throw the old warhorse a bone.

"Well?" Lou asked Paul. "What do you figure?"

"God, that's one big slab of humanity."

Lou acknowledged this was so, but said, "Often the worst you ever absorb is one good punch: the one that knocks you cold. Most guys find it hard to keep hitting a man who's gone unconscious—the skin goes slack, no tension to it, like punching a gutted fish. I've found there is an innately human resistance to such violence."

The glasses-wearing schizo overheard Lou and said, "That guy's a pro, too—he won't hit you any more than he needs to."

"Listen to Garth here," Lou said. "He's been around."

The schizo gave Lou a smile so grateful it was sickening. Only then did Paul realize where he'd seen him before: that first day at Lou's gym, the beaten fighter who'd shambled in to take a few licks at the heavybag before Lou stopped him. *Ease down, Garth,* he remembered Lou saying. *You did good last night. Real good.*

"So," Lou asked, "are we on?"

Not long ago, the prospect of fighting a man like Tommy would have made his bowels quiver. Tommy was huge and scarred and looked exactly what he was: a tough veteran fighter in the Thunderbird Layne mold. But when Paul searched the place in his heart where stark fear once held court, he found the court was empty.

"I want to fight him," he told Lou. "I do."

They met in a circle of stacked bales. No headgear, no mouthshields or gloves. Paul felt his heart as a discrete presence in his chest.

Tommy considered the guy: young, not a whole lot older than Robbie. But a lot of his youth had been sucked out. He looked like the lone survivor of a nuclear Armageddon: missing teeth and acne scars and worst of all the haunted look Tommy had seen in far too many fighters.

A true fighter's handshake was always soft. Perhaps this was because their hands were tender after months of punching bags and mitts and opponents. Or perhaps, after doing so much damage in the ring, they possessed not the slightest desire to do any damage outside of it— even so much as may be delivered through a stern handshake.

Paul and Tommy shook hands very, very softly.

"I'm sorry for what comes next," Paul said.

"What do you got to be sorry for?" Tommy chucked Paul on the shoulder. His smile was somehow ashamed. "I'll take it easy on you."

"Please don't."

The first punch struck Paul in the shoulder. There was no *oomph* to it: were it possible to throw a well-intentioned punch, Tommy had done so. But it was enough to unbalance him and he stumbled back, then rocked forward into Tommy's chest. Tommy leaned on Paul, a forearm

on the back of Paul's neck forcing his head down and making it tough
to draw breath. Paul was staring at his own belly button while the huge
fucker hammered at his ribs—not too hard, just enough so he'd feel it.
He felt his ribs shrink around his lungs, the staccato thump of his
heart, the sensation of being closer to his body than he'd ever known.

Tommy's forearm slipped off Paul's neck. Paul reared up and lanced
a right hand at his head; Tommy angled away and the blow hit the side
of his throat, his own right hand rising between Paul's arms to catch
him under the chin. Pain blossomed inside Paul's skull, not a flower but
gardens of the stuff, a pain like searing-hot rivets sprinkled on his scalp.

Tommy was stunned when the guy didn't go down. That Kilbride
kid would have broken to pieces but this guy just smiled, blood climbing the cracks between his teeth. He's infected, Tommy thought, same
way poor Garth Briscoe is infected.

Paul swung and missed, then Tommy hit him with an anvil fist.
Tears flooded Paul's eyes as a sharp note of pain danced across his face
and hit the center of his brain. He was hit again, harder than he'd ever
been hit before: nose compacting, capillaries bursting. The world went
red and Paul fell through that redness as though in a dream. The floor
rushed up to meet him. He watched a dark spot of his own blood
shape itself into a fan, then a butterfly, glistening and soaking into the
ripples and knots of the floorboards.

The bell rang.

Paul staggered to his corner like a man on a three-day drinking binge.
He was grinning.

Lou helped him onto the stool. Paul's face was like something Goya
might've signed his name to: Neanderthal-like swelling above his
brows and one tooth jarred from his gums, suspended on a strip
of skin.

"Hold on." Lou reached into Paul's mouth and, with a vicious twist, yanked the tooth out. "Swallow more than a pint and you'll be sick," he said as blood gushed into Paul's mouth. "What the hell—not like you're liable to grow another set, right?"

He used ferric sulfate to cauterize the bloody hole in Paul's mouth. Paul swallowed convulsively, the acid scorching his esophagus.

"I'm trying to go easy. But he's a glutton."

Reuben soaked Tommy's head with a wet sponge. "What did you expect? Last time you fought a feeb, now you're up against a punch pug."

"Masochist," Tommy corrected.

"Keep leaning on him. You don't owe any a these jerks a show."

"What if he won't go down?"

"Then you have to make him go down."

"I might really hurt him."

"Christ, Tom—how else do you picture this ending?"

It ended thirty-three seconds into the second round. And it ended like this:

Two men warred in a starkly lit ring, the whistle of their fists a death song. Paul experienced a wholly perverse joy in the feel of another man's hands upon his body—even in violence. Tommy found the soft spot under Paul's heart with a tricky uppercut; Paul gasped as if a crowbar had been spiked through his chest.

Tommy saw the opening: the kid let his guard fall each time he threw a right hand. Make it quick, Tommy thought. Make his world go black.

Tommy planted his feet and sat down on a right uppercut that rose from his waist like a Stinger missile shot from a hayfield silo.

The punch missed by an eighth of an inch.

Consider that distance for a moment.

Your own index finger, say. At the base of your nail, where the nail plate meets the nail bed—where nail meets flesh—that whitish half-moon. It's called the lunula, after the Latin *luna* meaning *moon*. The lunula should be no more than an eighth of an inch thick at its broadest point; a little thicker if your nail has been manicured, the cuticle pushed down.

Tommy's punch missed by a lunula. By a ladybug's wing. An eighth of an inch. But more crucially it missed by a lifetime, or several. It missed by Tommy's forty-three years and Reuben's forty-five, by Paul's twenty-six and Rob's sixteen. It missed by all the possibilities that existed in the split-second before it missed and by all that might conceivably have been afterward.

When Tommy's fist sailed past his chin, Paul stepped away and struck back instinctively. Tommy's jaw was clenched: the maxillary artery running from tip of skull to base of throat was crimped, blood collecting at his temples.

It was a lucky punch, the sort you'll see if you watch enough fights. Paul was in the right spot, Tommy the wrong one. The angles worked in Paul's favor and against Tommy. Everyone in that place knew who was the better fighter; not a single bet had been placed on Paul to win.

A lucky punch, is all. It happens.

Paul felt as though a very small, very ripe grape had burst under his knuckles.

Put it another way:

They say every substance that appears solid is, at its most basic level, not solid at all. Everything is composed of atoms, a nucleus orbited by protons and electrons. Massive distances separate protons and electrons from their nucleus: imagine the moon circling the Earth, or the Earth orbiting the sun, and you get the idea. They say if you remove all those empty spaces and squeeze everything together, the Empire State Building would fit into a teaspoon—a spoonful of pure matter weighing roughly 19,800 tons.

Paul's punch hit Tommy like the Empire State Building dropped from a teaspoon.

The instant the punch landed, as Tommy's eyes rolled involuntarily back in his head, Paul wanted to take it all back, as if the punch were an angry word he could revoke. *Sorry, sorry, I didn't mean that.* They were fighting, yes, trying to knock each other out or force surrender, but the sound of Tommy's skull hitting the boards—a horrid fracturing noise like a squashed snail—broke whatever spell he'd been under and now Paul could only watch as Tommy tried to stand up but failed miserably, blood coming out his nose as he stared around with a queer disoriented smile. And when Tommy fell, reaching for Paul because he was the only thing to reach for, Paul was there to catch him. He cradled Tommy's thick stalk of neck, his dense lifeless weight like a sweating sack of cement. Tommy's head lolled, eyes wide open, tongue jutting past the flat black gumshield.

Seconds later Reuben shoved Paul out of the way and knelt beside his brother. He mopped blood with a towel but there was so goddamn *much* of it and it wouldn't stop coming. The sweat on Tommy's arms was ice-cold and his head looked all wrong; Reuben was sick to his stomach wondering if everything inside was busted and if it was only the unbroken skin holding the works together.

"Call an ambulance!"

"That's not how it works," Manning told Reuben. "You take care of your own."

"Take care of him how?"

"Any way you can." Manning crossed his arms. "Anywhere but here."

Seven minutes later Reuben and Tommy were in the backseat of Fritzie Zivic's Cadillac El Dorado. Zivic's foot was tromped on the gas pedal and cold night air whistled through seams in the frame. Tommy's head was wrapped in towels; Reuben had cut holes over the nose and mouth so he could breathe. As the miles clicked off, the towels became redder and redder until Reuben's lap was soaked.

Six minutes later Tommy was strapped to a gurney wheeled through the Emerg doors at Mount St. Mary's Catholic hospital. The admitting nurse was Helen Jack—bespectacled Frankie Jack's youngest daughter. She told Reuben to calm down and tell her what happened.

"Tommy . . . he fell down a flight of stairs."

She shook her head. "Oh, Reuben."

Twenty minutes later, after an X-ray revealed the base of Tommy's skull to be severely shattered—the medical term an eggshell fracture—the beeper of a Buffalo-area neurosurgeon went off. Tommy received a blood transfusion. The towels were cut from around his head with surgical shears. His eyes stayed open the whole time. Heart rate: forty beats per minute. Tommy's HMO coverage was inadequate but Helen Jack was able to hustle the paperwork through.

Thirty-seven minutes later a bonesaw cut a window into Tommy's forehead. The portion of skull covering his frontal lobe was removed to allow his brain room to swell. His gray matter turned a creamy shade of pink from oxygen exposure. Tommy's face remained serene; a vague smile touched his lips. EEG readouts indicated brain function next to nil. Cerebral blood flow a trickle. Neurological activity proportional to a Stage 3 coma victim.

★

Rob was in his bedroom when the telephone rang. Racing downstairs to the kitchen, he caught it on the fourth ring.

"I'll be there in fifteen minutes."

"I'm not calling from Macy's, Rob."

His father had never called him Rob before. Not once in his life.

A gypsy cab dropped Rob off at St. Mary's Emerg entrance. Reuben stood shivering under a cone of blue light near the doors.

"What happened?" Rob's dread was such that he could hardly breathe. "Tommy—?"

"He's alive." The past hours had shrunk Reuben, cored and hollowed him; Rob was afraid to touch his father for fear he'd crumble to dust.

In the Emergency room they sat on orange plastic chairs bolted to the wall. Reuben explained. Rob couldn't quite wrap his head around it. In his mind's eye he still saw his uncle as he'd been earlier that evening: shadowboxing the fridge, dancing on the tips of his toes with a loaf of Wonder Bread clasped to his chest. Rob could not conceive of Tommy as he was at this moment: in an operating theater five stories above, strapped to a steel table with a precision window carved in his skull.

"Who?" he wanted to know.

"I don't know," Reuben said. "Some guy. A kid. Never even seen him before."

"What do we do?"

"Nothing else to be done. We wait and see."

The hospital surged: nurses hustled down the halls in response to code greens and yellows and blues; orderlies ran cases of blood mixture to the dialysis ward; a janitor guided a doodlebug over the floor. Few paid any mind to the man and boy sitting on the bolted orange chairs. Their tragedy, whatever it might be, was unexceptional.

10

The taxi eased through the wrought-iron gates, following the drive up to Paul's parents' house. A taste of early spring: stalactite-thick icicles dripping on the eaves, patches of brown lawn under the melting snow.

Last week a letter from a local barrister's office was delivered to the boxing club. Paul's uncle Henry had passed, it informed him; the will was to be read next week at his parents' estate, and could he please attend.

He checked himself in the cab's side-view mirror. A twisting slash on his cheek was healing badly, its puffed edges the same blue-black as a dog's gums. He hadn't slept well since the fight, suffering nightmares in which he fought great shadowy shapes the height of power poles that came at him with barbed-wire fists.

Three people sat in the living room: his father and mother, plus a young man dressed in wool pants and sweater. The estate lawyer, Paul assumed. His parents held recipe cards, as if they'd prepared speeches.

The young man motioned to a straight-backed Tiffany chair. "Paul, please take a seat."

"It's a shame about Uncle Hank," Paul said, sitting. "What got him—high blood pressure? Lord knows he loved his salty snacks."

"Your uncle is alive and well." The young man spread his palms, an apologetic gesture. "Max Singleton, Paul. I'm an interventionist."

"Oh, this is cute."

"Calm down." Singleton's air was that of a scientist handling a highly unstable element. "We're just here to talk, Paul."

"Does Uncle Hank know about this subterfuge?"

"That's neither here nor there," Max the Interventionist said. "Your parents are worried, Paul. The situation is grim, maybe, but not beyond hope. This afternoon you're in range of death; tomorrow you can be in range . . ."—dramatic pause— ". . . of *life*."

"Seriously?" Paul appealed to his folks. "This guy is serious?"

"We're here to help, Paul," Singleton went on. "Will you let us do that, Paul—will you let us help?"

Paul didn't care much for the constant repetition of his name; must be a tactic they taught at the Interventionists' Academy. "Ah, what the hey."

Barb Harris, demure in a black silk blouse, snatched a Kleenex from a box on the coffee table. "Don't be so flip, Paul." Jack Harris sat beside her in a charcoal-gray suit. They looked like a couple of funeral mourners.

"Mr. Harris," Singleton said. "Start us off."

Jack shuffled his recipe cards and swallowed. Paul noted the sunken rings around his father's eyes, the four-day growth of beard.

"Son, I always thought we were decent parents and made the right choices more often than not, but clearly we've let you down in some critical way. I've watched you fall apart and cannot for the life of me figure out why. There seems to be nothing I can do to help—you won't *let* anyone help. I'm afraid for you, Paul. Deeply afraid."

"Oh, come on—"

"You seem to believe I wanted you to follow in my footsteps . . . and maybe, thinking back, okay, I did want that. But I don't care now— you don't want to work at the winery, fine. Do anything you want, just so long as you're safe. I mean that. Absolutely anything."

"But . . ." Singleton prompted.

"But you've got to quit this self-destructive quest you're on. This . . . jihad. You need help, son. A car is outside—will you let us take you someplace so you can get better?"

"What, you got the paddy wagon waiting? Men in white coats ready to chase me across the lawn with butterfly nets?"

Singleton made a motion as though he were tamping down a patch of soil—*calm down, Paul, calm down.* "Mrs. Harris," he said, "you go on."

"Paul, I want to let you know how much I love and admire you. But I'm scared that if you don't stop this abuse and turn yourself around you will not be with us much longer. I can't stand thinking you are not in a safe place; whenever the phone rings in the night I'm terrified it is about you, telling me you're dead. So please, Paul, give me back the wonderful and caring son of whom I've always been so proud. A car is waiting outside—will you please accept the help that is being offered and get treatment today?"

"This car," said Paul, "where would it take me?"

"The treatment center is top-notch," Singleton assured him. "A secluded country estate, rambling meadows, cool valley streams, a four-star chef . . ." Paul thought Singleton would whip out a brochure. ". . . the best specialists trained in the treatment of various mood disorders—"

"Are you gay?" Barb blurted. "Is that it, Paul? You feel passionate for men?"

"What your mother's trying to say," said Singleton, "is that sudden interest in hyper-masculine activities is frequently indicative of a latent homosexual drive."

"The posters in your room," his mother went on. "Those . . . *surfing* posters."

"So, what, being gay is a *mood disorder*? Are you gonna cart me off and straighten me? Would it be better if I was gay—I mean, would it make this any more palatable? Okay, fine, I'm gay. Gay as a French foreign legionnaire!"

"See?" Barb spread her hands, apologizing for her son's behavior the way she might for a senile dog with a penchant for biting the mailman. "It's like I said—he's disturbed."

"Oh-ho-ho!" Singleton gave a ghastly chuckle, the chuckle of a man who'd just witnessed a ten-car highway pileup and was trying to wring a drop of hope from the tragedy. He cast his soothing gaze upon Paul. "Nobody's disturbed here, are they?"

"What do I know? You're the professional."

"That's right—I'm the professional. And I say nobody's disturbed."

"I'm sold," Paul said amiably.

"Why are you doing this?" his father wanted to know. "Why take punches just to prove you can? Why suffer just to suffer? That's how animals do it, Paul—no, animals have more sense."

"Because . . ." Paul was staggered a bit by his father's question. ". . . people need to suffer. People need to feel pain and experience want and get smashed apart if only to fix themselves."

"Do you have any idea," Jack said, "what you're asking of us? A son asking his parents to let him go through hell in hopes he might come out of it a better man? Who says you're going to come out better— who says you don't come out scarred and irreparable? We can't let you do that. It goes against every single parenting instinct; it goes against basic human nature."

"And is it our fault?" Barb said. "Our fault you didn't suffer enough? What should we have done—daily beatings to strengthen your constitution?"

"Mrs. Harris—"

"No, really, I'd like to know. Would you have rather we'd locked you in the root cellar, fed you bread and water—would that have been suitable?"

"Let your parents know how you're feeling," Singleton told Paul. "Let them in; together we can help."

"Do any of you remember that killer whale, Friska?" Paul said after a moment's consideration. "She performed at the amusement park down in Niagara Falls. This animal-rights group held a rally to free her a few years ago. A bunch of protesters chained themselves to the park gates, and they had this giant blow-up whale with a lead ball and chain clapped to its dorsal fin. The park agreed to set her free; they drugged her to the gills and flew her to Vancouver Island and dumped her in Queen Charlotte Sound. But the thing is, this whale, she was born and bred in captivity. Her whole life she's fed, cared for, protected. She was out of shape, bloated, and sickly. She didn't know how to protect herself. Her life was this tiny pointless world where all she'd ever done was perform tricks when the trainer's whistle blew. Maybe she dreamed—if whales dream at all—about her natural place in the world, the ancestral sea. But even so, would she really have understood?"

Max the Interventionist opened his mouth to interject. Paul shut it with a look.

"I think of her limited world blowing up in those new unknowable depths," he went on, "the strange fish and new waters and her not even having a concept of those depths, not knowing the language of any whale pods she might meet. That sudden, violent explosion of her world, lawless, lacking the parameters that had governed her existence: just bubbles and seaweed and storms and freighters and volumes of blue water that went on and on forever. A tuna boat found her floating near a wharf. She was drawn to sounds she understood: machinery, motors, human voices. Her belly was slashed open. She got chewed by a boat's rotor blades, or maybe killed by other whales—or by creatures much smaller than her. Her tongue and lower jaw had been eaten.

"They winched the body in and buried it in a whale-sized casket. Over a thousand people at her funeral. A picture in the paper: a giant half-moon-shaped coffin lowered into the ground. The caption went, *Noble burial for a noble creature*." Paul laughed, a brittle hack. "Burying a whale. How unnatural is that?"

"Paul—" Singleton said.

"Shut up and let me finish. I think about the whale and wonder—who's to blame? The amusement park for keeping her penned up all those years? The protesters for freeing her? The more I think about it, the more I come back to the idea that it was *nobody's* fault. The whale was born in captivity, the trainers loved and cared for her, the protesters were doing what they thought was right. Everybody's heart in the right place. But the reality is this poor whale adrift in a place she doesn't understand, scared shitless and so fucking *witless* she didn't last a week on her own. But what if she'd been given a chance to strengthen herself so that she might survive?"

"Paul," Singleton said, "all these fears and regrets can be worked through in therapy."

"Jesus Christ," Paul said, "did you hear a word I said? I don't have any regrets!"

"But first you need to admit you need help," Singleton overrode him. "Will you do that, Paul—admit you need help? Will you let us *help* you?"

"You knew the answer to that the minute I walked in here."

Singleton nodded. "I'd like you to set your credit and bank cards on the table."

"Why?"

"Your bank account's been frozen." Jack Harris looked impossibly weary: a man crossing a desert on a mission whose purpose he could not recall. "The cards are in my name."

Barb's needless clarification: "They aren't yours, Paul."

"They aren't, are they? I can't lay claim to any of it. Nothing stands in my name. None of it's mine."

He fished the cards from his wallet and laid them on the glass-topped coffee table.

"They're yours again," said Singleton. "Anytime you'd like. Just let us help."

Paul looked at his father and mother sitting on the couch, hopeless and confused. "Why didn't you ever let me suffer?" he said. "Just once, let me struggle?"

"We're your parents," Barb said. "We love you. How could we let you suffer?"

He went to his bedroom to gather a few things. The room smelled musty and tomblike, a scent peculiar to places long absent of human habitation.

His mother poked her head through the door.

"Is it okay?"

"Come on in."

Barbara sat on the edge of the bed. "Was it really so bad, Paul? The life you—the lives we had together?"

"It wasn't bad," Paul told her, "just fake and empty. All the people I knew, guys I went to school with—what stories did we have? You and

Dad, Grandma and Grandpa, their parents and on back—you have stories."

"You really believe that, don't you? That everyone who came before had it rough. Sorry to tell you, kiddo, but it didn't happen that way. I was a farmer's daughter, your dad a farmer's son. Our parents weren't rich but there was always enough. Christmases, birthdays . . . god, I had a *pony*. And my dad fought in the war, yes, but with no choice. Was he courageous? I'd like to think so—but he was courageous because the situation called for it. Circumstance can make a hero out of anyone."

"Or a coward."

She smiled sadly. "Is it worth it, Paul—to suffer your whole life just to prove you can?"

Paul could not tell her his deepest fear: that his suffering would always be insufficient and never enough to ensure any lasting happiness. "Do you ever think of the old house we lived in, before Dad bulldozed it? You ever think, what if we'd lived there forever?"

"Sometimes I do," Barb admitted. "But our life . . . we've moved on." She fixed her hair and said, "We could get you counseling, Paul. You could stay here with us, or we could rent you a place, and you could see a therapist. I've heard Prozac—"

"Mom, I love you and I love that you're trying to understand what I'm going through, but . . ." He hugged her, kissed her cheek, held her at arm's length with his hands on her shoulders.

Barb reached into her skirt pocket and produced a tinfoil packet. "Hold out your hand."

She dropped two small objects into his palm. Whitish yellow, the size of corn kernels, each tapering to a pair of reddened tips.

"I called Faith, the girl you were out with," she said, "the night . . . that night. She told me the bar you'd been at. I went the next day and hunted around for hours until I found them."

Paul picked one up, rolled it between his fingers.

"Mom, is this—are these—my *teeth*?"

She nodded, her entire being swollen with hope. Did she really think it would be that easy? Like his teeth were the wave of some magic wand and—*poof!*—everything went back the way it was? Paul turned them over in the light, realizing, with dawning awareness . . .

"Oh my god—these aren't *my* teeth!"

"Sure they are," Barb said quickly. "Who else's?"

"No, they aren't," he insisted. "They're too . . . big, or something. Too yellow. This one's practically *brown*." He saw the tiny lead plug. "It's got a filling! I never had a cavity in my life!"

"Maybe you did," his mother reasoned. "Maybe you forgot."

"How do you forget that?"

"You've been hit in the head a lot lately."

But they were obviously not his teeth, which brought up the obvious question:

"Mom, who the hell's teeth *are* these? Where in god's name do you find *teeth*?" Paul's mind reeled. He saw his mother rummaging through Dumpsters behind the dental clinic. Creeping through windows to snatch molars from beneath sleeping children's pillows. "Did you buy them? How much does a tooth *go for* in today's market?"

Barb was weeping now, sniffling and holding her head.

"I thought . . ." Her chest hitched. "Thought maybe . . ."

"Hey, calm down." He laughed a little—getting over the initial shock, he saw it was the craziest, most impetuous thing his mother had done in years. He was oddly touched.

"What are you laughing at?"

"Nothing." He stifled another chuckle. "It's nice, really. A very . . . nice gesture."

But his mom was not to be consoled. Tears turned to sobs. She sat on the bed, rocking.

"Oh, come on. Really, I love them. Look."

He selected a tooth—an incisor by the looks of it—and jammed the pointy root ends into a gap in his gum line. The prongs pierced the soft skin; Paul shoved hard with the pad of his thumb, socking it into the pocket of flesh. It looked like a fang.

"See?" he said. "Peachy. Good as new."

He grabbed another tooth—a canine?—grasped firmly, and drove it into his lower gums. He caught a glimpse of himself in the dresser mirror: the tooth, large and brown as a Spanish peanut, jutted from his mouth at a coarse angle. This one looked like a tusk.

"I *vant* to suck your *BLOOD!*" he bellowed in his best Nosferatu accent. "Blah! *Blah! Blaaaaaah!*"

Paul collapsed into uncontrollable giggles with blood bubbling over his lips. He found the whole scene uproariously funny.

He wiped tears from his eyes. Barb regarded him with an expression of stunned, horrified awe. The room was silent save the pitty-pat of blood on the floorboards.

"I'm sorry," he said. "I thought maybe . . ."

But Barb was already up, running to the door and slamming it behind her. Paul heard her stockinged feet thumping down the staircase, ungainly in flight.

He spat another mouthful of blood and wiped his lips on the pillowcase. On the dresser sat a framed photo of himself on the afternoon of his high school graduation. He smiled under his mortarboard, as did his folks on either side of him. Paul struggled to recall himself at that age, that boy's dreams and needs and fears. He wondered how his then-self might've reacted had his now-self shown up on that sunny afternoon years ago, crashed the graduation ceremony all cut and bruised and bloody. Would then-Paul have been sickened and ashamed—or fascinated? Perhaps he would've viewed his future self as a different species of creature altogether, one whose life bore no resemblance to his own.

Paul waited while the whore—her name, she said, was Adele—paid for the room. The A-1 Motel: owing to a string of dead neon, the marquee read simply A MOTEL. Niagara Falls, the red-light corridor. Streetlights along the quay cast their brightness upon the frozen Niagara River, a blue-gray sheet stretching to the rocky escarpment of New York State.

He lacked any clear recollection of how he'd gotten here. He'd borrowed five hundred dollars from his father's dresser before leaving the house, but since he had no means or intention of repaying it, *stolen* was the more accurate term.

Adele came out dangling a key from its plastic diamond-shaped fob. She was young and skinny as a guitar string. *I've seen more meat on a butcher's blade*, Lou Cobb might've said. She led him up a rusted staircase to a small clean room on the second floor and sat him on the bed.

"I got to say you're not looking so hot, cowboy." She drew a circle around her lips. "Your teeth are all shot to hell. Couple of them look too big."

The teeth his mother had "found" were still lodged in his gums. They didn't hurt that badly, though to leave them in much longer was to risk infection. "They were a gift."

"For the man who has everything, huh?" She flipped her hair— a strangely girlish gesture—then squeezed Paul's crotch. "I'll go wash up."

The bathroom door shut. Running water, splashing water. Paul removed his shirt and stood bare-chested before the window, considering the reflection of his body. The flesh over his ribcage was an ugly bluish-yellow mottle. It still hurt to breathe.

The name of the man who'd done this damage was Tom Tully; Lou had given him the name after much prodding. An ex–pro boxer. He and his brother shared a small house in the Love Canal district of Niagara Falls. Tom Tully was at Mount St. Mary's hospital, comatose fifteen days now.

Paul often thought about Tom Tully. What sort of person was he? He'd visited the local library archives and hunted through old *Ring* magazines. He'd dredged up an article: SAMMY "NIGHT TRAIN" LAYNE & TOMMY "BOOM BOOM" TULLY SET TO TANGO ON HOLMES/COONEY UNDER-CARD AT MSG. A photo: Tully looking impossibly hale beside a cigar-chomping manager. A trial horse, the scouting report said. Loads of heart, little skill. Takes a mean punch.

For the past few days Paul had taken a cab over the river. He idled across the road from the row house off 16th Street. Everyone looked so different. Nobody wore suits or carried briefcases. Everyone took the bus. Though a mere forty miles separated Paul from his childhood home, the distance seemed much greater. Paul Harris and Tom Tully—he wondered, were their lives in any way similar? The prospect gnawed. If they'd met outside the ring, somehow by chance, might they have been friends? Paul remembered the bigger man saying he'd take it easy on Paul. He remembered Tully's awkward, shamed smile.

A trial horse. Loads of heart, little skill. Takes a mean punch.

The whore, Adele, was singing. A sweet voice. She stepped into the room with a towel wrapped around her head and another draping her body.

"So," she said. "Ready to rock and roll?"

Paul realized, somewhat abruptly, that he had no desire to fuck this girl. He wondered if he could ask her to get dressed and leave so he could catch a few hours' sleep.

Adele stared at Paul, fascinated with his body: the lumps and abrasions and bruises. She leaned back on the mattress, a slatternly pose, running her bare feet over the puke-green shag. Paul retrieved his handwraps from a coat pocket and sat beside her.

"Give me your hand."

Gently, the way he'd been taught, he wrapped this whore's hand. Holding firm her wrist, he felt the birdlike bones pulse under her skin. The wraps were filthy, stinking of sweat and blood. Adele didn't seem to mind. Paul worked slowly, applying gentle pressure, testing his handiwork. Again he was struck by just how young she was: the rosy, fresh-scrubbed complexion of a high school girl. He considered asking her to leave—but perhaps her being with him tonight was the lesser of so many possible evils.

"What's your name?"

"Rex," Paul told her. "Rex Appleby."

Adele offered him a soft smile. "And what do you do, Rex?"

"I'm the last good cop on the force. If you have a problem, if no one else can help, and if you can find him, maybe you can hire . . . Rex Appleby."

When Adele's hands were wrapped, Paul set them back in her lap. He knew he wanted something from her—not sex, not comfort or intimacy, any of that. *Contact*, was all. Not loving contact, or even professional tenderness. Something more forceful that would leave him scarred.

He heeled off his shoes, unbuttoned his jeans and shucked them. He removed his underwear and stood before her naked.

"You sure got a big dick."

Paul knew she was lying: his cock was a runty wrinkled thing sunk so deep into his crotch it almost looked like a second belly button. She was no different from the stylist who runs her hands through a balding customer's hair and remarks how lustrous it is.

She was tall: they met eye to eye. Her lips were almost colorless, her mouth big and hard and brutal enough to chew right through him.

Her shaved pussy had a starchy, ruffled look, like the collar of a Victorian gentlewoman's dress. In the room's sulfurous light she looked like a young man. Her breasts so small, slender body roped with taut muscle. Like a teenage boy.

Paul pulled bills from the pocket of his jeans and placed them in the Gideon bible, between pages in the Book of Leviticus.

Adele smiled. "What is your pleasure, sir?"

He considered her and sighed. He could only make a fist and slug his thigh. Adele intuited something in this gesture—his need was as naked and undisguised as the buzzing neon M through the parted drapes.

She said, "I can do that."

They stood close but not quite touching.

"Well," Paul said softly, "what are you waiting for?"

The first blow glanced off his forehead. The room was so dark, visibility so poor, that he did not see it coming. Adele's fist had some serious steam behind it: fragments of shooting light spun before his eyes like formations of burning birds. He was still grinning stupidly when a second punch, this one much harder, rocked his jaw.

Paul tripped backward, startled and unbalanced. His thigh rammed the bedside table, knocking the lamp off as his feet swung out from under him. His skull slammed the wall and he dropped to the floor, crushing the lamp: the cheap cellophane shade crumpled and the light bulb burst with a powdery *pop* to drive eggshell shards of glass into his ass.

Her hand twined in his hair, dragging him up. Her lips pressed to his ear, breath stinking of sour bananas: "Like that, don't you?"

Before Paul could reply she slugged him in the belly. Twin whips of snot spurted from his nostrils. She punched him under the chin, an unforgiving uppercut that shut his mouth. His new teeth collided. One shot straight up into the air. He swallowed the other one and fell back on the bed.

When the cobwebs cleared he propped himself on his elbows and found her kneeling between his spread legs sucking his cock. She bobbed up and down, her hair—yellow like greased wheat—fanned over his thighs. Her tongue was small and pink, hot and wet, and she kept flicking it over the tip of Paul's hard cock as she sucked him off.

"Wait, now," he said, groggy but alarmed. "My god—!"

She took a swing at him with his cock still in her mouth, clipping his chin, and he fell back again. She grasped his hips, sharp painted talons digging deep into his ass, thick strings of saliva hanging from her lips as she bent to inhale his dick, taking the whole of it into her throat. She gagged around its size, a barfy-burpy sound. Paul had never felt anything like it. She kept pumping the shaft, impaling her mouth on it while at the same time slipping one finger between his legs, between his ass cheeks, pressing that finger against his asshole, circling, rubbing, and he tensed a bit before relaxing to let that raw skinny finger slip up inside him and he squirmed, helpless as an infant as she worked his cock, finger pressing his prostate, and it felt as if his every nerve center had been dynamited until she abruptly removed her finger from his ass and punched him in the kidneys so hard he retched.

She clambered atop him, straddled his hips. She punched him in the face—he could have avoided the blow but elected not to. Brilliant stars pinwheeled across the dark space between his eyes and the ceiling. She gripped his cock, rubbed the head over her clit. He was bleeding now, a ton of blood spilling from his torn mouth and ass. She ground her pussy against him, thrusting and bucking and slipping his cock up into her, riding him bareback as Paul idly contemplated the many diseases she might be infested with before realizing he didn't give a damn. Her pussy was tight and wet, not loose and used as a first-time customer might suspect.

She grabbed the bible off the bedside table, laid it flat on his face, and smashed her fist into the cover. His nose cracked. She slapped his forehead with the Good Book, as if she were a revivalist preacher and he a possessed worshipper speaking in tongues. In the brown light she regarded him with an interest best described as clinical—a specimen pinned on a dissecting tray.

She slid his cock out of her and stood at the edge of the bed.

"Come on." She was panting like a dog. "Let's see it."

Paul jolted off the bed and hit her as he might a tackling dummy, shoulder driven into her stomach, shoving her back. He had her up against the wall with his mouth hot on her neck, kissing and licking and sucking, hands propped under her ass lifting her a few inches off the ground. She guided his cock into her and he thrust up, slamming into her like the pump arm on an oil derrick, her long legs clamped around his hips, and she was kissing him now, biting his lips, one hand wrapped around his neck and the other clenched into a fist punching him lightly in the jaw, and in a high trembling voice she whispered, "This is great. This is really, really . . . *great*," and the realization that she was enjoying it, that the rough goings-on had penetrated her hard whorish soul, flooded Paul's heart with a bizarre species of joy and he orgasmed uncontrollably, the world blanking out for a few seconds, and all he saw was this endless sheet of gray-blue ice as his knees buckled and he slipped out of her. He slid down the slender plane of her body, exhausted and trembling, until his lips came to rest on the bony swell of her hip.

She was breathing heavily. "Was it good for you, Rex?"

Before Paul could say a word she brought a knee up into his chin. His head snapped back, then he didn't know a thing.

When he came to, Adele was gone. So was the cash in the bible.

In the bathroom he managed to tweeze most of the light-bulb glass from his ass with his fingers. He splashed cold water on his face and crotch and in the mirror surveyed the crazed geometry of his face.

A few fresh lumps and cuts. One of his testicles had swollen to the size of a racquetball; a violet spiderwebbing bruise spread over his ballsack. It was hard to distinguish one injury from the other: they all blended, cut-to-bruise-to-scab-to-bump-to-bruise-to-cut, red-to-black-to-purple-to-yellow-to-pink-to-blue. It had become impossible to recall where he'd absorbed them—in his mind they had merged into one single catastrophic injury.

He pulled his lower lip down and bared what remained of his teeth. "Booga booga."

From the motel he made his way toward Mount St. Mary's hospital. He followed snaking streets and narrow alleyways, crossed bridges spanning iced-over streams on his way to the place that he realized, deep down, he was destined for all along.

He bumped into a guy as he crossed the Rainbow Bridge. His fists instinctively curled before he got a look at the guy's face in the yellow glow of the bridge lamps.

"Jesus," he said. Then, "Hey."

It was Drake Langley, his old prep school chum. But Drake looked nothing like he had: he wore an old army fatigue jacket and sported a clean-shaven skull. And apparently he'd rediscovered how to walk without assistance: the dog-headed cane was nowhere in sight.

Drake was missing a handful of teeth. The dome of his skull was grooved with long slits stitched with catgut. His face looked odd. After a moment Paul realized that his eyebrows and eyelashes had been shaved off.

"How's it going, man?"

"I'm all right," Paul said. ". . . you?"

"Fuckin-A great."

Drake said he'd moved out of his parents' place and was holed up with "a pack of hardcore animal rights activists" in an abandoned house on Paper Street.

"PETA is a little dog with a big bark," he said. "We're a little dog with a mouthful of razor blades. We *bite.*"

Paul was distressed at the mania in Drake's eyes: skull cored out like a jack-o'-lantern, flickering candlelight dancing behind his eyes. Drake showed him the contents of his shopping bag: boxes and boxes of Eddy matches.

"Do you know," he said, "that if you stuff a PVC tube with enough permanganate, Sweet'N Low, and match heads, you can blow up just about anything?"

"I didn't know that," Paul said. "No."

Drake caught something in Paul's demeanor and got agitated. "Know how they skin a fox at a commercial fur ranch? They slit it right here," his fingers made slashes at his own crotch, "and pull its skin off. It's *alive* when they do it. When the skin's off they chuck the skinless body in a plastic barrel. They don't even slit its throat. You know what a fox with no skin looks like? A newborn baby. A bloody squirming baby. Picture a barrel full of babies, Paul."

"I've got to get going, Drake. Nice to see you."

Drake grabbed his wrist. "Hey," he said softly, "thanks, man. I mean it."

Now Paul stumbled down a white-walled corridor with hospital beds lining the walls. He was shivering, having walked fifteen blocks without benefit of a jacket. His teeth hammered and clashed.

The room at the end of the hallway was spare and antiseptic, its lone window inset with steel mesh. Tom Tully lay on the nearest bed. Shirtless, white EKG disks plastered to his shaved chest. The crown of his skull was swaddled in layers of surgical gauze, below which his eyes stared, wide open, at a spot on the wall.

Tom looked so small and frail, so badly—*shrunken*. His skin was drawn tight to the bones of his hands, making them appear grotesquely clawlike. Paul pictured a scarecrow with a tear in its belly, straw guts bleeding out in a blustery farmer's field.

Gummy matter had gathered at the sides of Tom's eyes. Paul took a Kleenex from a box on the shelf and dabbed at the sticky accretion. Tully's eyes didn't blink.

A wave of panic, near-hysteric in scope, washed over Paul. The skin tightened over his head, stretched so taut he was sure it would split to reveal the vein-threaded dome of his skull. He wanted to grab Tully and shake the daylights out of him; wanted to scream *WAKE UP!* into his sweetly smiling face.

"I'm . . . sorry," Paul whispered, his mouth so close to Tully's head that the downy hairs of his inner ear quivered. "I never saw it happening like this. I never meant to hurt you this way—it wasn't ever about that."

A young man came in. He carried an orange cafeteria tray, setting it down. Seventeen or so: a high school senior, maybe. Not that big, but a strong, compact frame. Dark, short-clipped hair. Eyes the same cornflower blue as Tom Tully's.

"Who are you?" he asked Paul.

"I'm nobody. Just visiting. Who are—?"

"Robbie. Rob. He's my uncle."

"I'm Paul. Were . . . are you close?"

"He's my uncle," Rob said again.

They stood across Tom's body. An accordionlike breathing bellows rose and fell. Narcotics dripped through a catheter into his spine.

Rob said, "What are you doing here?"

"I just wanted to see how he was faring."

"So you've seen him."

Rob's fists clenched and unclenched; brachial veins pulsed down his biceps. Paul set himself in a defensive stance, figuring the kid might leap across the bed.

"You look like shit."

Paul picked at the crusted blood on his lips. "It's been a long night."

"You crawl out of a Dumpster?"

The kid was goading him—he had every right. Paul picked a condolence card off the bedside table, skimmed it, and set it back.

Rob shifted from left foot to right. Antsy, ready to explode. "Where are you from? I've never seen you before."

"Across the river."

"You're a . . . Canadian? Were you fighting to make ends meet?"

"Would that have been any better?"

"Were you fighting for anyone?"

"I was fighting for someone. Myself."

Paul pictured the way Tom Tully had fallen: heedlessly, like a trench coat slipping off its hanger to the floor. He pictured Tom Tully with blood coming out his ears and recalled the rush of pure power that flowed through him at the sight; power born of the knowledge he'd reduced another human being to a thoughtless slab of meat, erasing every trace of history and memory and dream. And while he couldn't quite reconcile the hideous selfishness of these thoughts, neither could he deny he'd harbored them.

"So you didn't need the money?" Rob asked.

"Money's never been an issue for me."

Rob looked at Paul and peeled away the new muscles, bruises, and missing teeth to catch a glimpse of Paul as he'd once been: frail, monied, fearful.

"Can I ask you something?" Paul nodded; Rob went on. "Are you rich?"

"I was never rich. But my parents were."

"So that, with my uncle . . . proof of something?"

"I needed to know what I was capable of," Paul told him. "To know I could walk into a room and know that nobody in that room could . . . fuck with me, I guess."

Rob gave a look of such seething hatred it shocked Paul. "I've heard spoiled rich kids do a lot of self-centered things, but that takes it."

He went to the door and shut it. After a brief hesitation he dragged the chair over and lodged it under the doorknob. He crouched on the floor, his posture that of a baseball catcher. For a full minute he sat that way.

"My uncle was a solid fighter," he said finally. "This shouldn't have happened." He raised his head and stared at Paul with those blue eyes of his. "I want to hurt you, Paul. I think . . . I think I more or less have to. And I think you want to be hurt."

"We both know a place. How old are you?"

"Old enough."

"If you think it'll answer anything. Maybe I owe you." Paul smiled sadly. "I don't want to hurt you." Then, with perfect honesty: "Or maybe I do."

11

Robert Tully dreamed he was in Sharky's on Pine Street. The bar was dirty and dark and narrow, jammed between an off-license bettor's and the Pine Street theater, where a roll of dimes bought you a half-hour in the peepshow booths.

The bartender finished polishing a glass and faced Rob and Rob was surprised because the bartender was him, Robert Tully, only twenty years older.

"Heeeey," Old Rob said, recognizing his younger self. "Look at you, Champ."

Old Rob was fat in the way a lot of ex-athletes were fat: grossly and awkwardly so, as if after the years of training their bodies ballooned up out of sheer confusion. He set a glass of soapy draft before his younger self.

"God, it's good to see you. Me." He smiled. "Us."

"I can't drink this," Rob said.

Old Rob dumped it down the well. "Not old enough, are you? And still training. Stupid, stupid me."

Rob thought something was the matter with his older self: the shambling gait, the slurred speech like a man kicked awake in the middle of the night. And somehow childlike: it was as though his ten-year-old self was trapped in the body of his forty-year-old self.

Old Rob said, "Will you look at our hands."

Their hands were the same size; evidently, Rob did not have another growth spurt in him. Old Rob ran his finger over a scar running the length of his own left index finger.

"Hey, hey, hey," he said excitedly, "remember where we got this? South Korea; they flew us over to fight the Asian champ. The water gave us the trots so Dad filled the water bottles with chrysanthemum juice. God, that taste—*flowers*. We knocked the champ out but split our finger to the bone. Remember that?"

Old Rob saw his younger version's left index finger was as yet unscarred. "Oops. Let the cat out of the bag, didn't I? Stupid, stupid me."

"Please, stop saying that."

A pained expression came over Old Rob's face. "I'm sorry—I mean, I'll stop." He reached out to touch Rob, but he couldn't quite bring himself to. "You look so good. Strong, you know? And all that hair."

"You look good, too."

"You're not just saying it?" Old Rob was pleased. "I like to keep myself in the mix."

"You're still fighting?"

"Not professionally." He touched the side of his right eye. "Detached retina. First time my sight came back; second time, too. Third time . . ." He shrugged. "My license got revoked, but I found other places."

"I don't want to know about them," Rob said.

Old Rob wiped away the ring of condensation left by the glass. He was so goddamn *servile*. "No saying you have to," he said. "Maybe this life, my life, isn't yours."

"I hope not."

His older self got that pained look again; he wrung the rag out and folded it into a neat square. "The fight's a tough thing to leave behind." His shrug indicated that this was not an excuse, this was the plain fact of it. "They say every fighter dies twice: once when he takes his last breath, the other when he hangs up the leathers. And that first death— that's the bitch."

"But," Rob said, "I don't like fighting."

"You get to like it." Old Rob smiled in a confused way. "Smart too late and old too soon, huh? Everything passes so quickly."

The telephone woke him up. Probably his father, calling from Top Rank wondering why he was late for training. But Rob hadn't really trained for weeks. Not since Tommy.

He threw on sweats, grabbed his jacket, and set off down the street. A machine-gun wind hammered his body. He did not know where he was headed: an aimless trajectory through deadeningly familiar streets, no terminus or friendly port of call. All he saw were the hard, unflinching angles of a city he now wandered as a stranger. A sense of unremitting hopelessness descended upon him. The realization that other families suffered tragedies on such a scale as to reduce the sufferings of his own to a pitiful dot did nothing to allay his sense that a cosmic injustice had been perpetrated. His family asked for so little: a little house, a little money, a little respect, a little, ordinary life huddled together as an odd but workable unit.

Others had so much. Their wants were modest. Was it too much to ask?

He wound up at Kate's house. Seven-thirty on a Saturday morning, the neighborhood still asleep. He packed a snowball and hurled it at the transformer box bolted to a power pole.

"Tully?" Kate's head occurred in a second-floor window. "Jeez, Rob . . ."

"Did I wake you?"

"I was awake," she lied. "Everything all right?"

"Copacetic."

"I'll be down in a minute."

She came out wearing her powder-blue shell and unlaced boots. Crumbs of sleep in the corners of her eyes; a tuft of hair sticking straight out like a unicorn horn. "Fine morning for a walk."

They moved together down Niagara Street. A fire burned somewhere to the north: columns of blue-gray smoke rose over the flat shop roofs. Kate hummed a tune under her breath—high, peppy notes—and kicked pebbles from her path.

"How's your pops doing?"

"Tommy's coverage isn't great, so Dad's battling the insurance company. But it's not like they can pull the plug, can they?"

"No," said Kate. "That would be unethical, or something."

They passed Loughran's Park. Rob and Kate used to come here with Tommy when they were kids. Tommy would sit on the benches with the housewives while Rob and Kate played. He became a park fixture, an ox of a man with his smiling crumpled face. The housewives tried to teach him to knit, but his hands were huge and scarred and he never did get the hang of it.

"I met him," Rob said.

"Who's that?"

"At the hospital. I caught him visiting Tommy."

"Why was he there?"

"Felt guilty, I would say."

"Well, sure. Two guys in a ring, neither expects it to turn out that way." Kate puffed air into her cupped palms. "Big guy?"

Rob was too embarrassed on Tommy's behalf to give a truthful description: the raggedness, the *toothlessness*. "Big guy," he said. "Very rough-looking."

"Tommy never should've been there," Kate said. "Or your dad. It was a stupid thing to be mixed up in."

"Boxing's all Tommy's ever known. It's what my family's always done."

They crossed a baseball diamond. Rob stepped in old boot tracks pressed into the cold mud, idly wondering if he knew the person who made them.

"My father," Kate said, "was a big asshole. That's how Mom refers to him—The Big Asshole. Steps out for cigarettes one day when I'm three days old and never comes back. Talk about your abandonment clichés. He was a selfish man—but in a way it took guts to do what he did. Leave it all and never look back. Step out into the world with nothing. Of course, it was cowardly, too—walking away from his wife and kid, leaving us in the lurch. I don't know . . . cowardly and gutsy at once, if that makes any sense."

Rob gave a long sigh and looked away from her.

"You don't even like boxing," she went on. "Not like that's any secret. Your greatest problem stems from your not going after what you really want in life."

"And so what?" Rob felt himself getting tight inside; iron bands clapped around his skull and rocks started growing in his chest. "Who loves their job—who has that luxury? You think my dad likes hauling his ass out of bed at two a.m. to bake bread, or your mom loves clipping the stems off marigolds, or Tommy loved driving a forklift? No, they do it because it's their duty and you don't shirk that. Everyone has obligations; why should I be above that?"

"Yeah, but whose obligations?" She stopped and looked at him. "For a tough guy, you sure let yourself get shoved around a lot."

The whole point wasn't worth arguing, especially with Kate, who had honed her skills on the school debate squad. Still, he couldn't quite let go. "At some point you need to start being sensible about things. Take an adult frame of mind. Stop writing poetry and hunting up and down a beach with a metal detector."

"At least Darren has dreams and they're his own. His mom's a toll-taker but he feels no need to be one himself."

"Let's drop it—"

"You want out of here as bad as he does."

"Maybe so," Rob said. "But how can you escape without a plan that makes any sense? Boxing makes sense. I can make it work."

"That doesn't matter," she said. "It's not your own plan."

Rob lacked the energy to go on with this, and besides, he knew she was right.

"You'll make a great boxer," she told him, "whether you want to be or not. We all know that." She paused, then added, "But it takes guts to step away from the safety of the world you grew up in. I'm not saying the life you leave has to be a bad one—maybe it's just not right for you, personally. Any other way and it's not really your life, is it? Just the one someone else thinks you ought to be living."

They rounded back to Kate's house. They talked about trivial subjects: a spring-break road trip to Daytona Beach, the prom's lame "Under the Sea" theme.

"Mom and I are stopping by the hospital this afternoon," said Kate. "Mom's baking those sugar cookies Tommy loves. She thinks the smell . . ." She shook her head. "Maybe I'll see you."

Rob set off down 16th toward the Fritz.

He thought about what Kate said—about how being good at something shouldn't dictate the course of your life. He didn't love boxing, but he had talent and aptitude. His fists were a ticket out of this place, the tenement houses and blood banks and boarded shopfronts, no more of this scraping by, plenty of cash for fancy cars, eye-popping mansions, fine wines. He could save his father and Tommy from all this—it was within his power.

Or was it? Maybe it was each man's duty to save himself.

Fritzie Zivic answered Rob's knock in slippers and a housecoat. Murdoch squatted at Fritzie's heel, his old eyes focused on Rob.

"Young master Tully." Fritzie smiled sadly, scratched his backside through the housecoat's frayed material. "How you holding up?"

"Fine, Mr. Zivic. I need to talk."

"Tommy's debts? I cleared the books. Your uncle's such an awful player it makes me sick to think about collecting."

"Thanks." Rob was touched by this unexpected kindness from a man not known to dispense favors. "But that's not it."

"It's not, huh? Well, you'd better come in."

He led Rob down the front hall into the kitchen. Murdoch trotted behind, taking sly nips at Rob's boots until Fritzie hollered at the splenetic old beast.

He set a beaten coffee pot on the burner and sat in the chair opposite Rob. Rubbing his unshaven, blocklike chin, he yawned and asked what was on Rob's mind.

"You go to those fights. You were there for Tommy."

"Well, I do, I do." Fritzie's head nodded slowly, his hard features etched with some embarrassment. "And yeah, I was there when Tommy . . . drove him to the hospital, didn't I?"

"Take me next time."

"And why's that?"

"Does it matter?"

"If you looking for my help, yeah, it does."

Rob laid out his reasoning without meeting Fritzie's eyes. Once he'd finished, Fritzie spoke.

"Revenge, uh? Men have fought for less." The old Croat became pensive. "Let me tell you a story. Years ago, before you were born, this guy went around leaving refrigerators in parks and playgrounds. Your dad ever tell you about this?"

When Rob shook his head, Fritzie went on. "This guy would pick up fridges at the dump—the old kind, right, with the locking latches. He filed the safety catches down and left them where kids played. At night he'd leave them; the next morning, bright and early, there they were. Like an invitation."

Murdoch made a couple of circles underneath the table, snuffled morosely, and plopped down at Fritzie's feet.

"Now the good thing was, nobody was killed. Some kids hopped inside and mucked around but none of them ever shut the lid. But this whole town was terrified—meetings at city hall, a park patrol, and every old fridge at the dump filled with cement. They never caught the guy. But there are people out there like that; the type you don't quite believe exist until you see proof of it—like an open refrigerator next to a swing set.

"The point I'm driving at is this: every time I go to that place where your uncle got hurt, I think of those fridges. A lot of the guys don't look like anything—desperate bums and drifters, most take their beating and off they go. But you can never tell the scorpion from the frog; you never know which one's gonna sting. I think of those fridges because some a those guys are like that—they look harmless enough so you climb inside and muck around and it's not long before you're locked inside and down to your last breath."

Fritzie poured himself a cup of coffee. He sipped, his eyes holding Rob's over the rim of the mug, then said, "Now the question you need to be asking yourself, Robbie, is: do you think Tommy would want you doing that?"

"You're saying you won't take me?"

After a pause: "You're how old?"

Rob lied. "Eighteen."

"Old enough to make your own choices. Not my place to stop you. What I'm asking is, do you feel it's worth it?"

"I couldn't tell you," Rob said, honestly. "But I can't see my way clear of it any other way. What do I want—retribution? Is that what Tommy would want? I don't know. But nothing else seems to answer anything."

Fritzie sat down and knitted his hands together on the tabletop. "Robbie, let me ask you one thing. Is this going to be enough for you?"

"I don't catch your meaning."

Murdoch pawed his master's leg; Fritzie lifted the dog up and balanced him across his knees. Murdoch glared across the table at Rob, who had not received a more malevolent stare from man or beast.

"Look at your uncle or the pugs at the club—hell, look across the table: all of us single, no kids, no money, nothing to hold on to."

"My dad—"

"Your dad's no fighter. Your dad is . . ." Fritzie bit his lip. ". . . something else. Boxing's a dream, Robbie, and a sweet one. But the dream takes everything; you got to feed every ounce of your life into it. Like a heat shimmer on a stretch of summer tarmac—you can chase that damn thing forever without ever catching it. And one day you wake up and see you've fed that dream everything and it's no closer than it was years ago."

Fritzie kneaded the ruff of Murdoch's neck. "Your uncle and I did pretty good for a couple of neighborhood guys. Tommy fought at Madison Square Garden; I ate a fifty-dollar steak at the same table as John Gotti after a fight. But what's any of it amount to—an hour, a week, a month where you're king shit? Nah. The best thing about fighting is getting into that ring and you look the other guy in the eye and say, For the next ten rounds let's bring something out in each other—something we didn't even know we had. Show me what I don't know about myself. *That's* the juice of boxing." He kissed the top of Murdoch's head. The beast growled. "And if that's not what thrills you, you shouldn't be boxing. Not worth the risk—and I don't just mean getting hurt. Look at me. I got this vicious old mutt and when he goes I'm going to fall to pieces. I got nothing else."

Rob could think of nothing to say but, "He looks fairly healthy."

Fritzie smiled gratefully. "You think? Anyway, what I'm asking is, will you be able to walk out of that place when it's over and be kaput?"

"I hope so."

Fritzie nodded. "Fights go next Thursday night. You're here, I'll take you."

"I appreciate it, Mr. Zivic."

"Don't take it the wrong way when I say I hope to see not hide nor hair of you come next Thursday."

Suppertime at Mount St. Mary's hospital. Orderlies hastened down the halls with trays of Salisbury steak and lime Jell-O, or IV pouches of nutrient-rich Meal in a Bag.

Reuben Tully sat beside his brother's bed reading a sheet of paper. Withered balloons and wilted flowers. The room smelled too sweet.

He glanced up. "Where the hell were you this morning?"

Rob said, "I wasn't feeling up to it."

"I don't give a shit if you felt up to it or not. You be there. We need to maintain the basic routines, okay?"

"What's that you're reading?"

"Fucking insurance companies," said Reuben. "Jackals. Blood *suckers*. They're claiming since Tommy never made a living will . . ." A brief glance over at his brother. ". . . stupid, stupid . . ." And back to Rob. ". . . they say his care is technically governed by the state. It means that once Tommy's been declared—oh, Jesus, what was it?" He skimmed the letter. "Right—*a persistent vegetative state*. If that happens Tommy becomes a ward of the state, which means he goes on the organ donor list, first come first served. Whatever's left is donated to science."

Reuben tore the paper up. "No way is some government ghoul harvesting my kid brother's guts. No way is some medical school prick hacking up his head. I'll die first."

Tommy lay still. The EKG machine beeped fitfully; every so often the green line trembled, indication that a semblance of Tom Tully yet existed. His arms were pocked with needles—needles to feed and medicate and drain him.

Rob said, "Why did you let him?"

"Why'd I let who do what?"

"Why didn't you stop him? Tell him how stupid it was, or refuse to go along with it?"

Reuben looked as if he'd been stabbed in the heart. "You think I didn't say that—Christ, Robbie, you've been there, you've *heard* me say that. A thousand times I told him how stupid it was. I told him right up to the day it happened."

"But you were never forceful about it. You talked; that was all."

"Listen: this wasn't my choice. If I'd had my way, Tommy would've been finished years ago. All I could do was be there to see he didn't get hurt."

"But he got hurt."

"And you blame me." Reuben nodded, taking it in. "Maybe that's fair—I blame myself. But then each man acts according to his own wishes. My brother, not my slave."

Reuben dipped his fingers in a cup of water and wet Tommy's cracked lips. "Your uncle never learned how to throw a punch right. Purely an arm puncher; no hips. Couldn't dance for the same reason. But he took his body and his talent as far as they could go. A lot of it was for me. I was his trainer and he knew that if he ever hit it big I'd be right there beside him."

"And isn't it a trainer's job," Rob said, "to protect his fighter?"

Reuben ignored him. "We used to talk about what we'd do if Tommy were the heavyweight champ. I think we both knew it was a pipe dream, but where's the harm? We'd go out for a big Italian supper and put every other nickel in the bank. "And we didn't have the sort of relationship where . . . we knew each other too well—you take things for granted. He was always there so he's always gonna be there. What were the last words I said to him? Something practical, I'm sure: keep your chin down, plant your feet. Christ. Should've been, Fuck all this, we're out of here. I should've been the older brother. The protector."

Reuben's fingers dipped and wiped. Rob became aware of a very strange sensation looking at his father's hand: the paleness of it, bleached from enriched flour. A baker's hand. A breadmaker's hand. A hand nothing like his own.

"He's coming through this, Robbie. You still believe that, don't you?"

Watching his father and uncle together under that harsh hospital light, Rob felt himself pulling away. A dark hole opened and a massive force pulled him down a vast corridor at such velocity he thought his skin might get sucked off, huge pressure tugging at his arms and legs as his father and uncle dwindled, all sense of intimacy gone and Rob not fighting it at all.

His hands were clamped tight on the chair's armrests—not in fear, but rage. Rage at these two men, mere specks now, who'd been charged with his upbringing; rage that all they'd ever told him was that fighting was the only way to find a little space for yourself in the world. His whole life funneled, focused, preordained. How else to settle matters except through violence? It was all he'd been taught. His anger swelled, magnified beyond any point of reference or comprehension: a billowing mushroom cloud, a towering inferno, a brilliant supernova.

12

Two men drove the southbound QEW in a rattletrap Ford.

Paul Harris wondered at the chain of events that had brought him here. To him, it seemed life unraveled as a series of minor decisions. And it could begin almost without your knowing it: one moment your life followed a predictable path down well-lit streets, the next it was careening down dark alleyways. Momentum becomes unstoppable. A snowball rolling down an endless hill until it was the size of the world itself.

Lou asked Paul how he felt. Paul said he felt fine.

"Don't look so fine."

Paul's face was as expressionless as the face on a coin. "Don't worry about me."

The dotted median strip flickered, a luminous white line in the side-view mirror. Lou cracked a window—the kid plain *stunk*—to let the cool air circulate.

"What was it you said you did before this—something business-y, wasn't it?" When Paul nodded, Lou said, "Ever think about heading back to that?"

"Are you kidding?"

Lou shrugged. "Let your body heal up, buy a nice set of false teeth. Figured you'd enjoy looking at your face in the mirror and not seeing a plate of dog food staring back."

"Since when did you start giving a shit?" Paul asked him.

"Since never," Lou said, honestly. "A temporary lapse on my part."

Fritzie Zivic drove down narrow streets past boarded shopfronts and fire-gutted buildings. American flags hung from poles in rigidly frozen sheets; faded stickers covered rust-eaten bumpers: GOD BLESS THE USA and SUPPORT OUR TROOPS and BLESSED BE.

Staring from the passenger seat, Rob Tully was overcome with a consuming need to be different—different in every conceivable way—from all this. To be rich where all he saw was poverty. To find sophistication where all he knew was crassness. Grace where all he saw was ignorance. Girls with platinum hair extensions and three-inch fingernails gabbing outside Sparkles Nail Boutique. An old black man wearing a snap-brim fedora behind the wheel of a shiny white Mustang 5.0 ragtop. Teenage boys passing brown bottles of Cobra malt on the curb outside Wedge Discount Liquors.

"Just so we're clear," said Fritzie, "if things get ugly, I'm stepping in. I'll wave that white towel. That's the price of this ride."

Murdoch cut a toneless fart in the backseat: a low wheezing groan like a bungling musician hitting a flat note on his accordion. The car filled with a reprehensible stench.

"You sour, ungrateful mongrel," Fritzie said dourly.

The lights of the city faded. The Cadillac wended down dark country roads. Rob's heart beat in a regular rhythm. His course of action was settled. Fritzie slotted an eight-track cassette into the player; Frank Sinatra sang "I've Got You Under My Skin."

They pulled off the main road and parked along a barbed-wire fence. Bars of cold even light cut between the barn's slats: in the darkness the light appeared to be slanting up out of the earth itself.

Manning stood beside the barn door. Ankle-length duster coat parted slightly, the butt of his Remington shotgun resting on the toe of one boot.

"Who you brung me, Fritzie?"

"Amateur fighter from out my way. Robbie Tully."

Manning set his sharp eyes upon the young fighter. "I heard of you. You're hot shit."

"I just want a fight."

"Plenty safer places to find one."

Fritzie said, "He's got a specific fight in mind."

Manning nodded. "Big fella went down last time—that was a Tully, no? We run a blind draw here, so strictly speaking it'd be a beggary of the rules. But rules can be bent to clear room for a grudge."

The space under the barn's peaked ceiling was packed to capacity. The crowd was a mix of Canadian and American, their country of origin distinguished by the coffees in their hands: white Dunkin' Donuts cups for Yanks, brown Tim Hortons for the Canucks. Some wore T-shirts bearing tough-guy phrases: PAIN IS ONLY FEAR EXITING THE BODY and YEA, THOUGH I WALK THROUGH THE VALLEY OF THE SHADOW OF DEATH I SHALL FEAR NO EVIL, FOR I AM THE MEANEST MOTHERFUCKER IN THE VALLEY.

Rob made his way through the crowd to a shadowed corner. A lot of eyes on him: *Is that Rob Tully, the top-ranked amateur?* He found a hay bale and scanned the fighters. They stood on the fringes, some singly, others with their backers. All of them scarred or disfigured or broken in some way. And their eyes—the newer ones had this look of sheer psychic terror. The older and more mutilated showed no emotion at all: faces a fretwork of scars, eyes blank as a test pattern. Then there were those hovering in the middle ground, neither new nor old: they had the look of men who'd realized their lives were irretrievably lost and they could only await the inevitable passage into the final stage.

Rob unzipped the duffel and removed tape, sponge, and gauze. He'd never actually taped his own hands—his father was always there for that. He ripped off lengths of tape and hung them off his trunks. He centered a strip of sponge on his hand but it kept slipping off his knuckles.

Fritzie materialized from the crowd. "Let me help with that."

Rob pressed the sponge flat across his knuckles while Fritzie taped. "You go second, Robbie."

"You're up second," Lou told Paul.

Paul held his hands out, palms up. Lou centered Paul's left hand on his knee, flexed each finger, then began taping.

"Remember me doing this for you the first time you came by the gym?" Lou said. "Just another silver spooner, I figured. Gave you a week, tops." He shook his head. "This kid you're fighting—Robert Tully. Only about the biggest thing to come out of Niagara Falls since . . . well, forever. He's also the nephew of the man you knocked silly the last time out."

"You don't say."

"I won't build castles in the sky for you: godly intervention aside, he's gonna kick your ass. Tell you another thing—I won't be throwing in the towel."

"That's a good thing, Lou. I'd probably end up killing you, you did that."

Paul stared at a dark knothole in the floor. He stared at that knothole, that cavelike spiderwebbing knothole, until he fell into it. Inside the knothole all was dark and quiet and calm. Inside he could think. *I am a machine*, he thought simply. A machine of unforgiving angles and unshakable geometries, titanium and bulletproof glass and ballistic rubber and dead metals. A machine assembled in a work area completely free of human presence, riveted together by preprogrammed robotic arms, altogether unfeeling. Without name or face, lacking a past, lacking dreams or memories. A machine feels no mercy. A machine cannot be broken by fear. *I am a machine*, he thought over and over, and over and over. *A machine a machine machine machine machinemachinemachinemachine*—

At some point Lou was saying, "You're up."

Two men stood in the center of the ring.

Between them stood Manning. He ran down the rules.

"Fight ends when one man goes down and stays there. One guy's gotta go down to end the round. Keep it clean—no eye poking or biting. That's sissy fighting."

Manning stepped aside. The fighters came together. Their upper bodies were candle-white after the sunless winter months. Paul leaned forward until their faces nearly touched. Rob did not pull away.

Paul said, "I'm really sorry about all this."

Rob's first punch—a venomous straight right—struck Paul's forehead, splitting the flesh between his eyes like the blow from a fifteen-pound hatchet to bring forth blood in needle-thin pulses. Rob saw it in slow motion: his fist rocketing from his chest shoulder-high to pass over his opponent's guard, the flex of ligament and snap of tendon, impact sending a mild shiver down his arm and the guy's face opening up, blooming like some bastard weed, a bone-deep trench cut down the middle of his forehead.

Rob watched the guy—his name, he remembered, was Paul—reel back, brain obviously scrambled, eyes wide. His knee had barely touched the pine boards before he was up. He shook his head, red drops flying every which way.

As Paul came on again, if anything, Rob felt vague disappointment: *this* guy hurt Tommy? Like Fritzie Zivic said: takes one lucky punch. Rob was also puzzled by Paul himself: what drove a man to seek out a place like this, to fight so maniacally, so recklessly—and to what end? They circled. The united voice of the crowd boomed like subterranean thunder beneath their feet. Blood coursed down the sides of Paul's nose and off his chin. Someone tossed an empty mickey into the ring: it shattered with a glassy tinkle, silver shards sparkling the boards like chipped ice.

They met violently. Rob lashed out with a left hook. Exhibiting more grace than Rob would have credited him with, Paul ducked back and, rooting his left foot like a stump, threw a wicked right cross. The punch slammed Rob's abdomen above the hip. A flash of white-hot pain exploded in his gut. He backed off, gagging, bile burning his sinuses. His vision was studded with shimmering dots; he retreated jelly-legged as Paul followed up with a crushing right hand, smoking it straight through Rob's frail defense and smashing his mouth.

A cataclysmic *bang* filled Rob's skull, the sound of a .44 Magnum discharged in a broom closet. He felt himself falling, but, as in a dream, was helpless to check himself.

He came to slumped against a hay bale. Dry stalks itched the knobs of his spine. The soft tissue inside his cheeks was badly cut, pink rags hanging in his mouth. He couldn't hear anything and for a brief span was gripped with a sickening surety he'd gone deaf.

Then he caught his own shivering exhalations and came to realize that the crowd had gone silent in disbelief. He spat blood and touched his upper front teeth, unsurprised to find them loose in their moorings.

Fritzie helped him up. "Want me to stop it, Robbie?"

"You better not."

★

Paul leaned forward on a bale, elbows balanced on knees. His overall demeanor was that of a dog, a fighting dog, pit bull or rottweiler, waiting for his trainer to release the fetters.

Paul waved Lou's hands away from the forehead wound. "Let it bleed."

"You're gushing all over the place. That blood will blind you."

"I don't care. Leave it be."

The crowd was absorbed in funereal silence. Manning's son swept the busted bottle from the fighting surface.

Paul glanced at the other corner. The kid had regained his senses. He didn't appear fazed or scared—surprised, was all. Paul came to confront what he'd known all along: he was going to lose this fight, lose it badly. That suited him just fine. It was beyond winning or losing now. It was about the desire and willingness to approach the world with fists raised, always moving forward. To give everything of yourself without hesitation or fear.

★

Rob came out cautious the following round. His guts ached and broken points of fire danced across his vision, but his legs were steady.

Paul came on like a dervish, throwing hook after hook, lunging after Rob with ungainly strides. Blood ran unchecked down his face, into his eyes and mouth.

Rob snapped left jabs at Paul's upper arms, driving his knuckles into the solid flesh of the biceps. Paul's arms dipped and Rob's fists flashed, jabs peppering Paul's brows, cheeks, nose. Paul couldn't protect himself: he might as well try to shield himself against a sniper's bullets fired from a faraway bell tower.

The rough adhesive on Rob's fists left slashing burns on Paul's face. Rob wondered why he kept *smiling*. Or not a smile, exactly: an oddly blissed-out expression, as though he were in the midst of a pleasantly confusing dream.

The smell of cowshit and sawdust sweated up from the floorboards as Paul's face swelled under Rob's relentless assault. Blood vessels burst under the pressure of skin slamming bone, blood pumping from ruptured veins to collect in pouches like hard-boiled eggs inserted under his skin, erupting like oversize blisters under Rob's fists. Paul tottered, he wove and stumbled, he refused to go down. He threw punches blindly, not seeing Rob anymore, throwing for the doubtful possibility of contact or perhaps the sheer joy of it.

Rob only wanted Paul to go down and stay there. His hands were covered in blood and he didn't know whether it was his own knuckles splitting and bleeding or if the blood was all Paul's.

Voices in the crowd:

. . . never seen the likes of it . . .

. . . scrawny faggot's gonna need a casket before long . . .

. . . drop that chickenhead, man! He's neck-deep in hurt . . .

They collided in the middle of the ring and stood toe to toe, just winging. Paul felt like a man facing a barrage of rocks soaked in kerosene and lit on fire. Rob finished with a vicious right hook that sent Paul down onto a bale. Brittle straw puffed up from under him and the bell rang while he struggled to find his feet.

★

Lou had never seen a face like it. A Sunday matinee horror show.

Paul's lips were split so deep down the middle they were like four lips instead of two, the pink meat drooping in rags. Eyebrows broke open over the high ridge of bone, wounds so wide it was as though a pair of tiny toothless mouths were leering through the bristly hairs. One eye puffed completely shut, a fleshy ball the size of a baby's fist.

How long had the round lasted: three minutes, three and a half? So little time, really, for such a sickening transformation.

"Paul," Lou said carefully. "You need to listen to me. You can't go on fighting this way. Let me clean you up a bit, at least."

Lou wet a towel and wiped. When Paul's face was clean Lou saw it was hopeless: the cuts were too deep, too long, too numerous. Adrenaline chloride wouldn't do it, ferric acid wouldn't do it, a goddamn *staple gun* wouldn't do it. He could debride the deepest ones and razor the puffed flesh around that eyeball to give him some relief, but why bother? The kid didn't want to be helped.

"How do I look?"

Lou said he looked like an elephant had shit him out sideways. "And you're gonna lose the fight to boot. No other way this ends."

In a voice so low Lou had to strain to hear, Paul said, "And you think I didn't know that from the start?"

Fritzie yanked Rob's trunks open and splashed cold water over his groin. Rob saw all the sweaty, booze-flushed faces standing like flowers in morbid arrangements and behind those faces the fighters waiting in pockets of shadow, their bodies shivering with terror or anticipation, and beyond them the discolored barn walls rising to a rotting roof through which he glimpsed the vaulted emptiness of the night sky.

"Just go in there and put him away, quick," said Fritzie.

"I hit him as hard as I've ever hit anybody. He's not going away."

"Then hit him harder."

Rob gazed across the ring. Paul stared back. Rob was repulsed by the damage he'd inflicted. Paul smiled—a gruesome sight—and his eyelid closed over his working eye: a wink.

For a moment Rob thought Paul had been blinking blood out of his eye, but no: a wink.

The revelation was startling in its clarity: none of this had been about Tommy, or about him, and never had been—this was something else entirely. Tommy lay on a hospital bed, fighting for his life— and why? To afford this guy a means of restoring some semblance of purpose to his pitiful fucked-up life. Fury settled, a small black stone behind Rob's eyes. Spoiled selfish brat, winking at him. Spoiled selfish brat with his purposeless, futile, fucked-up life.

"Cut the tape off my hands," Rob told Fritzie.

"Why the hell you want that?"

"Because I want to feel it."

I'll kill him. The notion arose from nowhere. *It's what he wants. So give it to him.*

"He wants to feel it, too. I owe him that."

"You don't owe this guy a thing."

"No," Rob said softly, "I owe him that."

When the bell rang for the third round, Paul was thinking about his last vacation.

He and a few university friends had stayed at a five-star resort outside Havana. They'd lain on the beach drinking mojitos served by nut-brown cabana boys, laughing at their silly white outfits that made them look like plantation butlers. At night they'd gone to discotheques and hit upon the local women, pinching asses or grabbing tits until one reared upon Paul and slapped his face, but he'd only laughed thinking the sting on his cheek would be gone the next morning but her life would unfold in the same sad unremitting pattern until one day she died. He thought of such episodes, the indulgence and cruelty and extravagance and wastefulness. It seemed his whole life was a patchwork of similar events, one callous escapade stitched onto the next. He did not know how to make amends for any of it, to balance the karmic scales—was it possible? But the throbbing ache of his hands, the swollen fiery confusion of his face: this was good. If a man were to give enough, suffer enough—maybe. And so he craved this pain, the knowledge and atonement only pain could bestow, particular, intimate, and entirely personal, that pain washing over him, washing away his every wrong.

The next punch struck him square in the face and skidded him back on his heels. He took a knee, balancing on his knuckles; then, with a great shuddering breath, he stumbled in Rob's direction again.

He swung and missed as another blow spiked the knot of nerves where his jawbone met his skull and shocked the upper left half of his body into mute numbness. Another blow, then another and another, so fast his body could register the pain only after the fact, the way you'll hear the crash of thunder moments after lightning has split the sky. He took a murderous shot in the gut and his bowels let go with a mordant note like the groan of a ship's hull. "You reeking *prick*!" someone yelled and Paul was surprised at how quickly he'd moved beyond frustration or shame ...

... as Rob's rage built, cyclical and combustive, firing like the pistons of a supercharged engine. The thing facing him was nothing but a bag of skin and bone and gristle and blood and Rob wanted to inflict as much damage upon it as was humanly possible—as was *inhumanly* possible—smash and bash and crush and wreck until nothing of value remained.

The sack of meat shambled forward. Rob rained blows upon it. The air shimmered with blood. A few spectators looked away . . .

. . . Paul came on awkwardly. Equilibrium shot, he moved as though his knees and hips were packed with rusted ball bearings. He couldn't tell if he was smiling. He sort of hoped he was.

Rob's fist found his jaw and a cherry bomb exploded in the tin cup of Paul's skull. Warmth ran down the inside of his leg and he had no idea what it was but still it was oddly comforting. He was hit again and orange lights burned like sunspots before his eyes, initiating wild riots in his head until one of these spots mushroomed, bright as an A-bomb, blinding and beautiful and so incredibly alive and as he fell a claustrophobic blackness replaced that light, the airless dark of a deep sea cavern, then he came to on a bale of hay with spring stars shining through holes in the barn roof.

Lou's face swam above him. His features were a mask of wild panic. His mouth formed words but Paul couldn't hear anything on account of the cycling roar that filled his skull.

Lou started waving his arms. "No," Paul said, though he couldn't hear his own voice. Lou's lips moved; he might have been saying *Crying blood.* "Don't care." Lou's lips moved again: *Skull filling with blood.*

"Don't care."

Shit yourself—

"Don't care."

Die here—

"Don't . . ." Spit a sac of blood. ". . . care."

★

"This guy . . ." Fritzie was baffled. "I never seen anything like it. What is that guy anymore—a punching bag, that's it."

"He's got to quit," Rob said. "He's got to cry uncle."

"He's not gonna do that. There's something the matter with him."

"Then we keep going."

"And you're sure you want to? Don't exactly look it." Fritzie wiped under Rob's eye. "That's not sweat."

Rob swiped his cheeks furiously. "Tell someone to ring the bell."

A profound sense of peace settled over Paul. The workings of his mind flattened out; his thoughts disintegrated. Like he was on a plane on a clear cloudless day, staring out the porthole window as earth ceded to ocean: the houses and roads and buildings, the patchwork quilt of farmers' fields, all that variation giving way to a smooth blanket of water—green closest to shore, the white curls of Queen Anne's lace turning to deepest blue and, where the water ran deepest, flat ongoing black . . .

. . . while Rob's was consumed with visions of slaughter. His hands felt hardened, lumps of rock, and his wish was to drive them into Paul's face, across the bridge of his nose or into his mouth, dislodge the rest of his teeth and slam his fist, the whole of it, deep into Paul's mouth, down his throat, choking him, or instead cleave his skull, crack it open like a fleshy nut and destroy the core of his brain. To step through those barn doors was to enter a realm of violent imperatives and so he let his fists go, beating a merciless tattoo on this creature who stared balefully with his blood-filled eyeball . . .

. . . Paul could no longer feel his arms or legs. He felt isolated from the fight: as though another man was taking the punishment while he stood nearby, watching. He saw two men in a series of frozen moments, the sort of stylized postures glimpsed in ancient Greek friezes. It resembled less a fight than an aggressive coupling, yet there was an odd deference: *May I place my hand here? May I set my leg here, between yours? May I, May I, May I* and their bodies melding, fists enveloped by the other's chest or face, arms and legs and heads uniting, flesh bonding until they became a united whole, this faceless sexless creature that might haunt a lunatic's dreams ...

... until a hard stroke finally sent Paul to one knee. He could not see the boards under his feet. Blood dripped from his face, dripped from all parts of him. He raised one hand, that hand trembling uncontrollably, and touched his face. He felt something beneath the skin, incredibly hard. Harder than bone, even. He pushed three fingers deep into the most gaping wound and touched these alien contours. New ridges and planes that did not feel human—not entirely so. If his body were to be hit hard enough, long enough, if it absorbed enough punishment, maybe this soft outer layer would slough away to reveal whatever lay beneath. Imagine a cocoon, a pupating bug. The prospect entombed itself in his mind. If he could just weather the storm he would emerge as something infinitely stronger, harder, more meaningful. No weakness, no fear, no misery or rupture or death.

Paul came forward again, not protecting himself at all, walking straight into punches. The smack of meat on bone snapped off the high wooden beams and a queasy fan yelled, "Stop it. God, just ... *stop.*" The two men in the ring heard nothing: not the fans, not the lick of fists or the sound of their own breathing. For a crazed instant Paul wanted to simply touch Rob, to hold and breathe against him, to taste his wounds and know his skin.

And when neither man could punch anymore they stood at arm's length, strength sapped, holding on to each other: from a distance, it looked as though Rob was teaching Paul how to dance a slow waltz.

Paul's mouth opened. A single word passed over his broken lips: "Please ..."

Rob did not understand what he was asking.

Was it:

Please, stop.

Or:

Please, more.

Paul's eyes rolled back in his head as he slipped through Rob's arms, falling senselessly the way a toppled mannequin falls. Rob made an instinctive grab for him, but Paul was too bloody and Rob too exhausted and so he simply fell.

The bell did not ring; there was no need. Men climbed over the bales and bent over the stricken fighter with something approaching reverence. When they rolled Paul over, the shocking bloody imprint of his face remained on the boards. He was unconscious but his eyes were wide open. Someone might have placed two fingers upon his lids and drawn them shut but nobody did.

Lou lifted Paul's head and hooked his hands under his armpits.

"Careful," he instructed Fritzie, who'd taken hold of Paul's heels. "Get him out to my car."

The night was still. A low white fog rolled across the fields, thickening toward the tree line. Rob moved over sedge grass stamped flat by cattle hooves. His fury had evaporated as rapidly as it had risen, and in its place remained sickness and self-loathing. He was horrified by his actions—the savagery of them. He'd seen the bloody imprint of Paul's face stamped on the raw pine boards. The sight had provided no solace or peace, only emptiness and desolation more incurable than he'd ever known.

A fine cool night and Rob walked between heads of cattle, their heaving flanks, the pungent animal smell of them. He had glimpsed in himself a malice of purpose he'd never known and it terrified him. *I'll kill him. It's what he wants.*

The fence post was the circumference of a dinner plate. Rotting at the top, slim wooden stalactites he could snap off with a finger, but going solid toward the middle. Moonlight winked off the rusted points of barbed wire twined around it.

Rob asked himself: Can I break them all?

The first punch was tentative: it wasn't the pain that frightened him, but the finality of his actions. The next punch was harder; the post vibrated like a tuning fork. Wire tore skin. He threw his fists with as much venom as he could summon, dug his feet into the cold earth. The crisp *tok tok tok* of fist on wood gave way to mushier, meatier sounds until at some point his right hand—the dynamite right, his father called it—crumpled, delicate jigsaw bones shattering, and though the pain left him gagging he did not stop. His hands became a blur of ever-expanding and ever-darkening red, blood in the air, blood and skin stuck to the post and the bones of his left hand splintering with a tensile shriek and bone visible now, thin glistening shards jutting through sheared flesh, but he kept hurling them.

He dropped to his knees as the sound of his blows echoed across the field. His head rested against the post. The cool wood felt so good on his skin. His hands looked like bags of suet tied to the ends of his wrists. A few fingers hung on strips of skin at lewd angles. Rob curled them under his chin and cried. Softly at first, then with building intensity.

Fritzie found him hunched there. "We loaded that guy into the car. He's beat up pretty bad, but he'll be okay."

Rob's chest hitched; his body shook. Fritzie knelt beside him.

"What's the matter, Robbie?"

Rob uttered a wail of such resonant grief that it shocked Fritzie. Rob kept his broken hands curled under his chin: Fritzie could not see what he had done and so could find no sense in his despair.

"The hell's the matter with you?" Fritzie was truly perplexed. "You won, Robbie. For Christ's sake, you won."

13

L ou swung onto Highway 406 and exited off Geneva Street. He wound the car down Queenston, through staggered sets of stoplights and into the Emerg drop-off at St. Catharines General. "Hey," he said. "Hey, man."

Paul cracked his good eye, saw the well-lit bay and the glowing red cross above the sliding glass doors. "No."

"Be sensible. You need stitches—your face is . . . it's fucked up."

"No . . . hospital."

"Fine, if you want to be an idiot. But we are doing something about those cuts."

Lou parked in a shadowed alcove near some medical waste bins. He opened his medic's kit and pulled out a roll of Steri-Strip, a 24 mm surgical needle, two packs of Ethicon braided sutures, and a vial of high-viscosity Dermabond.

"Never met a fighter more obstinate." He cut lengths of Steri-Strip and stuck them to the dashboard. "I got no anesthetic, either—they only give that stuff to, y'know, *licensed practitioners*, the type you'd find twenty feet back that way."

Lou gripped Paul's chin and angled his face into the dome light. Pinching split lips of meat together, he moved the needle through Paul's cheek. Fresh blood rolled down Paul's chest and onto the upholstery.

When the gashes were closed he ran beads of Dermabond over them; the torn flesh met in thin red crescents, like the stitching on a pocket. They would scar up, but Paul would never look quite right again. His face was pulled out of shape, skin tight in some places and slack in others.

Lou said, "Should I take you home?"

"Where's that?"

Lou sighed, said, "So where am I taking you?"

"I don't care."

Lou put the Steri-Strip and Dermabond away. The air between them was thick and warm like in a tent.

"I was riding my bike home one time," said Lou. "This was as a kid. I saw this accident: a pickup truck hauling one of those mobile stables or whatever—those things you truck livestock around in. Both were smashed up. It was late, but a few cars had pulled over. There was a horse; must've been riding in the stable when it crashed. One of its legs was broken and almost torn off. It moved down the embankment between the trees and it stood there. People went to their cars and found whatever—chips and crackers, sugar packets, apples—and crept after the horse, making the stupid sort of noises people make." Lou made a clicking sound with his tongue: *cluk cluk cluk.* "But when they got close, the horse would bolt. This kept on for some time: the pack creeping after the horse and the horse bolting, busted leg swinging. I was young, but even then I knew what it wanted. Do you know what that was?"

"Don't tell me," Paul croaked. "That little horse grew up to become . . . Black Beauty."

"That horse didn't want to live anymore. Not all creatures want to die in the light, surrounded by friends and loved ones. Some just want to crawl into a dark quiet space away from everyone and die alone."

"Do you think you're being subtle?"

Lou turned the key and gunned the engine. "I don't want to see you around my gym again, Paul. You're not welcome anymore."

Jack Harris's study was a large oak-paneled chamber off the sunroom. It was furnished according to a clichéd *Better Homes and Gardens* ideal: a huge mahogany desk, bookshelves lined with imposing hard-covers, a pipe rack without a single pipe—bizarre, as his father didn't smoke. As a kid, Paul once spent the better part of an afternoon tilting the spines of each and every book, convinced one would spring a door leading to a hidden chamber; his childish suspicion had been that his dad was a superhero. Now Paul moved as quietly as possible, not wanting to wake his parents; he was shirtless and bloody, having nearly impaled himself while scaling the estate's spiked wrought-iron fence.

The safe was hidden behind a Robert Bateman painting. The combination was Paul's birthday: 07–22–79. He'd looted it many times, figuring his father would never know—though of course he had, just as he had known about his drunken forays in the winery and a dozen other indiscretions.

The light snapped on. His father stood in the doorway in a brown housecoat.

"What are you doing?"

"What's it look like?"

"Like you're stealing."

"Better call the cops."

"Don't think I won't."

Paul turned to face his father. Jack Harris recoiled at the sight. That face—like a rotted mummy risen from its sarcophagus.

Jack walked past his son and sat in the overstuffed chair behind the desk. Whoever had stitched his child possessed no more skill than a deli butcher. When he could not look anymore he laid his arms on the desk and rested his head upon them.

"We can't do this anymore."

Paul's knees buckled; his body slid down the wall until his butt hit the carpet. The study was warm and smelled of his father. He could fall asleep right here.

"This whole situation is destroying us, Paul. Your mom and me. And I know it's not your intent—maybe you think what you're doing is justified or that you have no other option. But we can't go down this road anymore."

"You shouldn't feel that way, Dad. Not your fault."

When Jack looked up, his eyes were swollen but he wasn't crying. "Oh, no—whose fault is it, then? It's never been my practice to pass the buck, but at least it's easier than admitting you fucked up your son's life."

Paul dearly wished he could somehow console his father but the answer was too big and required too much of him so he said nothing.

"At first I was scared for you," Jack said. "Now I'm scared of you. Never thought I'd be scared of my own kid."

"The point was for me to stop being scared."

Jack nodded, as though this answer at least made sense to him. "The world is full of hard men—a lot harder than you'll ever be. And you're bound to run across a truly hard man—then what?" When Paul did not reply, Jack said, "It's like anything else in life: a ladder, but those rungs, they keep going up. You'll never find any peace until you come to grips with your place on it, or else kill yourself trying to climb to the top."

"I need money," Paul said flatly.

Jack rose from his chair and spun the safe's dial. He grabbed two stacks of bills and tossed them on the desk.

"Get on up," he told Paul. "Take a seat."

Paul dragged himself up and sat in the chair opposite his father. Jack poured scotches from a decanter and set one in front of his son. Scotch dribbled down Paul's split lips onto his chest.

The money lay on the desk between them. Two crisp stacks. Jack sipped his drink, tapped the crystal rim against his teeth.

"Ten thousand enough?"

"It'll do."

A few years ago a worker's arm had been torn off by a tilling machine. By the time Paul and his father arrived on the scene the young worker was lying on earth gone dark with blood. Jack had made a tourniquet of his belt and held the man until medics arrived. He'd saved the man's life—and yet Paul never forgot that look on his face. Under the obvious care and worry, he'd glimpsed a mind calculating how this accident might affect his enterprise. A look of bottom-line pragmatism.

And was that same pragmatism at work now? Paul thought of how lizards will sever their own tails when attacked, forfeiting some vital part of themselves in order to survive.

"You know, I have to laugh," Jack said, "because in a lot of ways you're a better man than you were. I'm sitting here looking at you all . . . *mulched*, and still I think that. Not that you were ever a bad kid. Ineffective, I'd say. But then I looked at your buddies, sons of guys I did business with, and you all sort of came off that way. You weren't ahead of the curve, or behind it. You were just . . ."

"One of the pack."

"I guess as much as you want your kid to distinguish himself, you're happy enough to see he's the same as everyone else."

Jack poured another scotch. Paul noted the sunken bags under his father's eyes and a three-day beard furring his jowls. "I don't guess you realize how . . ." Jack searched for the right word. ". . . how *insulting* all of this is, do you?"

"Insulting to who?"

"To me. To every man who goes down the traditional path."

"That's not the point at all—"

Jack cut him short. "You're saying the only way to be a man is your way. Throw yourself into a meat grinder and claw your way out. You're saying my way of being a man—work a steady job, support a wife, a kid, try to carve out a life for all of us—you're saying it's useless and proves nothing."

"I'm not saying that. I'm only saying it doesn't appeal to me."

"Suffering for the sake of suffering—we didn't raise you Catholic, did we? And you could have gone your own way at any time, but you were scared to. Like you said."

"That's true."

"Scared of what, Paul?"

"Of everything."

"And after all this what's really changed?"

"Everything else."

"Has it?" Jack slid the money across the desk; he pushed down on the stack with his fingertips, forcing Paul to pull it from under them. "Strikes me as a pretty familiar dynamic."

"This is the last time. And I'll pay you back."

"Don't worry about it. This isn't a loan."

Jack had the air of a man who'd come to an awful realization: that nothing he might do for his son, here and now or tomorrow or the next day, would really matter. The realization that a man could spend his whole life climbing onto crosses to save people from themselves, but nothing would ever change. And finally, the understanding that all human beings—even fathers, even sons—were each as alone as dead stars and no amount of toil or love or litany could alter by one inch the terrible precision of their journeys.

"I'll need my passport," said Paul. "And something to wear."

"Your mother holds on to passports. In her files upstairs."

"I don't want to wake her."

"Your mom," he said, "isn't living with me right now. This . . . what's been happening . . . hasn't been easy on her."

"I didn't know. I'm sorry."

"Nothing to be done for it now. She'll be fine—your mom's a strong woman."

Jack led Paul upstairs. Signs of neglect abounded: a collection of neckties looped around the banister, a stack of dirty dishes at the top of the stairs. "Maid's got the week off," he joked.

The bedroom was a pigsty. Heaps of soiled clothes. Greasy Chinese takeout boxes. Jack hunted through Barb's dresser, found Paul's passport, and flipped it to him. He snapped on a light in the walk-in closet and found something to fit Paul.

"Might be the first suit I ever bought." Jack held it up: cream-toned polyester with wide, winglike lapels, a black open-throated shirt, white vest, white pants. The sort of thing John Travolta wore in *Saturday Night Fever*.

"I think it's what they call vintage." Jack ran his finger down a lapel, yanked it back as though cut. "Get a load of those flares—sharp."

"It's spiffy," Paul said. "I've got to go, Dad."

"Places to go, people to see, uh? Can I ask you something, Paul? Was I . . . your mom and me . . . . were we . . . ?"

"Whatever you may think, none of it is your fault. I don't blame you for any of this, and I don't think there's anything you could have done to stop it. I am what I am because I made myself so. You did the best you could with me and that's all I could have ever asked. I have no excuses for what I am or what I've done or what I've put you through."

"Need to borrow a car?"

"That would help."

"You know where the keys are. Can't promise I won't call the cops the second you're gone to report it stolen."

"You can't save me, Dad."

"And I know that, son."

14

Reuben Tully paced his brother's hospital room, acridly awake. Tommy had been moved to a room with oatmeal-colored walls; he shared it with five—*five!*—other patients. The ringing splash of urine in bedpans so loud it sounded like someone pissing directly in your ear. Even the meals were crappier. Discount Jell-O. No Name tater tots. Next thing you knew, they'd wheel Tommy's bed out into the hallway.

Reuben sorted the day's mail. Bills, bills, bills. Tommy's employer wasn't kicking in a cent to cover hospital costs: the accident occurred off-premises, so they weren't liable.

Kate arrived with coffees. "Thanks," Reuben said, taking his cup. "Any idea where my unreliable lug of a son is tonight?"

Kate went over to Tommy; gently, she smoothed the lank hair across his forehead. "It's strange," she said, "he looks so restful."

"Robbie?" Reuben said.

"I talked to him this morning."

"Oh, he still talks? News to me. I can't get two words out of him."
He took note of the look Kate was giving him and said, "What?"

"This isn't easy for anyone, Reuben."

Reuben bristled. "How am I supposed to make it any easier, he
doesn't talk to me?"

"That's Rob's problem. He doesn't say what he feels."

"So, what—he's telling *you* how he feels?" Her noncommittal shrug
made Reuben's hackles rise. "You've been here less than a minute and
already you're getting on my nerves. And what's with this 'Reuben'
stuff? What happened to Uncle Ruby?"

Kate flipped him a look: spare, flat. "You know, Rob would never
say this, so I guess it falls to me—"

"And what's that, Kate?" Reuben challenged. "What is it he'd never
say?"

Then Fritzie Zivic was saying, "I brought him here directly," and
both Kate and Reuben saw Rob in the doorway, Fritzie standing over
his shoulder.

Rob's hands, Reuben thought. *Something's the matter with my
son's hands.*

Zivic held his hat to his chest like a policeman come to deliver grim
tidings. "I didn't know what he was doing till it was a done thing."

Rob's hands were bundled in a grimy towel. The towel was dark.
The towel was red.

"What's happened, Robbie?" Reuben struggled against a rising tide
of dread. "What have you done?"

Rob seemed to have aged dramatically in the hours since Reuben
had last seen him. The skin ringing his eyes was of such shocking
whiteness Reuben felt as though he were staring into the headlights of
an approaching vehicle.

The towel was drenched. The towel was . . . *dripping.*

"Rob . . ." Reuben touched his son's shoulder. "What . . . ?"

Except he knew. From the moment he glanced up and saw his son in the doorway—*knew*. Where he'd gone, what he'd done, and why. For Tommy's sake, yes, but more than just Tommy.

And how long had Reuben known—really *known*? For years. The evidence had been everywhere: in his son's every forced acceptance and grudging nod of consent, every time he'd pulled a punch to spare an opponent or took a punch where he could have given, the forlorn and defeated air with which he laced his boxing shoes. Of course he'd known. Why else would he have been so unrelenting? To push Rob past the point of resistance, after which he'd settle into his role. Jesus, nobody was taking his *life* away: he would box until he was thirty, maybe thirty-five. Reuben would manage him carefully, bring him up the right way so he could retire with his brain intact and enough money to spend the rest of his days in comfort. On the streets he'd hear "There goes the Champ!" and he'd die knowing that part of him would remain on this earth—in the record books and archived footage—forever. This was Reuben's plan: a wise and reliable plan. A plan for the future. The family's future. And yet always he'd known, in the greater part of his mind and soul, that his son had never accepted his role.

Reuben and Kate guided Rob to a chair and sat him down. Rob stared, with a gaze of deep absorption, at the halogen lights overhead. Slowly, with great care, Reuben peeled sodden toweling away.

"Oh, my . . . oh . . . oh . . ."

What they saw resembled nothing so much as what might be found clogging the filter of a slaughterhouse sluice grate. Meat. Red and flayed and broken meat. Everything tangled up, enmeshed, no one part all that distinguishable from the next. Reuben marveled, with knife-edged sickness, at the fortitude it must've taken to commit an act of such desperate aggression against oneself.

"My god, Rob . . ."

Reuben could not take his eyes off his son's hands. What if they healed that way, skin grafting and bones setting into a scarred lumpen ball? Would they ever be right again? Not right enough so he could box—there was no way he'd ever step inside a ring again—but right enough to grip a pencil? To tie his own shoelaces?

"I'm sorry," Rob said. "I'm so . . . sorry."

"Sorry? No . . . you don't have to be sorry. You don't ever have to be sorry."

"I didn't . . . couldn't do it. For you and Tommy and everyone I wanted to but I couldn't anymore and I'm so, so sorry."

"It's okay," Reuben said even while he felt his whole world collapsing, all the things he'd striven for coming down around his ears. "It'll be okay."

Reuben set his arms around his son's shoulders. Rob's every muscle tensed; his entire body quaked. Reuben had no idea as to the precise sequence of the night's events, what his boy had been through since they'd last spoken. He only wished he'd known of Rob's intentions: if not to stop him, then at least to have been there for him—his father, instead of some neighborhood bum like Fritzie Zivic. Christ, what were they going to *do*? Rob was a smart kid, hardworking, but college? No way could he afford it. So what were his options: pouring concrete, snaking toilets, hammering two-by-fours. The same ones open to every go-nowhere do-nothing slug in town. For a soul-destroying instant Reuben pictured his son at the bakery with a bag of enriched flour on his shoulder. Flour in Rob's hair and ears, gathering at the sides of his eyes.

"You didn't have to do this," he said. "You could have told me."

But was that really true? Perhaps there was no other route his son could have taken: only an act of this magnitude—an act of zero recourse—could steer him off the path he'd been set upon. Bonds of family are the fiercest, and can only be broken by the most extreme strokes.

"We'll be okay." If his words lacked conviction, at least his voice was steady. "We'll figure all this out." He touched his lips to Rob's forehead. "You need a doctor. Kate, stay here."

Reuben shot Fritzie an unforgiving look as he shoved past him out into the hallway. "I'll go with your dad," Fritzie said meekly. Murdoch padded into the room and sat by Tommy's bed; he started to chew on a dangling IV tube.

Rob could still feel the lingering wetness of his father's lips on his forehead. When was the last time his dad had kissed him—as a baby?

Kate's expression was caught somewhere between dread and wonder. "You've destroyed them," was all she could say.

"I'll never box again."

She smoothed the sweaty hair on his forehead. Though the sight of his hands obviously made her queasy, she smiled.

"What are you smiling at?"

"Nothing. They look awful, Tully. A busted jigsaw puzzle."

"You're still smiling."

"I know I am. I'm sorry. I don't know why."

Rob found himself smiling as well. Still in shock, he figured. He glanced at Tommy and wondered what he might make of all this, were he awake. Then he thought of them in their little house on 16th Street. Sitting on the porch with his uncle on a warm summer's night: a cold soda, the fireflies and stars. Brief, sure, but then the good times always seemed too brief. Who was he to ask for any of it over?

"Do you want me to get you anything?" Kate asked.

"Just sit with me, okay?"

His hands were blazing. He heard the whisper of Tommy's breath. He sat with his uncle, each man in his own place.

Both of them waiting.

15

Paul drove the QEW north toward Toronto. He'd taken his father's Corvette Stingray—why the hell not? The highway was empty and quiet; Lake Ontario swept off to the east and night-long valleys twisted west to the escarpment. Over the Burlington Skyway, past Stelco smokestacks pumping effluvia into the charcoal sky. He tuned the radio to NEWS 640: *Earlier tonight, an explosion rocked the InoDyne Animal Testing Center in midtown Toronto, leaving four dead. A rogue animal rights group has claimed responsibility for the blast. . . .*

He felt queasy and pulled over, jerking the door open in time to puke a stream of yellow gruel over the breakdown lane. Three great heaves from the gut. For thirty seconds he stayed that way, his body leaning out over the dirty slush, but that was it. He was empty.

The Corvette skirted the city on the Gardiner Expressway. The slender spike of the CN Tower, the bleached bubble of the SkyDome. Three o'clock in the a.m.; spider legs of pale pre-dawn light skittered over the horizon.

Pearson airport sprawled across a flattened scrim on the city's western edge. Shark-colored planes eased down on gentle trajectories to meet halogen-lit runways.

Paul parked in the short-term lot and killed the engine. He grabbed his father's suit off the passenger seat, tossed the keys under the seat, and set off toward the international terminal.

Once inside he made a beeline for the nearest restroom. He shucked his clothes and donned the button-down shirt, trousers, and flared jacket. He stuffed his old clothes in a trash can and kept only his sneakers, rinsing them under the tap to wash away the blood.

He considered himself in the mirror. The suit made him look like he'd wandered off from a Captain & Tennille theme party.

He grabbed a handful of toilet paper, wet it, and wiped his face. The paper clumped and shredded; bits snagged on his stitches. When he finished he looked, if not presentable, then at least human. Grabbing the stacks of money off the countertop and stuffing one into each pocket, he headed into the terminal.

The departure board loomed above the ticket counters. Destinations ticked past: Beijing, Kuala Lumpur, Sydney, London, Moscow, Barcelona, São Paulo, Caracas, Monterrey.

Eenie, meenie, minie, moe, catch a tiger by the toe . . .

Edinburgh.

. . . if it hollers . . .

Cairo.

. . . let . . . it . . . go . . .

Napoli.

. . . eenie . . .

Tokyo.

... meenie ...

Rome.

... minie ...

Kabul.

... moe.

The girl behind the Thai Airways counter clocked his approach with a mixture of professional decorum and abject horror: a wretched ghost in a cast-off leisure suit who wouldn't have looked out of place haunting an abandoned discotheque.

"I'd like a ticket to Bangkok. Your earliest possible departure."

The ticket agent cleared her throat and asked mildly, "Will that be round trip?"

"One way."

Her lacquered fingernails tapped the keyboard. "Our next flight departs in one and a half hours. Business or personal, sir? The Customs officials will need to know."

"Ever seen a guy more in need of a vacation?"

The ticket cost $3,400. He paid cash and headed toward the departure gates.

"Sir?"

"Hmm?"

"You're bleeding a little."

The terminal was deserted. A janitor guided a miniature Zamboni across the floor, leaving strips of wetly polished tile. Through soaring plate-glass windows he saw mail jets and freight carriers taxi into lit bays. A family dressed in Hawaiian beach finery was sprawled over some padded benches. Paul wondered whether he'd be allowed through airport security. He was a little beat-up, sure, but it didn't make him a flight risk—did it?

He lay out on a bench and slipped into an exhausted sleep and dreamed he was on a trawler.

It was nighttime; penlight stars winked. He stood on the gunwale but could see no horizon, no line where water gave way to sky. The water was shiny as patent leather and so depthless he felt a touch of vertigo.

"There you are."

A man clambered up a ladder from the engine compartment. His face was squarish, knotted, weather-roughed. White powder had dried to a crust around his eyes.

"You were expecting me?"

"I was, eventually," the captain told him. "Wasn't sure what you'd look like—it's tough to tell from the inside."

"I'm sorry—inside what?"

The captain walked to a boom jutting off the starboard side. He picked up a tin bucket and dipped it over the side. When he set it on deck Paul knew at once that it wasn't water in the bucket. Too dark, syrupy, and red.

"Inside of you," the captain told him. "Your heart."

The vista reconfigured to fit this understanding. No horizon: only the curved rim of Paul's aortic chamber. What he'd mistaken for stars were gleaming white nodules lodged in the meat of his atrial walls. The opening and closing of his pulmonary valves created soft waves. Like being in a massive undersea cavern.

Paul placed his hand on his chest: not the slightest tremor.

"My own heart." There was no reason to doubt it. "Am I dead?"

The captain considered it, then shook his head. "Neither you nor I would be here, that was the case."

"How long have you been . . . ?"

"As long as you've been," the captain said, simply.

"And are there others like you," Paul asked, "in . . . other parts of me?"

He shrugged, as if Paul had tendered the prospect of life on remote planets. He bit the end off a cigar, spat the stub overboard, and lit it with a wooden match.

"I'd really rather you didn't," said Paul.

"This?" The captain indicated the cigar. "My friend, it's the least of your worries."

A winch was attached to the boom and the captain cranked it; wet rope wound over a metal drum. He cut Paul an exasperated look. "Pair a broken arms?"

Paul took hold of the winch. The currents were stiff; he was sweating before long.

"What are you fishing for?"

"Not fishing," the captain told him. "Dredging."

A net rose from the dark bottom of Paul's heart; the captain swung the boom and spilled the catch over the deck. Amidst the pulpy tissue and clotted blood monstrous shapes flapped and heaved. They were white, whatever they were, whiter than the nodule-stars, eyeless, face-less, boneless as jellyfish. It wrecked Paul to know such things existed somewhere within him.

"What," he struggled, "what are they?"

The captain's features creased with disappointment. "Hoping you'd be able to tell me."

They held no universal shape, no unifying properties at all. Some were large, others quite small. If anything, they resembled shreds of animate blubber. Paul imagined a huge formless mass rotting in a lightless cavern of his heart.

"Nothing you'd want to eat," the captain said. "No nourishment at all." He lowered his boot onto one. A wet *squitch*. "They're not at all hardy and happy enough to die. Hell, seem only grudgingly alive in the first place."

"And . . . this is what you do?"

"All my life." He peered down at the abominations. "All my life."

"I'm sorry," was all Paul could think to say.

"I've been hauling up a lot less lately. Used to, I'd bring up four or five nets. Now, only one and it's not even quite full."

"Do you think that's a good thing?"

He gave Paul a warm smile. "Makes my job a helluva lot easier, leastways."

The creatures died quickly. Some melted; others calcified and sifted into powder; the rest turned to flakes that blew away over the gunnels. Soon there was no indication they'd ever existed.

Paul woke up on the terminal floor. The family dressed in Hawaiian shirts was looking at him strangely and Paul wondered if he'd been screaming in his sleep. Then he remembered the dream, those flapping blubber-creatures, and felt sick in his own skin.

He found a restroom on the terminal's south side. A few stitches had popped; blood wept through the Dermabond seal. Stripped to the waist, he blotted his face with toilet paper. He blotted too hard and popped another stitch. He leaned over the sink and let himself drain.

Paul stepped back and considered his reflection. His torso was splotched with purple bruises and scored with gloveburns. Destroyed but still standing. Beaten and bashed and bloody, but there he was.

With his right foot set slightly before his left, his body turned at such an angle as to present as spare a target as possible—*turn yourself into a pane of glass*, as Lou would say—Paul began to shadowbox. Flashing out the left hand and puffing short breaths—*tsh! tsh! tsh!*—the sound echoing sharply off the tiles. He executed the Fitzsimmons shift and threw a right hook at his reflection. He was warming up; the sweat was flowing. He felt loose and agile and strong.

He threw punches and thought about it all. Thought about the kid, Rob, and about his uncle, Tommy. Thought about Lou and about Stacey. Thought about his mother and his father and felt nothing but gratitude and love.

Five jabs in quick succession—*ts-ts-ts-ts-tshh!*—right hook, right hook, left uppercut, step back bobbing on the tips of his toes, sneakers squeaking. He considered how it all started as a simple desire. To banish weakness and inhabit strength. Develop those defensive mechanisms he'd never used. The porcupine, its quills. The scorpion, its sting. He juked and feinted then lashed out with a right hand, knuckles grazing the mirror. Drops of blood-tinted sweat wicked off his brow.

Why didn't you ever teach me to be a man?

He'd wanted to ask his father this question last night. Yet he realized his father *had* taught him how to be a man—a man for this time and era. Where before the teachings had been learned in fields or factories or foxholes, Today's Man learned in lecture halls and boardrooms. Where before men wore coveralls or buckskins or the colors of whatever side they fought for, Today's Man wore herringbone jackets and loafers, his nails were manicured, his hair smelled of nectars. His father had taught and he had learned. Those lessons had held him in fine stead until his path crossed with Yesterday's Man with his bloodlust and quick fists and old ways; only then did he realize that all he'd been bred for was useless. Perfect in his element, fragile and susceptible outside of it. And a man can't live in a vacuum—not his whole life.

Paul wiped his chest and armpits with toilet paper, donned his shirt and jacket. He stared into the mirror. Who was that person staring back?

It was . . . well, it was him. For better or for worse—him.

He was as unlikely a candidate for all this as you were liable to find. Or else he was the ideal one: a man whose life had always been primed for cataclysmic change. Or maybe there was no ideal candidate; perhaps the reasons for taking the road less traveled were as diverse as the histories of those who ultimately chose to walk it. And why not him? He came from good strong stock. His ancestors were farmers and before that sharecroppers and before that hunters. His bloodlines were fierce and he felt that fierceness in his own blood.

Follow anyone's family tree back far enough and you'll find warriors.

It wasn't that he thought he'd become a better man; he didn't feel like a Phoenix risen from the ashes of his former self. And yet there was a former self, a person who existed once and existed no more. So if he stood for anything at all, it was as a testament to change.

That full five percent change. A whole new person.

And consider if he'd never tried at all. Never fought, never suffered, never given all of himself. He would have spent his whole life wondering, just like any of us. And one day he might have woken to the awful realization that no choice he'd made had been his own, that his life had been plotted and planned and he'd followed it all by rote. Woken up still scared of every little thing. Woken up with no knowledge of his limits.

"I'm coming to your town. Last of the ramblin', russlin', tusslin' fighting men." The mirror reflected the sly irony in his smile. "Lay out your best, your fiercest men. Let's toe a line in the dirt."

Paul Harris butted his fists together, turned from his reflection, and exited the washroom toward Customs.

ACKNOWLEDGMENTS

My deepest thanks to my wonderful agent, Sarah, and to my supportive and diligent editor, Helen. Also to Jack Hodgins and Greg Hollingshead, who edited early drafts of the book at the Banff Writing Studio. Also my constant first reader, my father, and my mother, who read the manuscript—not because it was her cup of tea, but simply to support me.

Those of you who come to find anything of value between these covers, be assured that these people had something to do with it.

And as for the rest of it . . . hey, that's on me.